Praise for Wendy

WENDY LOU JONES

I was born and raised in West Sussex and moved to Birmingham to study Medicine at University, where I was lucky enough to meet my husband. We now live in a little village in Herefordshire with our two grubby boys. I discovered a love of writing not long after my youngest son started school. And if you were to ask me what it was that made me make the switch, I'd tell you quite simply, that it started with a dream.

http://wendyloujones.weebly.com/

@WendyLouWriter

The Summer We Loved

WENDY LOU JONES

Harper
impulse
we've got the love

Harper*Impulse* an imprint of
HarperCollins*Publishers* Ltd
1 London Bridge Street
London SE1 9GF

www.harpercollins.co.uk

A Paperback Original 2015

First published in Great Britain in ebook format by Harper*Impulse* 2015

A catalogue record for this book is
available from the British Library

ISBN: 9780008124762

Automatically produced by Atomik ePublisher from Easypress

Printed and bound in Great Britain

*To my fellow guinea pig loving editor, Charlotte,
whose refusal to let me off easy during the creation of
By My Side meant I fell in love with Peter too.*

Prologue

So Adam had done it again. Twice now he had found love; binding himself to a woman 'till death do us part'. He made it look so easy, stood up there in front of the congregation, eagerly saying 'I do'. Peter Florin couldn't think of anything worse. To have your own happiness bound so tightly to another's that you had no choice but to feel their pain? No. That was not an option he was willing to pursue.

Still, a wedding was a wedding: plenty of women in fancy frocks, drinking merrily and expecting to be flirted with. You couldn't knock it, really. His eyes scanned the guests at the church, rapidly surveying the offering. Had her. Had her. Ugh! Won't be having her. His gaze came to rest on Kate's friends a few rows ahead of him: Flis, Jenny and Soph.

From what he had heard, Soph was off the market now. Flis still held a torch for him, he had known that for a while, and although not exactly his type, he would keep her in mind just in case. But then there was Jen. Jenny Wren. He hadn't had much to do with her yet, and looking at her now, he couldn't imagine why. Her skin, where it rose up the back of her neck, was like cappuccino silk. He licked his lips. As he watched, she turned her head to whisper to the friend next to her and Pete could see the light dancing in her eyes. Yes, he was going to enjoy this.

Before he could deliberate much further, the organ started up, breaking his reverie, and the congregation began to stand. It was over.

Throughout the dullness of the small talk and speeches that followed, Pete kept Jen firmly on his radar. He smiled across at her when she caught his eye and relished the faint blush of crimson that appeared in his wake. Everything about this was wanton anticipation and, beat after beat, it was building.

Outside, it was a warm summer's evening. Kate and Adam's reception was being held in a marquee on the back lawn of an expensive hotel, and in the aftermath of the meal a disco was slowly warming up on one side of the tent, leaving the tables being cleared on the other. In the relaxed atmosphere of the early evening, when groups of guests were milling about, catching up with old friends and relatives and congratulating the bride and groom, Peter Florin could be found leaning up against the bar.

He stood there watching her and nursing a fresh pint of beer. She was dancing now – an observer's sport, in his books. She had looked over at him once or twice and he had been busy studying her reaction. She liked him. This was good. Just being there that day, with Adam, had been hard for him; he would welcome a challenge, if only for distraction.

To amuse himself, Pete tried to determine her response as a lover just by looking at her. The big eyes, full lips and seductive moves spoke of a decadent sensuality and the sparkly earring in the top of her right ear screamed out 'rebel'. Yes, she was just what the doctor ordered. His smile kicked in. It was time to make a move.

Greeting Adam briefly as he walked up to the edge of the dance floor, Pete kept his eyes on the prize. Jenny's body was supple, and as it moved and swayed in time with the music, it was almost hypnotic. Her mysterious eyes caught him approaching and for a second he became aware of her, trapped, unmoving in his spotlight. His heart rate kicked up a gear in response, but his pace didn't slow. Closer still, he continued his appraisal. The short choppy

2

hairstyle gave her a pixie-like quality that echoed of mischief and fun. Yes, he had to have her. His skin was burning with desire, so much so that, for a moment, he wondered just *who* was dangling on the hook.

Jenny spoke to a friend whilst her eyes were fathoming him and then left the dance floor. She walked right past him and as she did, she smiled. Wham! Pete turned to watch her walking away from him and quickly recovered. Was he being seduced? It was a novelty for a woman to make him work for it, but it made a refreshing change and from the look of her, it would definitely be worth the play. He looked around him. He had better crank up his pitch.

From the far side of the dance floor, Pete waited for his cue. He wasn't a fan of dancing, but on some occasions, he realised, needs must.

A minute later, the DJ tapped the mic. "Would a *Jenny* make her way to the centre of the dance floor, please, as her Prince Charming is currently waiting there to dance with her."

Pete took a deep breath and loosened his tie a little as the message stirred through the crowd. All eyes were searching for someone called Jenny. It wasn't a common name, so Pete was banking on her being the only one. Fingers started to point and nudge and then he spotted her, being escorted by some friends, warily winding her way back over in his direction. He moved into the centre and waited.

The three of them were egging her on and then, as she approached the dance floor, the crowd slowly parted, until there was nothing left between Jenny and him but air. Pete revelled in the surge of adrenaline coursing through him. He held out a hand and the crowd held its breath.

With her cheeks glowing, Jenny responded, moving slowly closer towards him. The proud set of her chin and determination to hold his gaze impressing him even more.

The onlookers sent up a cheer and after a moment or two,

began to close ranks around them and then she was there, with him, her hand holding onto his.

She stood before him. "You could have just asked me," she said.

"Now where would be the fun in that?" he replied. The song changed and a slow dance was calling them. "Shall we?" he asked.

Moving her into his arms, Pete felt the thrill of a new chase. He winked his thanks at the DJ over her shoulder and then looked down at her, smiling. He knew if he had gone about things in his usual style she would have likely sent him packing, but this way he had her, and he wasn't about to apologise for that.

Slowly, he felt her body start to relax beneath his fingers. He could smell the warm spicy scent of her skin and her hair and took pleasure in the touch of her hand, still clasped gently in his. "Would you have said yes if I'd have asked you?" he asked her softly in her ear.

"Probably not," she replied.

"Thought as much." He left it hanging in his tone that he was feeling smug about this.

"You're not as irresistible as you think you are, you know," she told him, but her body was slowly yielding to his. He rejoiced at the sensation of her breasts pressing lightly against him, and the fact that her cheek was slowly falling towards his chest, but it was her eyes, now big and dark, that were calling her a liar.

Jenny jumped a little and pulled away from him. She picked her phone out of her pocket and looked at it. She paled. Looking around, Pete followed her gaze and spotted a man standing at the edge of the dance floor, staring shards of glass at them.

"I've got to go," she said and Pete stood back and let her walk away.

At the edge of the dance floor he saw the man dragging Jenny outside by her wrist. The man's frame was stiff, his shoulders hunched and his jaw was set firm. Pete was unsettled.

Pete walked over to a marquee window, watching them carefully. The man led Jenny out to a big oak tree in the grounds. The light outside was fading now, not black yet, but a dim, hazy glow.

An argument was happening. He couldn't hear it, but their body language was saying enough. Jenny Wren must have a boyfriend too, he thought. And she was in trouble now, because of him. So much for his sensual evening. He wanted to turn away and head back to the bar, but something inside him said, 'wait'. He noticed Jenny rubbing her wrist where the man had held onto it, as she tried to sort out the problem between them. He'd hurt her. Something distant was rising now, coiling up inside him like a viper ready to spring.

The man put his hand up to her hair and for a second Pete thought the worst must be over, but then he grabbed it hard in his fist and he could see Jenny buckling beneath him.

Charging outside, Pete's head was in another place, in another time. Rage was coursing through his gut, along with fear and hate and so much pain it terrified him. He was on the man in seconds. Grabbing his other hand and twisting it back until it seemed as though it might break. "Leave her alone," he hissed. Teeth bared, his eyes held the shadows of night. The man dropped his hold of Jenny, doubling over at Pete's feet. He tried, unsuccessfully, to free himself and Pete wrenched at him all the harder. "Do you know this guy, Jen?" Pete asked, not taking his eyes off him for a second.

Jenny sounded shaken. "H-he's my boyfriend."

"Your boyfriend?" When would these women ever learn? "And you let him treat you like this?"

"No."

"Has he ever hurt you before?" He still had the man whimpering in his grasp. Please let her not be a victim. He couldn't bear it. He'd thought her stronger than that.

"No. Well. Yes. Only once, though."

Shit.

From behind him, someone was calling his name. Daylight crept inside his darkened shell. He let his gaze sweep over Jenny to make sure she was okay. She was looking at him as she would

5

a mad man. He had to get out of this, get himself away.

He turned to the man, busy struggling in his grip, the contemptible bully now squirming on his knees. "She doesn't want to go out with you any more," he said. "So leave. Now. And don't ever think of coming back. She won't be seeing you again." He let the man go, pushing him away and then stood between him and Jen, who was by now busy picking herself up off the floor. Pete stood his ground as the man looked from one to the other. "Isn't that right, Jen?" he called back.

Her voice was shaky, but adamant. "Yes."

The man shot one last dirty look towards him and then, rubbing his hand and swearing under his breath, he turned and stomped away.

Pete turned around to Jen and noticed she was shaking. "Are you okay?" he asked. Her frightened eyes looked back at him, like a child's. He quickly shrugged out of his suit jacket and placed it around her shoulders. It swamped her and something about that picture appealed to him, making his heart quiver. "Come with me."

He walked with Jenny to a bench he spotted further down the lawn; it was tucked into a border of high flowers, partially obscuring it from view. He sat her down and then, sitting next to her, he tried to talk some sense into her. "Let me see your wrist."

Jenny was reluctant, so he carefully reached down and took it. Pink marks were rising all around it, making Pete's scalp prickle with anger. This girl loved attention. *That* much he *did* know about her. Surely she didn't have to put up with scumbags like that just to get it? "Why did you go out with him?" he asked.

"He seemed like a nice guy... at first," she told him. "Only yesterday he told me he thought he was falling in love with me."

Pete pointed at her wrist, now cradled back in her lap. "This isn't love, Jen," he said. He was trying to sound calm, although every fibre in his body was screaming.

Her reply was a soft, barely audible, "No."

He turned to face her, willing her to understand. "You're a

gorgeous woman, Jen. Why haven't you found yourself a good man yet? You're stunning and kind and fun. So what is it? Am I missing something? Because from where I'm sitting, I can't see anything to complain about."

Her expression was turning misty. Big, round, emotional eyes poured into him, penetrating deep into his guts. Adrenaline flared again. What did she want from him? No. He didn't do this. He was no good at emotional. He wanted to run from the need he saw in her then. He had said too much. Damn, but how to get himself out of this now? He had only been trying to settle her, to reassure himself that she was all right. That was all. He could do fun, he could do pleasure; emotions were off limits for him.

Pete stood up and searched for some means of escape. With relief, he noticed Soph and her boyfriend hurrying towards them.

"Guys."

"I know. We saw everything. How are you, Jen? Did that bastard hurt you?"

Pete remembered to breathe and gratefully seized the opportunity to get away. "You'll be all right now?" he asked her.

Soph put her hand on Jen's arm. "We'll take care of her."

"Great." What else could he say? Those mysterious grey eyes, now pink-rimmed with tears, looked up at him from the bench. They were studying him, as if they could see inside his soul. Like they could read every thought in his head. He needed to run.

Pete did his best to smile and then made for the cover of the party. Now what he needed was a shag. He needed escape. Mindless sex to take him away from all that was closing in on him.

He searched the dance floor. Who was still available?

*

That was where it had all begun, according to Pete, anyway. Jenny sat at her writing desk and tried to remember the order of things. She wanted to tell the story exactly as it had happened and had

7

interrogated Pete long and hard (or that was how *he* had seen it) to this effect. She wanted to show how it had *really* been, not just how people had seen it. It was important. She had to get this right.

Jenny looked up at the paperwork from the hospital, pinned to the notice board in front of her desk. She was on a tight schedule. If she was to get this all down in time, she was going to have to push herself.

She opened up her laptop and logged in. Listening to the hustle and bustle of life outside her window, Jenny let her mind wander back to a time when she had been less contented and she searched for a place to begin. In the end, she decided on five years later, after Pete's return to her life. That was where her story would open, because that was when the pining had stopped and action had set in motion the storm that swept in…

Chapter 1

I saw him again today, standing there, leaning against the wall. A set of notes hung casually in his hands, as he talked with the nurse whose patient he'd come to see. Did he see me? I don't think so. He looked, but I don't think he saw. His smile, as always, lit up the corners of my heart, but nothing was said, not to me. He must have asked out every nurse in the hospital at some point, either when he was here before, or since his return, but he never wanted me, not any more.

Am I that unattractive? Is it his reluctance to want me that's making me think about him all the more? I hope not. I hope I'm not that shallow; maybe I am. Kate seems convinced there's a decent guy lurking inside there, just waiting for someone to help him break out and I have to hope that she's right. Because I saw something in his eyes the day of the wedding, just for a moment. It may be buried a long way down, but I can hear its voice.

Jenny's brow crinkled as she let out a deep sigh and bit down on the end of her pen.

Whilst before he used to treat me like a little sister, now he barely acknowledges me. So here I remain, in limbo, waiting for him to notice me. And not in that wham-bam-thank-you-ma'am way he does with most women, but with something more, something deeper. I'm not a fool. I know that if he'd ever had any intentions romantically towards me he would have acted on them by now, but that is my hope, and for now, hope is all I have.

Putting her diary back in the drawer, Jenny slumped back down onto her bed. One of her friends had remarked once that her love life was rather akin to the rhyme for King Henry VIII's wives: 'Forgot to get divorced, should have been beheaded, lied, forgot to get divorced, should have been beheaded' and now *she* was determined to survive. No more married men conveniently forgetting to tell her about their other halves; no more players. No one. She was through casting her net and coming up with jelly fish: all softness and beauty on the surface, but with barbs that stung you underneath. What she needed now was all or nothing. Love. Deep, meaningful, overwhelming love that took hold of you by the guts and dared you to feel the pain. Love that sucked you in and devoured you whole, while releasing you to evolve into something bigger, something… wonderful. Until that happened, she was not going to fall again.

Jenny hugged Mr Rochester, her old, worn, and much-loved teddy bear, to her chest. For now he was going to have to be enough. And she turned out the light and settled down to sleep.

At ten o'clock the next morning, Flis appeared at the kitchen door for breakfast. She was also on a late.

"Lover boy not eating with us this morning, then?" Jenny asked.

Flis shook her head. "He's got a meeting in London today, so he didn't stop over."

"Anything important?"

"I'm not sure. He was a bit cagey last night, but I've got a feeling it might be a promotion."

Jenny looked up from her cereal. "Do you think he might have to move there?"

"I'm not sure."

"Would you go with him if he did?"

"In a heartbeat," Flis said, excitement lighting up her eyes. "Of course. And be a kept woman in the big city? Sounds pretty good to me."

"Sounds hideous, I'd say. Wouldn't you miss work?" Jenny asked, not at all convinced she could give up her independence so easily.

"No way. Why, would you?"

Jenny thought for a second. "Sadly, I think I would," she said. "I think I'd miss feeling like I belonged, that I mattered. I'd miss the people."

"Some more than others."

Jenny raised an eyebrow and Flis shot her a meaningful look.

"Oh, come on. You're not *still* harping on about Peter Florin, are you? That was years ago, Flis. You've got Robert now."

"I know, but Connie from Goodwood Ward got fooled by him the other day; it just reminded me. She's only been in the hospital a few weeks. Someone should definitely warn them. It should be part of the welcome pack: "Welcome to St Steven's Hospital. We hope you enjoy working as part of our team, but please, ladies, don't let the seductive charms of Dr Peter Florin fool you."

Jenny chuckled. "Look, forget about him, Flis. Pete was never going to be a keeper, you knew that. He's a womaniser. You need to get over it."

"I am, really." Flis gave Jenny her best 'sincere' look and then rested her cheek back down on her hand. "I had hoped for more than one desperate shag, though."

"Yeah, well, join the club. I'm sure there are a hundred nurses who all feel exactly the same way as you. And not just here, all over the place."

"You've never got caught by him, though, have you?" Flis said.

Jenny winced inwardly, sore at having been reminded of her virtually leprotic allure. Was she the only one left out in the cold? "Nope." She tried her hardest to sound smug. "He'll have to be quicker than that to catch hold of me. I've gone man-vegan."

Flis looked at her.

11

"Yes, I decided I'm done with manipulative, self-centred men." Flis looked at her, with eyebrows almost on the ceiling. "And, no, that doesn't mean I've gone the other way. I'm just not going to waste any more of my life dating losers." She picked up her bowl, washed it and placed it on the rack to drain. "I'm going for a run," she said. "See you in a bit."

Under the clear, blue sky, Jenny stepped out into the garden and started to jog. She felt the sun warming her shoulders. It was going to be a good day, she thought.

Closing the back gate, she made her way along the alley and out into the sun. Houses passed by as she headed off along her well-trodden route. She picked up the pace, winding through the streets, until she found herself out in the countryside, quiet and alone.

Jenny sucked in deep breaths, filling her lungs with the fragrant air of the soft summer breeze as she let her mind wander. Her feet beat a rhythm on the ground and she wondered about a holiday. She had thought about going on a writers' retreat in her time off at the end of the summer. It was something she had wanted to try for a long time, but had never quite found the courage to take the next step. Maybe one day, she thought. Probably just a pipe dream, anyway. Perhaps she'd just have a couple of weeks in the sun.

The daydream called out its want for a partner and Jenny remembered the look in Pete's eyes the first time he had said hello and spoken to her on the wards, almost six years before. She had thought he liked her back then, maybe he had, but ever since that day at Adam and Kate's wedding, things had changed. She should think herself lucky that he'd avoided her, having seen how little others got from him. But deep down she wanted to believe there was more to him, and to be honest, her vanity was smarting.

Her fondness for Pete had begun at the start. But in the early days Flis had been so besotted with him that she hadn't felt able to try. With the disaster at the wedding, everything changed.

Pete would check on her often, but his eyes never looked at her the same after that. At home, with Flis now feeling bitter, they had barely been allowed to mention his name, and then he had gone, off to other hospitals to gain experience in his job. And Jenny had thought that was that. Men had come and gone, but nothing remained.

But with Pete's return had come a rekindling of an old ember and a yearning to be loved... by him. Sadly, the words 'loved' and 'Pete' seemed such a laughable contradiction that she was resigned to the fact that it was a lost cause and she would just have to wait it out until he was gone once more, which, if rumour was true, would only be a matter of months now.

As field merged with hedgerow, fence post with stream, she drifted into a world of fantasy, allowing herself to imagine scenarios still unexplored. A first date, a first kiss, an evening spent hand in hand, arm in arm, touching, holding, feeling... She tripped and stumbled on a root sticking out of the ground and looked up. Where *was* she? Realising she must have lost her way, Jenny headed back the way she had come and rectified her route, finally continuing on her trail, relieved to have been alone and unobserved.

With her new resolution echoing in her mind, she decided to clarify her plan with the hope of easing her pain. "He. Doesn't. Want. Me. He. Doesn't. Want. Me," her thoughts sang back as her feet fell hard on the ground. And when the reality of that had finally hit home, she changed tack with a new voice. "I. Don't. Need. Him. I. Don't. Need. Him." It was something she had to learn, however hard the bite, for it was in *her* power to determine the rest of her life and she was not willing to be a doormat for anyone.

Staggering back home from a pace a bit more ambitious than usual, Jenny hit the shower and got ready for work. It was a double-edged sword, working on a surgical ward and being smitten with an emotionally stunted anaesthetist. The upside was that she got to see him far more than if she had worked on any other ward, but the downside was the same. Agony and ecstasy in equal measure.

Jenny stood at the nurses' station, listening to handover. All around her, work carried on as usual: trollies wheeled about, rattling cups and saucers, instruments and trays, and patients pressed their buzzers. Incessant demand. And then Dr Peter Florin breezed past and the world about her stopped. Jenny's heart trembled and she forced herself to focus back on the job in hand, but not before noticing the heaviness of his gaze and the thin set of his lips.

She had seen him like this before, years ago, when he first came to work at St Steven's. She had forgotten how his moods could flip like a light switch. Five long years he had been out of her life. But not any more. And now she had become one of those sad women who look at a man and think they can change him. Like she was so special that he would do anything just to be with her! She rolled her eyes at her own folly. Why was she always so weak when it came to him? Her heartbeat surged faster every time he was near. She had learned to be strong before, hadn't she? But strength hadn't brought her happiness. Could it eventually set her free?

The shift rolled by, mundane, nothing special, but that night Jenny felt uneasy. The fact that she was noticing little changes, subtle details about him, made it clear to her that her heart was still in peril. So to protect herself she made a solemn promise. Not until she was convinced he wanted her, *really* wanted her, not just her body, but *all* of her. Would she let him in? And she was determined to stick by this. She wobbled at the thought of a single night of unbridled passion with Pete, something so many others had known. No, she couldn't. She had learned the consequences of that one a long time ago. For her it had to be different. She had to be sure... should ever the occasion arise.

He was looking as though that cloud was back over his head again today, she wrote in her diary that night. How I wish I could brush away those cobwebs. Take him in my arms and feel his weight against me.

Turmoil raged within her. Her romantic heart beating wildly against her mind. Be strong, Jen, she thought. You mustn't forget. As Flis had found out, loss of hope would be far worse than this.

The next morning she was on an early and the ward was bedlam. The anaesthetist for Mr Hammond's list had failed to turn up for work and so everyone had been delayed while the doctors shifted around to cover them. Jenny checked the chart. Friday – am - Dr Florin. Pete was meant to be gassing that morning; it was *Pete* who hadn't turned up for work. Probably woken up in the wrong bed, she thought.

Jenny had hoped he'd have grown out of this behaviour by now, but it seemed not. She remembered he'd got into trouble more than once for having too many days 'sick' last time he was around. She wanted to be angry at him, shirking his responsibilities. It went against every principle she held to, but she couldn't. She would get Kate to have a word with him again when she got back from her holiday. The two of them seemed to get on well together. Maybe *she* could do something to sort him out.

That evening a group of nurses were planning to meet up in town and then head over to Helix for Maisie's hen night. Sadly, Jenny was starting to feel a little old to show her face in a nightclub, especially on a Friday night. She probably had ten years on the majority of those there, but she was happy enough to go for a drink beforehand.

Heather and Chloe, her two other housemates, knocked on her bedroom door. "Come on, Jen. We don't want to be late. Flis'll want to hear all the juicy gossip when she gets off work later. Hurry up," they called.

Jenny opened her door and beamed. She scrubbed up pretty well, even if she did say so herself.

"Wow, you look great," Heather said, just as a horn blared outside. The two young nurses squealed. "The taxi!" and they hurried out to get started on their evening.

15

Jenny stood in the doorway of the Swan Inn and looked around. She was wearing a short brown leather jacket, skinny blue jeans, heels and her diamond stud earring in the top of her ear. She spotted the group of nurses out celebrating the impending wedding and a cheer went up as the three of them joined in.

Jenny was enjoying the evening, having a laugh and a drink with the girls, and on the way to the toilets, she spotted a face she knew. It was Pete, but not the Pete she was used to. He was sitting in a dark corner, his eyes empty, lost somewhere in a world of his own. Gone were the smiles and charm of the daytime. His expression was dulled and his shoulders hunched. What could have happened? She had just decided to go over and talk to him when he looked up and spotted her. A look of defiance lifted his chin and he grabbed the woman clearing the table, hauling her onto his lap, and in the blink of an eye there he was again: the charmer, springing back into action. Jenny walked on. Of course, she thought. As if *he* would ever be lonely!

Later that evening, as the others made their way on to the nightclub, Jenny walked outside to catch a cab home, and standing on the pavement waiting for her ride, she looked back through the window and noticed Pete, still in the same place he'd been sitting all evening, his head, once again, hung over his pint.

It was a more sombre note she wrote in her diary that night.

Today his eyes were downcast and his features drawn, and yet still he had the power to turn my bones to jelly. I wonder what has happened. Why was he missing at work today and why was he all alone on such a lovely summer's evening?

Maybe I'm just kidding myself, looking for a reason to feel sorry for him. He could easily have been meeting some beautiful woman a little later on, for a night of fabulous, raw, all-consuming passion. Passion... with Pete. I bet he's good... He should be. He's had enough practice!

But he didn't look happy. Why wasn't he happy? He's gorgeous. He's got a body to die for, beautiful eyes, handsome and clever.

Everybody likes him. Why wasn't he happy?

If only Kate was here, instead of halfway round the other side of the world, she could have spoken to her about it.

Jenny put the cap back on her pen, slumped against her pillow and stared at the ceiling. So many of her friends had been happily married off in the past few years. She'd lost track of the number of weddings she'd been to. Only a few of them remained single now - a dying breed. Even fickle old Flis had a steady boyfriend. She felt old.

The hospital was full of pretty young nurses now too. Of course they weren't half so good at nursing, she thought, not like in her day. Training had been far better when she had come through, but they would learn.

Sharing a house with a couple of young nurses brought it home to her every day, the difference in mind-sets. If Pete was still single, *if* he was single, he was never going to look at her now. She thought back to all the stupid stunts she had pulled in her younger days, all in the pursuit of happiness. You couldn't win love. She had learned that now. You just had to wait and hope that it was given.

Still, it was only a matter of time until he would be moving on again. Then maybe she could try and find love in other places, in men who didn't make her stomach dance every time they walked in the room and who couldn't make her fingers tremble at the sound of their voice.

Time. Time was a cruel thing. In the years since they had first met, Pete had only managed to look more and more attractive. But he was the complete opposite of what she needed. 'Dependable' and 'committed' were not words to be associated with the dashing Dr Florin. Caring of his patients, yes. Brilliant at his work, maybe. But not reliable. Not solid. But with all his faults, and she knew they were many, Jenny still longed to make him happy, to watch those eyes shining with delight, to see him smiling back at her like they had done once before, a long time ago, and to tell him how much his words had meant to her.

17

Pete walked in and looked over her shoulder. "Where have you got to?" he asked.

"Just about to start on you," she said.

He winced. "Can I get you a cup of tea? I was just about to make one."

Jenny turned around and looked at him. "Tea would be lovely, thank you," she said. "Now push off. I can't concentrate with you hovering around, looking over my shoulder." She smiled.

"I'm going, I'm going," he told her and winked before he closed the door, and then she was alone again.

Pete didn't know what all the fuss was about. All he had done was offer to buy the girl a drink. There was no need to go all macho over it. Besides, she hadn't exactly said no, had she? In fact, she seemed quite keen on the idea of the two of them getting it on, he'd thought. So she had a boyfriend, so what? It wasn't like they were married, or anything.

Pete's elbow slipped and his head fell forward onto the counter, knocking him in the eye. Maybe he *had* had enough. He rallied, only to find a complete bear of a guy standing before him. Pete hoisted himself up, his vision beginning to blur. "Come on, now. I don' wanna figh' you." He attempted to pat the man on the shoulder, but his judgement was off and he only succeeded in shoving him in the chest, annoying him even further. The man stepped closer, snarling.

"I'n warnin yooou," he slurred, swaying. "I know martial ahts an' I'm a damn goo' boxer too." He reached over to take a swig of his drink, missed and managed to spill his pint along the bar, splashing the already angered man. The bear in front of him growled and from the beer-sodden haze, lights suddenly sparked all around him. Pain, like dynamite exploding in the side of his face, penetrated the cotton-wool cloak of his mind and he was wrapped in darkness.

Chapter 2

"Come on, Pete. Pete?"

A slap brought Pete round and he stirred, disorientated.

"Wake up, mate."

Pete squinted into the light and colours tore into him. A dark shape formed in front of what looked like… a ceiling. He struggled to pull the shape into focus and then realised it was a face he knew well. He beamed. "Jimmeeee! What're you doing here?"

James Florin picked up his brother and apologised to the staff and customers around him. He dropped a couple of notes on the bar and hoisted him up to standing. "Come on, mate. Let's get you home."

Outside the pub, James managed to persuade a taxi driver to accept them (for a premium) and wrestled his brother inside.

Pete's home was in an old Georgian building on the edge of town. It had been converted into flats at some stage, badly, without style or grandeur; a basic set of rooms, where doctors on various rotations stayed for the duration of their job.

At the front door, he rifled through Pete's pockets to find his door key.

"Ooh, cheeky," Pete teased, wobbling precariously against one arm while James struggled to open the door with the other.

He lugged him across to his bedroom and dropped him down

onto the bed. With a lot of encouragement, he managed to get a pint of water down Pete, and on him for that matter, and then he pulled off his shoes and covered him with his duvet. It was going to be a long night.

James picked out his phone and rang home. "Rach, it's me."

"Jamie, did you find him?"

"Yeah."

"Same again?"

"I think so. He's out for the count at the moment, but I'll speak to him in the morning."

"Don't forget to put him into the recovery position and then you really must try and get some sleep, sweetheart."

"I might nod a bit. But I think maybe I should stay awake," he said.

There was a pause on the other end of the phone.

"It's not his fault, Rach," he told her.

"It's not *yours* either."

"I know, but I have to help him. I owe him that much, at least."

"Still?" She let out a long breath. "It was all such a long time ago, Jamie. Haven't you done enough?"

"I'll ring you tomorrow," he told her.

"I love you," she said.

"Love you too. Give the kids a kiss from me."

"Will do."

James made sure Pete was safe to go to sleep and then settled himself in a chair beside him, ready to keep vigil for the night.

At five-thirty the next morning, Pete's body stirred to the chirruping song of a bird sat on the ledge outside of his window. A groan released the breath from his lungs and he pulled his hands to his head. James awoke from the brief, drowsy haze that had overtaken him just before dawn. He looked across. "Morning," he said, and waited for the light of comprehension to take form behind Pete's eyes.

"What day is it?" Pete asked.

"Saturday."

Pete lifted his head and peered at the light stretching in around the curtains. Apart from the relentless chatter of the birds outside, there was silence all around them. "What time?"

"Early."

Pete sucked in a deep breath and winced. "My head."

"Is as much as you deserve. In fact you're bloody lucky I showed up when I did."

Pete was confused. He was usually grateful for the blur that followed one of these binges, but this time there was nothing.

"It seems you decided to hit on some poor young woman waiting for her boyfriend at the bar."

Pete cringed and let out a sigh.

"Where are your pain-killers?" James asked him.

Pete pointed to his bedside drawer and James reached in, popped a couple out and handed them to his brother. He fetched some fresh water and then sat down again while Pete knocked back the tablets with practiced ease. There was a moment of silence between them.

"How long this time?" James asked him.

Pete looked up. His head sank back down again and he rested back. "Thursday night..."

James shook his head. "Why do you keep doing this to yourself, Pete?"

"I-"

"Had the dream?"

Pete opened his mouth to protest, but then closed it again. "Something like that."

James looked at him, his head shaking slowly. "Why can't you just let it go, mate? It's been *years*. Even Adam's managed to move on since then."

"Adam didn't kill anyone, though, did he?" Pete said, his tone flat.

James pierced his brother with a solemn look. "Neither did you."

Pete shrugged. "Semantics."

James rolled his eyes and let out a deep sigh. "The courts exonerated you of all responsibility, Pete. You weren't the one to blame."

"Wasn't I?"

"It was an accident. Shit happens. You can't carry on beating yourself up over this for the rest of your life. You're just throwing it away. It wasn't *you* killed in that car that night, you know?"

"Maybe it should have been." Pete closed his eyes and the dream replayed inside his head. Desolation swept across his face as the turmoil of the memory evolved once again. He couldn't get past it, try as he might. Sometimes he thought he had cracked it, but the dream just kept recurring, bringing it all back and refreshing the agony again.

His voice calmed, aware he had snapped at his brother and he shouldn't have. If it wasn't for Jimmy he would have nobody. "I'm not sure I can," he admitted, his voice barely more than a whisper. "I'm not even convinced I want to."

"You need to get some counselling," James told him. "I can't keep driving around bailing you out all the time. You need to get yourself some proper help."

Pete let out a puff of derision. "Nobody asked you to keep coming here." He winced and held onto his head. "How *did* you know?"

"It was Shane's stag night last night."

"Shit! I'm sorry. I'll call him. Tell him I was ill or something."

"I've already told him. But *you* can ring and apologise. When you didn't answer your mobile or your door, I started making my way around the pubs again. I got lucky. Third one this time. You're getting more predictable, Bro."

Pete let out a choke of unhappy laughter.

"Look, I don't mind for me," James told him. "But I think Rach would be happier if you stopped trying to drink yourself into oblivion."

23

Pete smiled and shook his head. "Tell her I'm sorry, won't you. And I *am* grateful. Really."

"It's your future I worry about," James told him, after the moment had settled again. "You've got some big exams coming up soon and you seem determined to mess it all up again. All that work you've put in. Don't throw it away like this."

"I know, I know."

"So you'll get some help?"

Pete took the path of least resistance. Not in a million years was he planning on sitting down with some poxy counsellor and spilling his guts to a random stranger, but his brother was looking at him, desperately concerned and with such grave fear in his eyes, so he nodded.

"Good. We'd better get some food into you before I get back home to my long-suffering wife and then you can start getting your act together and get things straightened out. You might want to give your liver a break while you're at it. And the female population, for that matter. There can't be many women you haven't been through left around here now, are there?"

Pete gave him a withering look and thought of the face that had pierced him with enigmatic eyes the night before, or was it the one before that? One of the few supposed to be 'off limits' (if Kate had anything to do with it). Jenny Wren: stunningly beautiful, bold and disapproving, devastatingly sexy and tantalising as hell. But she had witnessed the rage inside him. Her turbulent nature and mysterious, all-seeing eyes were unsettling to him. It would be dangerous to get too close to her. From the confines of his mind, however, the delicious taste of fantasy was a spectacular thing.

"One or two," he said.

Monday morning Pete was back in work and, on the surface of it, happy as a pig in mud. His consultant gave him a dressing down for his no-show the Friday before, but he apologised and managed to talk his way out of it, claiming a brief stomach bug, and all was forgiven (on the understanding that his lack of communication never happened again).

New faces appeared on the wards as a couple of young nurses joined the team and Pete was revived for the moment. He flicked his predator switch to "on", cranked up the charm and watched as fresh eyes turned dreamy; he was back on form.

Pete gassed and consulted with patients for different lists for the following day, and then he went home to his flat, where he had no need of bravado, except for himself.

For some reason he felt out of sorts that evening. He couldn't put his finger on why, but he was uneasy. He couldn't settle and he needed to; he had exams coming up, even his brother had mentioned them. He looked at the great pile of books crouching ominously at the side of his desk and he had every intention of working. He had an ENT list in the morning, so it would have been an ideal time to recap on the problems particular to that and the different strategies for dealing with them. But instead, he shoved a shepherd's pie in the microwave and flicked on the TV. Tomorrow night, he thought, when he was feeling better. It wasn't worth trying to study when you weren't on top form.

The following afternoon, Jenny was on a late, and the feeling on the ward, as she walked on, was seriously off. Red-rimmed eyes and softly spoken whispers crowded in on her on all sides. The new shift was quickly rounded up and taken into an empty room.

"I have some incredibly sad news to tell you all," Debbie, the nurse in charge, said. "This morning, we were informed that two days ago, whilst on holiday in the Caribbean, Mr and Mrs Elliott, together with their daughter, were lost at sea when the yacht they were sailing capsized in a freak storm. Their bodies have been recovered and there will be a funeral when they've been returned home. I'm sure we'll hear more nearer the time, but for now, that's all we've got. I'm very sorry."

Whatever was said after that, Jenny never heard it. What a way to hear about your friend's death. Debbie wasn't to know they'd been close, but... Kate was dead? No. Kate; her oldest friend and partner-in-crime. *And* Adam. Poor Adam, who had turned out to be such a lovely guy, surprising them all. And even little Selena... all gone. Maisie passed across a tissue. Jenny hadn't even noticed the tears flowing down her face until then. She took the tissue and dabbed at her eyes numbly. She couldn't process it, so she did all she could do; she worked.

Turning to the nurse in charge, her voice said, "Can we get on?" and she wandered out onto the ward.

The shift drifted by in a surreal daze, but that evening, when she walked in, Jenny found Flis sobbing her heart out on the settee. She walked over; they looked at each other and then folded up in each other's arms and wept. "I know. I know. It's so unfair," she said, pulling back and plucking a tissue to wipe her face. She passed one to Flis. "After all the good they've done for others, and just when it was all starting to come together for them."

"It just doesn't seem real," Flis sobbed, pulling another tissue clear to wipe her nose. "Adam had only just... And Kate... Our Kate." She shook her head. "All gone. It's just... It's such a terrible waste!"

They talked for a while, gradually turning the tide and reminiscing about the fun times they'd shared and then, with neither of them having much appetite, they put on a late-night chat show and stared at the screen, before drifting off to bed.

Kate is dead, Jenny wrote in her diary that night. Kate and Adam and Selena. What can I say? It's too tragic for words.

Jenny was off the following day, so she spent her time trying to keep her mind busy. She rang her aunt to see how she was doing. As her dearest relative, Jenny felt very protective of her. She had been the one who'd taken care of her since the age of 17, a time when she had needed so much and been granted so little.

Jenny got through all her laundry and stocked up on food and then, having no more chores left to do, she decided she would finally succumb and lose herself in Lorna Doone, a story she had always wanted to read but had never quite got around to. She didn't want to face her inner thoughts that night, couldn't bear to, so she just kept on reading until she fell asleep.

Thursday she was back in work and rumour was sweeping through the hospital that Dr Florin had disappeared again. This time Jenny *was* cross. At a time when everything seemed suddenly so vital, such a gift to be living, *he* had decided to bail out. He was probably skulking around somewhere with a bottle and a bad woman. It was as if he didn't even care. She knew the three of them had been friends, but so had she. The man had no backbone. How was he ever going to make consultant carrying on like this? He certainly didn't deserve to. Jenny was disappointed. There were Kate and Adam trying to do so much good with their lives and living life to the full, and they had been cut down in their prime and here *he* was just pouring it away.

Her mood got under her skin and she bristled at the thought of what he was up to, instead of what he should be doing, which was taking care of all those people on the wards waiting for him. The anaesthetist was the one they most relied on, the one whose very presence could easily calm their fears. "No good, womanising, beer-swilling…" She ran out of words, and it pained her to see him through different eyes.

But by Friday he was still nowhere to be found. Rumours were flying about. Some said he was lying dead in his flat, although Jenny noticed this was mostly put about by those whose hearts he'd broken. Had he suffered bereavement in the family Jenny wondered? Was he lying in a hospital miles away? Or had he finally been thumped hard enough by some boyfriend or husband and lost his memory? Wherever he was, and whatever he was doing, there wasn't one scenario that looked good for him.

A shadow had been cast over the staff at the hospital. One missing, considered reckless, and two lost for good. Time dragged by on every shift as the light and ease of everyday mirth was suppressed by the weight of their loss.

The funeral was arranged for the following week, and luckily for Jenny, she was free that day. Flis was working and the other two in the house were so new they'd barely had time to get to know Kate, or Adam, so she was going on her own and she was daring Pete not to show.

The day arrived and it was bright and sunny. As one of Kate's closest friends, Jenny found herself invited to Kate's parents' house before the service. As she approached, she sadly found no need to recheck the address. Curtains were drawn and flowers had begun to carpet the front lawn up the edge of the driveway. Jenny walked up to the front door, took a deep breath and rang the bell.

A gentleman introduced himself as Kate's uncle and showed her inside and Jenny looked round for someone she might know. More flowers attempted to brighten the inside of the house, but the lost looks on the faces there overpowered them all. She met Gloria in the hallway, a nurse she knew from A&E and they hugged. It was one of those brief, stoical hugs that dared not linger in case it broke the fragile façade and brought on the tears.

"Hi, Jen. I just need to quickly check on Lena." They walked the few steps to the living-room door and peered through. On the far side of the room was a young girl, about 18 or so, Jenny thought, sitting on her own among a selection of empty chairs, her eyes downcast. Gloria took a calming breath, paused for a second and then turned away. Jenny looked at her.

"She's had a tough time recently. I just need to keep an eye on her," she explained.

They walked further back, into the kitchen, where she was introduced to Kate's mum and Rebecca, her sister-in-law. Jenny offered her condolences and gave Kate's mother the same brief hug she had given Gloria. She stood back and tried to collect herself.

Another relative walked in and the family were distracted, so Jenny wandered over to the back window.

In the corner of the garden stood two men: the father and a

brother, she assumed. They were standing, locked in a powerful embrace that almost broke her heart. It was too intimate a moment to pry on, so she turned back to face away again.

Gloria offered to make her a cup of tea, but just as she was about to pour, word filtered through that the cars had arrived. It was time to go.

Not a single eye was dry by the time the service had finished, but in all the sadness and tragedy of the day, Jenny had not missed the fact that there had been one face that hadn't shown: Pete. And although she wanted to be angry at him, all she felt was pity. She didn't know him that well, but she knew he had been friends with both of them and unless he had a solid reason for not being there, she felt sure that he would regret missing the goodbye… one day.

After the interment, the congregation began to split up and Jenny started looking around for the kind couple who had given her a lift. She was just starting to believe they had forgotten and gone without her, when from behind a large yew tree at the side of the church, she spotted a flash of blonde hair. She took a step back and then prowled across to investigate.

The graveyard was virtually empty now, apart from one elderly couple walking slower than the rest. It was just her and the blonde figure behind the tree.

Jenny stepped around the corner and was startled by a figure she barely recognised. Drawn and pale, like a frightened ghost, stood Peter Florin.

Chapter 3

Jenny went to reach out to him, but he flinched away. "Pete? Whatever's the matter?" she asked him. "You look awful. And why were you hiding back here? Why didn't you come and pay your respects with the rest of us?" Her mouth moved again to scold him, but something in his demeanour made her hesitate. She looked into his eyes and saw the turmoil inside him. The guy was in torment and her voice fell to a whisper. "What is it, Pete?"

A woman appeared across the far side of the churchyard, calling and beckoning to her. "Jenny, dear, there you are. I'm so sorry. We got to the end of the road before we remembered we were meant to be giving you a lift. Hurry along! I've left Harold in the car with the engine running."

Jenny waved. "I'll be right there." She turned back to Pete and put her hand on his chest and felt his heart beating wildly beneath her fingers. His stare widened at the contact and, afraid, she let her hand drop away. She pulled out an old till receipt from her bag and quickly wrote her number on it. "Call me," she said. "Please. I want to help. You can trust me." And she stuffed it into his hand and hurried away to catch up with her lift.

Two things were troubling Jenny more than everything else that night, twisting and clambering at the corners of her mind. First, the disturbing sight of Pete, looking lost and alone in the empty graveyard, and second... the tiny coffin. So much was going on inside Jenny's mind, that the desperate loss of her good friend was getting overshadowed. She needed order, so she pulled out her diary and tried to make sense of it all.

The day was as awful as I'd expected, she wrote. Three coffins and almost 100 people mourning. It was both beautiful and terrible in one fell swoop.

And the tiny coffin. It was so small and sad. How I made it through that without falling to pieces, I will never know. After all this time. I thought I had buried it so far down that it was like a dream, but it still tore at my heart to think of it... of her.

I saw *him* there too – after. He showed up. His eyes hollowed out and his face drawn and grey. How could I be angry at such a sorry sight? I'm afraid for him, though. I think he might be losing it. I don't know what it is that's haunting him, but it's eating him up inside. Maybe all that flash exterior is just a mask for something far deeper going on. I hope he calls me. He has to. I won't be able to rest until I know he's okay. What a state he was in. If this turns out to be just a guilty conscience after sleeping in with a serious hangover, I'm going to kill him. Where has he been?

Oh, Kate, I need you. Pete needs you. Your mum and dad need you. You should have seen them today. I hope you did, them and everyone else, because then you would have seen how very much you were loved.

She couldn't go on. Words were swimming around the page, so she set down her pen and curled up in a tight ball, and wept... for them all.

Far across town, on a coach heading west, Pete sat looking at his reflection in the window. Barely recognising his features or the thoughts that lay behind them, he settled back in his seat, let his mind drift and was soon swallowed up by the memories that claimed him.

The next day on the ward, a sober turn of mood replaced the
saddened one of before. No one had seen anything of Pete, and
Jenny was starting to worry.

By Friday, whispers were circulating that he was going to lose
his position. And when there was still no sign the Monday of the
following week, Jenny made up her mind that she was going to hunt
him down. She had already asked around to see if anyone knew
what was going on. Flis seemed less than interested, preparing
to head off for a fortnight on holiday with her man; none of the
staff at work had seen him at all and now the scandal was starting
to take on new excitement. Only Jenny seemed to actually care.

She sought out Laura Engelmann, another anaesthetist, in her
lunch break and heard from her how little anyone in the department knew about what was going on. Pete hadn't been answering
his mobile and there had been no sign of him at his flat. She asked
about his friends and Laura pointed her towards Dave Matthews,
a surgical registrar, who seemed to know him better than most.
At the end of her shift, Jenny went in search of Mr Matthews, but
he was in theatre and wouldn't be free for hours, so she left him
a note and her number and went back home to wait.

He called her that evening, just as Jenny was finishing her tea.
She answered. "Hello."

"Is that Jenny White?" the voice asked.

"Yes."

"Dave Matthews. You wanted to speak to me?"

"Yes, thank you. It's about Pete. Peter Florin."

"Yes, I know. What did you want to know? Your note was
very cryptic."

"I'm just worried about him."

"Well, we all are."

"But is anybody actually trying to find him?"

"He's a grown man. I'm sure he's got his reasons for disappearing like this. He'll probably be with his family if something's wrong."

"But how do you know he's okay?"

"Pete can handle himself just fine, I assure you," he said.

"Look, I saw him," Jenny said abruptly, the frustration of beating her head against a brick wall finally getting to her.

"You did? When?"

"After the funeral. And he looked *awful*."

There was a pause at the other end of the line.

"He has... issues; don't ask me what they are, I've no idea, he doesn't say, but he does this now and again. Admittedly not for this long normally."

He paused again and Jenny could think of nothing else to say that might persuade him to help. She heaved a deep sigh.

"He has a brother who seems to look out for him," he said. "I met him once. If you're really concerned, I'm sure he'd be the best person to talk to."

"Do you have his number?" she asked, hope suddenly flickering to life inside her.

"Afraid not. But I think he said he lived in Teak. Yes, I remember, because it reminded me of the wood. It's a little village, or something, outside Upper Conworth."

Jenny wrote down the name and thanked him for his time. She had two days off before she had to be back in work and this was her mission: she was going to find Peter Florin, wherever he was, and try to sort out whatever mess he was in. She owed him that. He had been there for her once. He had seen her struggle and had given her the strength to pull through, to stand up for herself. It was he who had made her believe she was worth more. He had cared. And dear Kate had cared for him, and she had known him better than all of them. But it was down to her now, that much was clear, and she was going to find him.

That night she studied maps and timetables, working out her route, before finally searching directory inquiries for a Mr Florin in Teak. And it must have been a tiny place because she got lucky;

33

there *was* only one: number six, Stoney Cross, and two minutes later, Google had him pinned. She printed out a map and wrote herself directions and then made a bag ready for the morning.

That night she had a sense of real hope when she wrote in her diary.

When I return, I will have found him. Someone has to care where he is. He needs a friend right now. He was a friend to me once, when I needed it. I don't know why he's like this, but whatever he is facing, he obviously can't deal with it on his own. So I'm going to find him and I'm going to bring him back. Somehow. God, I hope I can do this. I hope I'm not too late. What if I am? What if he's...? No, I can't think like that. This has to work, because I just can't lose him as well. I can't. I won't.

*

There was a knock at the door and two little faces huddled in cautiously. "It's bedtime, Mummy," they said.

Jenny stopped typing and turned around in her chair. She looked at her watch. "Oh my goodness, so it is!" she said. Holding her arms out wide, the two little girls ran over and cuddled in. She lifted them briefly on to her lap and kissed them. "Have you brushed your teeth?"

"Yes," they chorused, showing her the tiny white pearls that she cherished.

"Absolutely dazzling! Would you like me to read you a bedtime story?"

Their dad appeared at the door and they looked at him. "Are you up to it?" he asked softly.

Jenny nodded.

"Just a quick one, then, and then your mum is going to have a rest before she sits her bottom down there and starts writing again." He looked at her then, with such adoration, that Jenny had to agree. She knew he was only thinking about her and so

34

she would let him care for her for a while, but not too long; the story was far from finished.

*

Jenny awoke with the birds. She was too excited to sleep. She wanted to be up and out of there. She wanted to find Pete, but the first bus didn't leave for another three and a half hours, so she rechecked her bag, added a packet of chocolate Hobnobs for emergencies and went for a shower.

Still three hours to go. She began tapping her fingers. What could she do until then? She pulled everything out of her bedside drawer and plopped it down on the bed. Junk. It was all junk. She spent two minutes trying to sort it through and then lost all patience and shoved it back inside the drawer again, cramming it down and forcing it shut. She didn't want to concentrate on something good in case she lost track of the time, so she couldn't read a book, but she couldn't think of how else to fill the time. Breakfast. She had to eat. Lord knows when she was going to get to eat again.

Pacing the floor with a muesli bar, she added her book and her MP3 player, in case the hours on the bus were long. She knew where she was going to start, but had no idea where the journey would end. Maps, purse, biscuits, bottle of water, wash kit and comb, spare pair of pants and an extra layer in case it turned chilly. All she needed now was a brass neck as wide as a mountain to go nosing into business she had no reason to be messing in. But this had never been a problem for Jenny; attitude and nerve were her speciality. She'd been an independent soul most of her adult life. She'd had to be, and they had helped her survive.

With two hours left to go, Jenny left the girls a note, checked her mobile, packed her charger and headed off to walk the three or four miles to the bus station. The weather was mild and the walk would do her good before a couple of hours cooped up in a stuffy old bus. So she'd be early; it didn't matter; it was nice out.

As the journey drew on, Jenny became more and more determined in her venture. Mile after mile of countryside passed by outside the window, and then finally, the bus pulled to a stop in Upper Conworth.

Jenny stepped out and found herself in a quaint old market town bathed in sunshine. People in the street went about their business, happy and carefree, or so it seemed. She pulled out her sunglasses and slipped them on before retrieving the directions from her bag. She checked the bus route to take her to Teak: the number 24. She had 40 minutes before it left, so she decided to have a bit of a look around and maybe get something to eat.

Not far into town Jenny came across a café serving an all-day breakfast. By now she was starving and her anxieties allayed for the moment, she tucked in to a fry-up and a nice mug of tea and then, map in hand, she made her way back through the town to find her stop for the next leg of the journey.

It was a slower trundle through the outlying villages before Jenny spotted the sign she was looking for. The bus stopped and she checked with the woman on the seat next to her. "Is this Teak?" she asked.

The woman nodded and Jenny made her way down the bus and stepped off. And it was only then, as the bus pulled away and she was left on her own in a village she had never known, that she started to feel anxious. The weight of her mission had seemed so important that before arriving in Teak she had been confident in her intrusion, but now... here... possibly only yards away from where Pete might be, she began to question herself.

What if he was fine and had just had enough of his job? What then? What was she going to do if it was a woman who had tempted him? How would that make her feel? What if his brother turned her away? And how small and stupid would she feel if he appeared at the door, happy as a child at Christmas and totally bemused to see her?

36

Jenny stood watching as the bus disappeared around the bend, and then, hoisting her rucksack onto her shoulder, she fished the instructions out of her pocket. She had drawn a rough plan of the village on the back of the timetable and she turned it around in her hand until she had her bearings and then looked up. Over there, she thought, and blocking out all worries for the time being she made her way up the road in the direction of Stoney Cross.

A postman walked by. "Good day," he said and Jenny smiled and greeted him warmly, but whether it was *going* to be a good day remained to be seen.

She passed a pub and took a left, then a right and followed the road to the end, to a small nook of houses tucked away around the back: Stoney Cross.

Nerves began to rise as she approached the front door of the house. She really hadn't given much thought to what would happen next. All she had known was she needed to find him. The rest, she supposed, would take care of itself. There were no cars in the driveway now. Was nobody at home? She took a deep breath and knocked. There was no answer. She looked around for a doorbell and found it, camouflaged against the frame of the door. She pressed it once. Still nothing. What was she supposed to do now? There was little point in getting all this way and then turning back at the first hurdle, so she sat with her back to the garage door, her face to the sun, and waited.

After a while she became thirsty and drank some of her emergency bottle of water. Feeling bored, she put on her headphones and listened to some music, and after that, the next thing she knew, a car was pulling up in front of her and two feet were stepping out.

Chapter 4

Pulling off her headphones, Jenny scrambled to her feet. She shoved everything back into her bag and then, searching rapidly for the right words, she looked at the woman beside the car. For a moment she considered running, but she couldn't, not when she had come so far, so she forced herself to stay calm and started by apologising.

"I'm so sorry," she said, taking a hesitant step forward. "I didn't mean to fall asleep on your driveway. But I'm looking for Mr Florin. Have I got the right address?"

The woman kept her children safely inside the car, out of the way of the stranger invading their privacy. She had obviously found little reassurance in Jenny's explanation thus far, so she added, "It's about his brother. He's gone missing."

The woman's face fell. Reaching back inside the car, she undid the children's straps and herded them towards the front door. "You'd better come in."

Inside, the little children kept close to their mother while they assessed the stranger trespassing in their lives. "I'm Jenny White," she told them. "I'm trying to find Dr Peter Florin. I work with him."

"How did you find us?" the woman asked.

"Dr Matthews, one of his colleagues at the hospital, told me he had a brother who looked out for him."

The woman rolled her eyes. "For his sins."

"And he remembered Pete had mentioned the name of the village where you lived."

"Ah." She held out her hand. "I'm Rachel Florin, Jamie's wife, and these two horrors are Joshua and Annabel." The children were still looking at her cautiously. "Please, take a seat. Can I get you a drink? You look a bit flushed. I think you might have caught the sun there."

Jenny felt her face. It was tight and hot. "A glass of water would be lovely, thank you," she said.

Rachel ran her a glass of water and dropped in a couple of ice cubes. She handed it over and led her children away to settle them down to play. Jenny looked around the room. It was a nice, ordinary kitchen in a nice, ordinary house. The garden was smallish and littered with children's toys and the fridge was covered with paintings. It was a home, and for a minute, Jenny recalled a similar scene in her early childhood with affection.

Rachel returned with a bottle of moisturiser in hand. She offered it up and Jenny took it gratefully and smoothed some on.

"It's a lovely spot you've got here," she said.

Rachel smiled. She was busy searching in a cupboard for something. She stood up again, with a toy in her hand, obviously relieved. "If you don't mind, I'll just…"

Jenny was very aware she had intruded. "No. Please," she said, and she kept her silence while Rachel sorted out her children, leaving her own mind space to think. How had she got here? What was she doing? Doubt was champing at the bit for free rein and she had to battle hard to remember the reason she was there.

Rachel was soon back and the two women sat down with a drink. "So how did you say you knew Pete?" Rachel asked.

"I work at St Steven's. I'm a nurse."

Rachel looked at her and nodded. "And… are you his girlfriend?"

"Heavens, no!"

Rachel smiled. "Good. At least you're not so likely to attack him with a carving knife when we do find him, then."

Jenny smiled at her and held up her hands. "I'm unarmed, I promise."

"So, how long has he been missing this time?"

Jenny was a little surprised.

"It's not the first time," Rachel elaborated. "A couple of days? Three perhaps?"

"It's been well over a week. Almost two, in fact."

Rachel looked a little more concerned now.

"I was hoping he was here with you. You haven't seen or heard from him, have you?"

"Not for a couple of weeks, no. Not since the last time."

Jenny quickly joined the dots. "The Friday before?"

"Did he not go back to work after that?"

"Yes, he did. For one day, maybe two. I'm not sure. And then he was gone again."

Rachel frowned. "I'd better ring Jamie." She picked up the phone on the table near by and pressed a button. It rang several times and must have gone through to an answerphone. "Jamie, it's Rachel, please ring home when you get this. Don't worry, we're all fine, it's Pete. I think he needs you." She put down the phone again and turned back to Jenny. She looked at her watch. "Have you eaten lunch? Can I get you anything?"

"No, I'm fine, thanks. I had a big breakfast in town."

"You don't mind if I get the children theirs?" Rachel asked, getting up to have a rummage about the kitchen for something to feed them.

"Of course not," Jenny said. "Go ahead."

Rachel pulled out some cheese and grapes from the fridge and reached for the bread on the side. "What made you think he'd come here?" she asked, continuing to make the sandwich. "He usually stays in Duxley."

"Nobody's seen him," Jenny told her. "I've asked everyone I can think of."

Rachel was quiet for a long while after that and Jenny wondered if she was going to say any more. She took the children their lunches and returned to the kitchen.

"He's not really as bad as he makes out, you know," she said, sitting back down at the table, opposite her. "Pete... He used to be such a sweet guy: a steady, good-tempered, respectful lad. This isn't the real him... At least, I hope it's not."

Jenny looked at her, eager to learn more.

"He lost someone a few years ago and he blames himself. It's changed him. And not for the better, I'm afraid."

Rachel asked Jenny a little about herself and then they talked about the kids, and after Rachel had settled the children in front of the TV and cleared up the plates, she began to look pensive. "They had a tough childhood, you have to understand. It's made them very close. James doesn't talk much about it, but I've picked things up over the years. As a family it's never discussed at all, but I know some of what went on and I think Peter took the brunt of it, being the eldest."

Just then James walked in and strode straight up to his wife, he kissed her and then asked her what she had heard. Rachel introduced him to Jenny and he turned round and apologised for not having noticed her before. He was shorter and darker than his brother, Jenny observed. The years didn't show as clearly, but there was a lot about them that was alike. James's eyes were darker, but still bright and striking and he was attractive in a quiet, more reserved, way. He had that same dependable calm that seemed to radiate from him; like you could tell him the worst and he would still find a way to help you, but no hint of the edgy flirtation of his brother's style.

Rachel suggested the two of them go into the kitchen to talk and she would keep the kids busy in the living room.

"Has something happened to Pete?" James asked, the moment they were alone and Jenny recounted all that she knew and waited for James to decipher. "Well, a funeral would probably be hard for him, especially so soon after one of his bouts, but…"

"Do you mind me asking what these 'bouts' actually are?" she said, hoping to finally understand what they were dealing with.

"He gets recurrent nightmares about the night he was involved in a car crash. It's something he finds hard to deal with, still, after all this time. Did he know the person whose funeral it was well? Or was it perhaps a car crash that killed them?"

"It was three people, actually," she told him. "One of my friends died on holiday… with her husband… and their little girl."

"I'm so sorry." He automatically reached out and touched Jenny's hand. He seemed so kind and sincere and Jenny felt immediately comfortable with him.

"I think Pete was friends with both of them too: Adam and Kate. Did he ever mention them?"

James's face became ashen. "Adam? Not Adam Elliott?"

"Yes. Did you know him?"

James pulled out a chair and called for his wife, who came hurrying in. She took one look at her husband, pale and concerned, and looked across at Jenny.

"What is it?"

James reached out for his wife's hand and squeezed it hard. "Adam's dead," he said. "He was killed on holiday with his new family. Poor Jenny here was friends with them."

Rachel turned to Jenny. "Oh, I'm so sorry. Then this can't be an easy time for you, either. It's very kind of you to think of Pete."

"He might well have done the same for me, once," she told them. James looked curious.

"Look, is there something I'm missing here?" Jenny continued after a minute of watching their expressions.

"You're certain he's not been at his flat?" James asked.

"Certain. The caretaker checked and his phone was still there too."

"And he's not languishing in some pub or other?"

"Duxley's not a big town. I'm sure someone would have seen

or heard something by now if he was. Please tell me whatever it is that's so significant about Adam. I may be able to help, or at least, if not, it might give me a clue as to his state of mind."

James indicated that she should sit down too and she did as she was asked.

"The night of the crash, the thing that started this whole crazy rollercoaster off, Pete was the one who was driving. It was Ali, Adam's first wife who died. He blames himself for her death – which he shouldn't – but if Adam has died, and you said he was friends with his new wife too, he's going to take that pretty hard. We need to find him. *I* need to find him."

So that had been the pain he had been hiding. Old conversations came flitting through her head. Something Kate had said about blame all made sense now. He needed her, and she hadn't come all this way to be pushed to the sidelines now. "We," said Jenny.

"No, you stay here. I wouldn't feel comfortable dragging you around a load of pubs and gutters in a foreign town."

Jenny thought she was quite capable of handling herself these days. She'd taken self-defence classes and tried hard to keep herself fit. That was part of why she ran. But she didn't want to get his brother off side already. "You think he'll be here?" Jenny asked him.

James shook his head. "No, but I've got to start somewhere if he's not at home… I'll get going. Should be easier to find him at this time of day."

Reluctantly Jenny stayed at the house and tried to distract herself, playing with the children, while they waited for news. She wasn't happy being left behind when she'd been the one to set the ball rolling, but he was James' brother, so this once, she would let him try and find him alone. But if that didn't work, she was determined not to be pushed aside again.

At a quarter to eight James returned. He looked tired and Jenny knew at once that his search had been fruitless. Rachel crept downstairs, whispering that the children were finally asleep and he softly headed up to kiss them goodnight.

They tried to eat that evening, but none of them were hungry. They picked at what Rachel had prepared for them, but when even *she* pushed the last of it away, they all adjourned to the living room to regroup and plan their next move.

"I'll go back out in an hour or so," James said as they settled down to rest. "See if I can find him in a nightclub. He might not show his face until it goes dark." Rachel squeezed his hand.

"What if he isn't here?" Jenny asked.

James looked thoughtful. "Have you rung home to make sure he hasn't shown up *there* yet?"

"No. Good idea. Excuse me." Jenny got up and made her way out into the hallway. Who could she ring? It had to be someone who would know, but wouldn't ask too many questions. Dave Matthews; he should know. She rang his number. "Hello, Dave, it's Jenny. I'm with Pete's brother, in Teak. There's no sign of him here so far. Has he turned up with you yet?"

"Um, no. Not as far as I know. But if you find him, you'd better let him know that it's not looking good around here. According to Laura, he needs to come up with at least a phone call and a doctor's note soon or he'll be out on his ear."

"Okay. Thanks, Dave."

"Good luck."

She walked back and stood in the living room doorway. She shook her head and then sighed. "I should be making tracks, actually. The last bus leaves in 20 minutes and I haven't booked a bed for the night yet." She smiled and walked out towards the front of the house to gather her things.

Rachel appeared in the doorway. "We haven't got a spare room, I'm afraid, but you're welcome to crash on the couch if you'd like. I've got some spare bedding."

Jenny hesitated. "Are you sure it's no bother? I'm quite happy to get the bus. I wasn't expecting to stay."

James walked over to stand next to his wife. "No bother at all."

"Well, if you're offering? Thank you; I'd like that."

44

James returned before the night was through, but once again there had been no sign of Pete and before they made up Jenny's bed for the night, the three of them made plans for the morning.

Rachel was going to hunt down a photo of Pete on the family computer and then James would take it in to work, print off a load of copies and drop them back home as soon as he could so that Jenny could spend the day asking around Upper Conworth, and only then, if she had no luck, would they call the police.

That night, as Jenny tried to get some rest, wondering how she had ended up sleeping on the settee in Dr Florin's brother's house, she started to fear the worst. Pete had looked so awful the last time she'd seen him. She should have done more. She shouldn't have left him on his own like that, in a graveyard, of all places. What if he had taken his own life? Her blood ran cold as the possibility of this hit home. She wriggled around, trying to get comfortable and thumped the pillow next to her head. Where the hell was he?

Pete woke up in a room he didn't recognise. His brain graunched slowly into life. Home. Yes, he was going home. Travelling around the country trying to run from his past had been no help at all. All he felt now was an overwhelming urge to go home, but not to his childhood house, to somewhere safe.

Swinging his legs off the bed, he rubbed his face, took a swig of water and swallowed a handful of tablets to ease the lightning in his head. His throat was raw. He hauled himself up on shaky legs and looked out of the window.

He was nearly there now. He didn't want to eat, he just needed to get there, and so he splashed some water on his face and got ready to check out. Weary, so very weary. It was time to stop running.

As the bus brought him closer to his old life, anxiety pierced him like an arrow through his heart. He told himself no one lived there any more, that it was just a memory of what had been, but he struggled to contain it quickly enough. His stomach wrenched, threatening to humiliate him, but he gritted his teeth and, breathing slowly, he managed to suppress his nerves and loosely regain some semblance of control.

At his stop, Pete alighted and stood there, rigid and still. Others got off the bus and circled around him, their expressions enquiring, wondering what he was doing. A tabby cat purred at his feet and curled around him and as he became aware, he was distracted from his dream world. He reached down to smooth its fur, tickling the creature behind the ear. A dog barked in the distance and the cat startled and scuttled away.

Pete took a deep breath and looked up. If there was any other way to do this he would not be within a million miles of this house, but he need to get to his sanctuary and the only way he knew was from his home.

He began to walk up the road, his breathing controlled, but his mind was drifting further and further away from him. He turned the last corner and there it was. A shiver coursed through him, even though the day was warm, and flashbacks of rows and fights flickered through his mind. His mother crying. His father leading with his fists. He closed his eyes, trying to block out the pain. He was a grown man now; his dad couldn't hurt him any more. His mother was safe and far away from here. He had protected Jim and fought for them all. But there had been nobody left to fight for him. Nobody, except Ali.

The door of his old house opened and his heart forgot to beat. A chill slithered around him and then a woman with a little toddler walked out into the garden. Blinking, he realised he had to move on. He didn't want to alarm them. But the woman spotted him and walked over.

"Can I help you?" she asked, with concern in her eyes.

"No. I'm sorry. I was just looking. I… I used to live here."

"Would you like to have a look around?" she offered, but her voice shook at the end, as if she was suddenly afraid of his reply.

She let her hand reach up, protectively cradling the child in her arms and her body weight shifted.

He had frightened her. Pete shook his head. "No, thank you." He smiled wearily and walked away. He was as much of a curse as his father had been. He would remove himself from her happy home. At least it *was* a happy home now, he thought. Or was it? Who knows? Most people had thought his home had been a happy one.

Two doors along there was a path that lead back between the houses to a street on the other side. And there, right in front of him, was Ali's house. He wondered if her family still lived there. Sadly *she* never would again, but she was close by.

At the end of the road was a gateway and through this was his release. He could almost taste it. With more energy than he had known in days, he climbed over the gate marked 'PRIVATE, NO ENTRY' and headed up the lane into the woods. Familiar trees and bracken showed him the way, as his memory led him home.

It was the place where they had hidden when life became too frightening, when his mum had begged them to run and hide. Torn in two, he had desperately wanted to stay and help her, but he had run and protected Jimmy instead.

Brambles snagged at his calves as he tramped further and further into the wilderness. Unseeing eyes caused him to trip and he fell, face down in the mud, winded and confused. With no power to move, he lay there for a long while, until the cold of the ground came calling and he heaved at his bones to stand up. His face was sore and he noticed a trickle of blood collecting beside a stone on the ground. He wiped at it and tried to move, stumbling again with the pain. His ankle. It was pounding with a fury usually reserved for his head.

Pete looked around, searching for where he thought it should be. Although familiar, nothing was quite the same any more and, spotting a fallen branch, he lifted it, broke the rotten twigs away and used it as a crutch. He limped on and finally he found it: the den.

It was a little fort they'd made when he was about eight or nine, stealing a hammer and nails from his father's shed to build themselves an escape. It had been their secret - their second home - something they had needed to block out the threat and the fear. Some days he had left Jimmy there alone for hours, as he crept back home to check on his mother. But it only seemed to make matters worse. If it was bad, the images would torment him and plague him with guilt and if he was caught, as he occasionally was, he would pay the price and Jimmy would be left by himself even longer. So, as the years went by, he learned to spend more and more time out in the woods, blocking out what might be happening in the house.

The den was worn down by time now, but still it was standing there. Tattered remains of bin liners peeped out, nailed around the inside to protect from the wind and the rain. It had been added to as they'd grown bigger and more able. They did their homework inside it and made plans and alibis, excuses for bruises on school days and a code to let each other know when to run. They would never have survived without it, or... perhaps... perhaps if they had faced the music, if *he* had faced the music, his mother would have left the man earlier? He thought about this. Had she, in trying to protect them, only prolonged the agony? Who could say?

He ducked his head and stepped inside, crouching to look around him and see what remained. Nobody had touched it. It was on private land. Whoever it belonged to either didn't know or didn't care. Gingerly he rested on an old wooden box they had dragged inside many years before. It held his weight. Scratches from their knives, writing words in the wood, still remained to be seen and he ran his fingers across them and remembered.

Shivering in the dank shelter of the moss-covered hideaway, thrown back in time to a place he had tried to forget, Pete rested his head back and tried hard to picture the happier times: him and his brother playing make-believe in their fort... with Ali. His body ached. He was so tired. Life was tiring, and it was cold.

Chapter 5

Jenny walked around the streets of Upper Conworth, stopping anyone who would talk to her, to ask them if they had seen this man. She showed them the picture of Pete and willed each one of them to recognise him. She left her number on the back of the ones she'd placed in the pubs around town, but it was useless. She had been at it for hours and nobody had seen a thing. He could be anywhere by now. Hell, for all she knew he might even have his passport on him.

With a sigh she sat down on a wall, knowing time was fast running out for both of them. She had to be back in work the following day and Pete might have already lost his job. Jenny had to get back that night and they still hadn't found him. People were looking out for him at home and she was sure someone would have rung her if he had turned up. She had to think. If *she* was upset and she wanted to get away, where would she go? Home? Not likely. A friend? She had tried all the contacts she knew. So it was back to first principles. He had left his phone behind, but he would still need a place to stay. He probably had his wallet and since he wasn't at home and he wasn't with James... Maybe she should have been checking hotels? Jenny jumped up and looked around her. Hotels and B&Bs. Where should she start?

She walked around, calling in on any establishments renting

rooms. Door after door was opened and shut, with nothing new to report. She grabbed a pasty from a baker's she passed on her way, as the day was slipping past her and her body needed fuel. She had almost given up when she finally hit on some luck. In a small B&B on the edge of the town centre, at last, a lady remembered him.

"Quiet guy. Yes, I think it was him. He didn't look well, though. He checked out this morning."

Bingo! Well... almost. So he *had* been there. Now she just had to find where he had gone. "Did he give you any idea which way he was heading?" she asked.

"I'm afraid not, dear. He didn't say much at all. Looked like he had the worries of the world on his shoulders. Is he going to be all right?"

Jenny looked at her for a second. "I hope so," she said and then, smiling weakly, she thanked the woman and left.

Standing outside on the pavement, she rang Rachel. "He's here," she said.

"You've found him?"

"No. But he stayed in town last night. I found a B&B owner who thinks she recognises him from the photo."

"Well, good, at least we know we're on the right track."

"Can you think of anywhere else I can try? I've done around town, hotels, pubs; James did clubs, er..."

"Have you looked around the park? It's just a thought, but he did hang around there a bit when he was a teenager."

"No, I'll take a look, but if he's not there, I really don't know what to try next."

"Jamie will be home in an hour. If you haven't found him by then, come back here and we'll reconvene over tea."

"Right-oh."

Jenny put her phone back in her pocket and looked for the town plan on a billboard she had spotted close by, to find her way to the park. There were two, on opposite sides, but she had to make a choice, so she headed off in the direction of the largest one and kept her fingers crossed for a result, but on the bus back to Teak, Jenny's hope was fading. The last bus from Upper Conworth was leaving at nine o'clock that night and it was already past four. Three hours was all the time she had left to find him before she would have to start making her way back home, defeated, having failed him.

James and Rachel met her at the door as she walked up to the house, her stride slowing with her approach. She looked up at them, deflated. "I'm sorry," she said and they hugged her. They brought her in to sit down and within minutes she had a hot cup of tea in her hand and a couple of Jammy Dodgers in her lap. Jenny looked at them and made a small smile.

"I'm sorry; they're all I had," Rachel told her.

"No, they're great. I haven't had a Jammy Dodger in years. I'd forgotten how nice they were."

At tea, they sat together, trying to come up with an idea of where Pete could be.

"What about any other family?" Jenny asked, very aware that this might be a difficult subject.

James answered. "Well we used to live around here when we were little, but Mum moved away not long after Dad left. She's in Oxford now. She works at the university. She's a lecturer in Classics."

Jenny could see the sun rising in James's eyes as his pride in his mother shone through. She smiled. "She sounds like a clever woman."

"She is."

"And your dad?"

His expression faded. "I wouldn't know."

Silence weighed heavily on them as Jenny regretted her last words. She tried to think of something else to say. "Was there someone who would look out for him living near your old home? Somewhere else he would want to go?"

"No. We generally kept ourselves to ourselves. There were friends, but they're all grown up and gone now."

And then Rachel had an idea. "Didn't you tell me there was a place you used to go to when you wanted to get away?" she asked quietly.

"Yes, but… that was just a den, really. A hut in the woods where we hid when…"

Rachel looked at him and then at Jenny.

"You don't think…?" he asked. "It probably fell down years ago."

"But it's worth a try."

Twenty minutes later Jenny and James were in the car driving towards his old neighbourhood. Anticipation held their thoughts as they approached the house that had been the family home.

He pulled up by the kerb and they got out. As Jenny watched, James just stood on the pavement, saying nothing, his eyes empty, like a door leading nowhere. She touched him on the arm. "I'll go and ask if anyone's seen him, shall I?"

Jenny walked up the garden path to the front door and knocked. A minute later a woman appeared carrying a toddler covered in food. "Can I help you?" she asked.

Jenny grinned and the woman noticed the state of her child.

"I'm sorry. We were just finishing tea."

"I won't keep you a second," she said and pulled out a photo. "Could you tell me if you've seen this man around recently?" The woman looked concerned. "Don't worry; he isn't dangerous. We just need to find him."

The woman reached for the photo. "Yes. I have. Or at least I think I have. It looks like him, but he was in a bit of a state. Frightened me a little, if I'm honest, but I'm pretty sure it was him. He stopped by here earlier today. He said he used to live here."

"Yes, he did. Do you know where he is now?"

The woman's face fell. "I'm afraid not. But he walked off in that direction, if it's any help." The woman pointed off to one side.

Jenny thanked her and returned to James, still standing on the pavement.

"Well?"

"He was here. Today. He went that way," she said, pointing down the road.

James nodded. "He's there."

At this revelation, Jenny was expecting a sudden burst of energy, but instead they walked sedately down to a pathway and into another street. From there they walked out until they came across a gate. "We can't go in there," Jenny said as she noticed James beginning to climb over.

"You can stay here if you want," he said. "I need to find Pete."

Jenny didn't need too many seconds to decide on her course of action and quickly hopped over the gate to catch up with James. The pace was picking up now and Jenny clambered over fallen trees and past deep fern gullies until they came upon an old tumbledown wooden shack.

A few paces off, James stopped and stared. He seemed miles away. Jenny arrived beside him and cautiously moved ahead. James reached out and held her back. "No. I need to do this," he said. His words were soft, but full of warning, and suddenly Jenny was afraid. What was she about to see? What could be so bad that she needed to prepare herself to see it? She held her breath as James approached the decaying cabin and carefully leant in.

James disappeared inside and Jenny was left to wonder at what he'd found within. Moments became minutes, minutes, hours as Jenny waited for the verdict on their search for Pete. When she could bear it no longer, she took it upon herself to go and look. There, inside the dingy, damp cabin, she found James, squatting in front of his brother, with tears slipping silently down his face.

Fear gripped her, as her gaze swept over Pete's hollow form, sunken eyes and dry, cracked lips. Jenny crept quietly in. The heat radiating from him in that rotten, damp hole gave her grave cause for concern. He might not be dead yet, but if they didn't get him out of there soon, he could be.

Jenny noticed a slight twitch of his hand and she stepped closer and touched his face. He was burning up. The smell of alcohol was pungent in the muddy, sweating melée that had become the man before her. Slumped in the corner of the den, with his long coat wrapped around him, Pete was drawn and pale and had lost a lot of weight. She called his name, softly at first. "Pete. Peter. Dr Florin. Peter, we need you. Wake up for me, Pete. Wake up."

She squeezed his hand. There was little response, so she dug her knuckles into his chest, as she had been trained to do. He winced and opened his eyes. He looked around, obviously trying to make sense of things.

"Jimmy," he murmured as his brother wiped his face on his sleeve and tried his best to smile. "Are you okay? Did he hurt you?" Pete's face filled with concern, but then his eyes began to close again.

James managed to pull himself together. "Oh, no you don't! I'm fine, Pete. Come on. Open your eyes. We need to get you out of here."

Pete's gaze focused again. It moved over to Jenny and his brow furrowed, seemingly unable to place her.

James tried to hoist him up as Jenny did her best to ignore the hurt his wary look was causing her.

"Come on, mate. Let's get you on your feet."

Pete tried to stand up, but fell back against the side of the cabin in pain. The wood creaked and clods of dirt fell down around them and Jenny feared for their safety. James asked her to grab Pete's other side and they tried again. "Up you get," he said.

Pete wobbled to standing as, with a body under each arm, they stooped to fit under the door. Somehow they managed to wriggle him out without completely demolishing the cabin and helped him slowly back to the road. James left them then, while he ran to fetch the car and Jenny held on to him, afraid to let go.

Jenny had seen people in far better shape occupying hospital beds and she was shaken to see him in such a bad way. Too heavy to hold on to, as his legs gave way beneath him, she let him slip to the ground and sat with her back to a fence post, propping him up as best she could.

Once they'd hauled him into the back seat of the car, Jenny phoned Rachel with the news and James drove them home as fast as he could. Jenny asked her to make up the settee again and have a doctor on route to tend to him.

They arrived back home just as Rachel finished. At the front door she met them. She looked at the car, where Pete was lying fast asleep across the back seat and turned to her husband. "Joshua's got chickenpox," she said.

James looked at her with a gaze already laden with worry. "Is he all right?"

"He's got a temperature. I said I thought he was a bit off the last few days. He's been a little sod, hasn't he? Now we know why. He's had some Paracetamol and I've been fanning him." James stepped past and hurried upstairs to see his son and Rachel looked over at Jenny, standing beside the car. Waiting. Weary. She walked over.

As they both looked inside the car at the man lying there, filthy and in need, Jenny already knew what she had to do. "I'll stay with him, if you'll let me," she told her. "I can take care of Pete and you can take care of the kids. They need you, both of you. Chances are Annabel will go down with it any minute too."

"But I thought you had to leave tonight to get back for work in the morning?"

Jenny nodded. "I think I'm going to be sick tomorrow, don't you?"

James returned to them.

"Jenny's going to stay and look after Pete," Rachel told him.

James looked from one to the other. "Okay. We'd better get him in."

"We need to strip him off," Jenny said as they laid him down on the covered settee. "He's soaked and filthy and burning up.

55

Feel him."

James volunteered to help and they peeled off his long coat, all muddy and ripped on the side. His clothes looked as though they hadn't been changed in days and, between the two of them, they undressed him and put the whole lot in the wash. A small bottle of spirits had been smashed in his pocket, revealing the cause of the stench. He had been lying in it. Luckily for him, the glass hadn't cut through to his skin. James fetched him some spare pants and they laid him out carefully on the settee.

Jenny gave him the once-over to check for any injuries, and bathed him with a flannel and bowl of warm, soapy water. She noticed the cut on his face and scratches on his hands. His arms seemed otherwise uninjured. Although her gaze lingered longer than it should, she tried hard to focus on the job in hand. His brother's presence there becoming her anchor.

Concentrating, she quickly assessed his injuries and noticed that one of his ankles was clearly swollen. "Looks like he's done his ankle in," she said. "Do you have any ice I could put on it?" She placed a couple of cushions under his lower leg and waited for James to return.

When it came to his groin, the two looked at each other, wondering who should tend to him. Neither was eager for the job, but in the end, Jenny conceded. "I'm a nurse, I've seen it all before," she told him and James nodded and turned away, relief obvious in his features. She was never going to be able to tell Pete she had done that.

That night, after the doctor had been, Jenny pulled the armchair up by the side of the settee and made herself comfortable to nod when she could. He had a nasty case of tonsillitis and a sprained ankle, nothing life-threatening, but he was dehydrated and under-nourished and obviously needed taking care of. They had no idea how much or how little he had had to drink. Had Jenny not been there, the doctor was going to try and get him admitted to their busy hospital, but having found him partially rousable and with a willing nurse on tap, he was glad to let her care for him at home instead, and they were to let him know if things remained grim.

Jenny set her watch to beep on the hour and each time she assessed his temperature and was pleased to see, by the early hours, it was improving. When it dipped, she pulled over an extra layer of blanket around him, and when it rose again, she used a damp cloth to cool his skin. He was sleeping peacefully, Paracetamol and spirits helping for now, perhaps, but he was going to hurt in the morning.

Jenny watched him, in the quiet times, when she was alone with her thoughts and his sleeping figure, and she studied the contours of his face and arms as he drifted through the night, sleeping the sleep of the righteous, ironic but fortunate, giving his body time to heal.

This man, who was suffering demons, was a beautifully muscled specimen. She slowly reached out and touched his arm and made contact with skin. The touch crept up her arm from the tips of her fingers to her chest as, with one eye on his expression, she stroked his forearm down as far as his hand and across the backs of his fingers. At the thought of his fingers intertwining with hers she steadied her breathing and noticed a flicker in his brow. She quickly pulled her arm away, scolding herself, as he sank slowly back into a steady rhythm. Jenny rested back in her chair and bit down on her bottom lip. She took a deep breath and quietly let it go. She was playing with fire. And fire burned.

Pete came back to life around a quarter to five in the morning. The first rays of sunshine were just creeping across the sky, teasing the echoes of dawn, when he looked around and found himself... in Jim's house. How had he got there? He was in the living room. He looked down and his neck hurt, everything hurt. He was on the settee, wrapped in blankets, *just* blankets. He checked underneath. He had someone else's pants on, and there was a woman sitting beside him. Jen. Something distant stirred his memory. What was *she* doing there? How did Jenny know his brother?

He rubbed his hands across his face and felt the sting of injury. His head was pounding and although familiar to him, this time, it seemed worse. He tried to sit up, but he was too weak. His neck felt swollen and as he tried to swallow, his throat was raw, slicing into him. He croaked and wished he had kept his silence.

Jenny Wren. The name kept echoing through his bleary mind. In Teak? His stomach cramped as he moved his head to look around, the room tipped and rolled and he closed his eyes again. He refused to throw up in his brother's house. Rachel would kill him. She wasn't a big fan of his as it was, and he couldn't blame her.

Noticing a glass of water on the coffee table, he reached over to lift it. The cool water flowed down into his guts and he revelled in its path until it hit his stomach. He took some deep breaths and rested his head back.

From where he was lying on the settee, he could see his nurse-maid curled up against the side of the chair. Her lashes fell long and dark across her cheek and her lips were flushed. Never in a million years would he have pictured this happening and if one good thing was going to come out of this, it was here, and now. He was going to enjoy this rare moment: waking up next to Jenny, a woman he hadn't slept with, and feeling no shame. He *hadn't* slept with her, had he? The days before were something of a blur. No. He couldn't have. He doubted he had been in a fit state to manage *anything* feeling the way he did.

Her skin was peaches and cream against the beige-coloured settee, her short, brown hair like feathers he longed to run his fingers through. She lay there, her delicate hands resting flat over the arm of the chair. Innocence, he thought, such tempting innocence. While she was asleep, that was. When she woke up, Lord help him, she would be formidable. Jenny was a strong, independent woman these days, who was not afraid to speak her mind. No, he would be in for it this morning, so he'd better make the most of the quiet time.

Her watch signalled the hour and Jenny's eyes fluttered open. She immediately focused her gaze on Pete and sat up in surprise. Suddenly neither of them seemed to know what to say. The intimacy of the situation seemed quite at odds with their acquaintance of before.

"How are you feeling?" she asked him, looking more than a little uncomfortable.

Pete raised a single eyebrow. Like hell, he thought. "Rough," he whispered.

She smiled.

"How…?" He wanted to ask her how she had got there, but it was hurting to speak. Still, she seemed to understand.

"We found you in the woods last night. And brought you home."

We? How had there even been a 'we'? "You?" he managed to croak.

This seemed to cause her some discomfort. "It's a long story."

Pete looked at his watch and raised a brow. It was early, very early and there was nothing else to do with their time. He wanted to know.

Jenny shifted uncomfortably and then, seeming unable to look him in the eye, she focused her attention on a wrinkle on her left sleeve and spoke. "Someone had to find you. I had some days off and nothing particular to do. You're in quite a bit of trouble, you know?"

He rested back. So she had drawn the short straw. Lucky old her. Having to spend her days off traipsing around the countryside after him. She probably wanted to make sure he got what was coming to him. He knew she wasn't a fan, always giving him those disapproving looks. And she had said he was in trouble at work? He wasn't surprised.

Looking around, he started to wonder why his brother wasn't looking after him. "Jim?"

"Jim? Your brother? He's probably passed out in one of the bedrooms upstairs. I heard them moving to and fro most of the night."

What was she going on about?

"The kids are ill."

Pete lifted his hands to his face and groaned. "I have to go," he whispered, more to himself than anyone else. He tried to get up, but his ankle hurt. He reached to touch it, but there was no strength left in him.

"You've hurt your ankle. But you're not going anywhere in that state, anyway."

She was wide awake now and her nurse's look was on her, determined and bossy. Good. It would help him ignore the disturbance she created within him. He could manage without her. Lord knows why she was here in the first place. He didn't need her help. He pushed off the last of his bedding and tried to stand up, but his limbs were shaking. "Damn it, woman, give me a hand here!"

Jenny pursed her lips and pulled her chair out, giving him room to move. "And you can keep your voice down." She pointed upstairs. "That lot got less sleep than *you* did last night. And their illness wasn't self-inflicted."

Ouch, her words stung more than his throat did from speaking. Pete looked at her and, if looks could kill, she would have been writhing on the floor. Who was she to sit in judgement over him? She knew nothing about him.

He tried walking, but it was too painful and he fell back against the furniture. His head hung. And she just left him there, for a second, anyway, and then she took over, bossing him back into bed and scolding him in that superior tone of hers.

"You need something to eat. When was the last time you ate? You look awful."

So much for bedside manner. Pete rested back, defeated and gave a sullen kind of shrug.

"Well it's too early for a full English. I don't want to wake the entire house. I'll see what I can find."

60

Five minutes later she was back in the living room with a plate of something ominous. "What on earth is that?" he managed to ask, his brow crinkling in distaste.

"It's the best I could do. Eat up. It'll do you good."

His face took on an expression he hoped would convey his disapproval.

"Oh, stop making such a fuss and eat it."

Pete brought the food to his lips. It smelled revolting. Gingerly he took a bite. Sickly sweet squelchy innards hidden inside two slices of bread. His stomach recoiled and he had to concentrate hard just to swallow. "What the-"

"It's a strawberry jam and banana sandwich. It'll sort you out. Until I can get you something more."

"It'll make me heave."

"Just eat it, you big baby. You men think you're so tough, but heaven forbid you get a bit of an infection and, in your case, no doubt a hangover too."

It certainly felt far more than a hangover to Pete. He felt as though someone had ridden a horse all over his body, taken a grater to his throat and then kicked him in the head just to make sure. He stared at her, trying to convey in his expression what it hurt to put into words.

But Jenny just shrugged. She handed him a pint of water. "Here, and you need to take two of these; they're your antibiotics. You've got tonsillitis. And here's some Paracetamol."

There were many things he wanted to say to her at that point, but none of them were pleasant. It was probably a good thing his throat felt as if he had swallowed a mouthful of barbed wire. He picked up the sandwich and did his best to eat it. "You're enjoying this, aren't you?" he managed quietly, as he screwed up his face to swallow the final bite.

Jenny grinned and then bit down on her bottom lip. "Just a bit."

As the rest of the house woke up around six, two weary parents appeared at the living-room door. They looked towards the settee and then smiled with relief.

"One slightly delicate, but still very much alive, brother," Jenny reported.

"Not for the want of trying," Pete growled. "She made me eat kiddy food."

"I didn't want to risk waking you up," Jenny explained.

Rachel smiled. "Thanks, Jen. I have to confess, I'm feeling pretty rough this morning. You were right, they're both covered now. We only got an hour or two last night. How about you?"

As the world started to wake up outside, Jenny realised she would have to call in sick. She took herself out to the back garden and phoned the ward, and in her best poorly voice she claimed a migraine. It pained her to lie, knowing the disruption she was causing, but she had to do this, for Pete.

Jenny breathed in the fragrant morning air and thought. Where did they go from here? Pete was alive, but still not well. He needed to get better, to get back to work, so he didn't lose his job, but he obviously still needed to confront what was troubling him. She walked back inside.

"I'll take Pete home with me," she announced to the rest of them.

"No, he can stay here. I'll look after him," James said.

"But you've got the kids to look after," she reminded him.

"And *you* need to get back to work," Rachel said.

Pete waved his arms in the air to get their attention. "I am here, you know," he managed. "I'm quite capable of taking care of myself. I'll go home."

The three of them just looked at him.

"There are four nurses in our house," Jenny continued, returning her gaze to Rachel and James. "One of us will normally be around and we can all keep an eye on him."

"I don't need anyone keeping an eye on me!" he bit out, wincing with the pain.

"Are you sure that'll be okay?" James asked, completely ignoring him.

"I'm sure," she said. But was she?

Pete bashed his mug down hard on the empty plate to make a loud noise. "I'm a bloody doctor. I don't need a gaggle of nurses keeping an eye on me. I'll be fine."

Jenny turned on him. "Like you were when we found you last night?" She snapped. She couldn't help it. Lord save us from doctors; they made the worst bloody patients of all!

Grizzles started emanating from above stairs. "Look what you've done now!" Rachel scolded and she shot Pete a scathing look, withering him on the spot.

Jenny looked at James. "I'll take him. If he can just have a bit more food and rest here until lunchtime? Get another dose of tablets inside him, and then if you could maybe give us a lift to the bus station in town, I'll get us a taxi the other end."

James agreed and walked back out to see if Rachel needed a hand and Jenny turned to Pete. "Get some rest," she told him. "We'll head back home after lunch."

Jenny wasn't sure how this was going to play out when they got there. She hadn't asked the other girls. She was just thankful when she remembered Flis was away. But at least they had found him. Now all she had to do was sort him out. With his co-operation would be easier, but without would work too.

But before they left James took her aside. "He's got finals in just over a month. He's already failed them once. I doubt, with all that's happened, he's put much effort in as yet and with his record and his problems, this could be his last chance. If he gets through, he can make consultant. If you have *any* sway with him, please don't let him throw it all away. Help him back out of this." And that was exactly what she intended to do.

Chapter 6

With his head leant against the window, Pete drifted in and out of consciousness the whole way back to Duxley. He was exhausted. At times he became aware of Jenny's arm or leg resting against his, and the feeling that grew inside him was at odds with the workings of his mind. She was his captor, his nemesis, the punishment for his sins, but his heart beat a little faster every time she was near. Her scent played games with his insides as her soft skin rested quietly against his own. He had struggled before with wanting what he could never have and never had it been harder than here.

As soon as he was back on form, he would be gone; she wouldn't see him for dust. They would both be safer that way. One night, that's all he needed; 24 hours of rest and care and he would be up and ready and out of there.

Work was another matter. Jenny had mentioned he was in trouble and he understood that he should be. He had messed them around more than once and this time had been a biggy.

His brother had come up to him before they'd left and told him he knew about Adam. He'd said he was sorry and understood it must be hard for him, but he had no idea. He wanted Pete to focus on his studies now. On his studies! What did it matter if he sat the exam or not? What was the point? He was kryptonite. If he couldn't keep safe those he loved – first his mother and then

Ali, and now Adam and Kate's little girl, Selena, his beautiful goddaughter – then what use was he to anyone?

The bus stopped and Jenny dug him in the ribs. "Pete. We're here."

Pete opened his eyes and looked around. He was back, and his problems were worse than ever.

"We'd better find a taxi," Jenny said and he stirred himself into action.

They made their way off the half-empty bus and stepped out into a warm afternoon. His body ached. Jenny took his bag as he was struggling to keep up, and in the end he had to rest on her shoulder to hobble the 50 yards to the taxi rank.

As Pete watched through the window, they moved through the streets and pulled up at a terraced house on a road about a mile away from the hospital. Jenny handed over the money, which, had he not been so exhausted, would have wounded his pride, and they got out. Pete lifted his bag onto his back and sagged.

Jenny rolled her eyes and yanked it off him again. "Give me that," she scolded. "And let's get you to bed."

"Promises, promises," Pete mumbled under his breath and Jenny threw him a look that could have withered steel.

Jenny unlocked the door and called out to see if anyone was home. A girl's voice answered.

"Where the hell have you been?" The girl rounded the corner from the kitchen and saw Pete standing there next to Jenny. "Oh."

"Heather. Yes. The prodigal son returns. I found him languishing in some ditch, miles away," Jenny told her. "He's in a bit of a bad way, so I'm going to look after him here for a few days until he's better. I hope that's going to be okay?" She put down their bags. "By the way, if anyone asks, I was in bed with a migraine today, okay?"

"Migraine. Right." Heather nodded.

"Come on, buster, let's get you up to bed," Jenny said.

"Can't keep her hands off me," Pete joked in his least-strenuous voice and Heather giggled.

Jenny stopped and looked at him sternly. "Okay, tiger, first ground rule: my lot are out of bounds. And you're not in any state to be promising anything. I should also warn you that *Flis* lives here too, so if I were you, I'd watch my step."

Pete groaned, reminded of his brief drunken liaison with her friend. A huge mistake. Kate had given him hell for that. And then to cap it all off, Flis had turned out to be as clingy as athlete's foot and it had all turned rather ugly. Kate. His smile fell. Kate was gone.

He followed Jenny up the stairs to her bedroom and stood in the doorway, numb to the world around him, except to the pain that was trying to sidle back into his mind. He needed a drink. Pete slumped down on the bed and looked around for his bag. He started to rummage through for his bourbon, searching faster, becoming increasingly frustrated.

"If you're looking for the booze, you smashed it. We had to pick the pieces out of your coat before we put it through the wash," Jenny said.

He growled and tossed the bag back down.

"Sit over there," she told him, pointing to her chair. "I need to get you into bed before you fall down. I don't want you hurting anything else. I don't think being a patient is your forte." She pulled out some fresh bedding and started to strip the sheets.

"What are you doing?" he asked.

"I thought you would prefer to sleep in a clean bed."

He tried to stand up. Why hadn't he thought of this earlier? If she was going to tend to him here, in *her* bed, where was *she* going to sleep? He wasn't having this. "No. I'm going home."

He tried to get up, but Jenny glared at him and pushed him back down into the seat. "You're going nowhere, mister. Sit. Down."

"I'm not throwing you out of your bed and having you nanny around after me. I can take care of myself."

"Obviously!"

Stubborn bloody woman. God, how he wished he was just a little bit stronger. He would... He would... What the hell would he do? He was a mess and he knew it, but he was damned if he was going to let *her* know that. He turned sullen. "I'm okay."

She gave him the sort of look that said, "I beg to differ," and carried on making up the bed.

"Right. Get those shoes off and get yourself on there. We need to elevate that ankle and get some more ice on it. And while you're resting up, I'll get us something on for tea."

Pete did as he was told, this time, purely because he had no other choice.

Twenty minutes after she had left him propped up on top of her bed, Jenny came back in and found Pete fast asleep. She didn't have the heart to wake him, so she sat on the chair and quietly pulled out her diary to catch up on what had been going on whilst she was away.

I found him, she wrote. He's alive. He's a handful, but there's nothing new there. I don't know when I'm going to have the chance to write in here again, but suffice it to say he's... I don't know. He's beautiful, but damaged; vulnerable, but fiercely independent. I can only think that he's lonely, and probably afraid, and although I know he's no good for me; that he's salt to my wound, I have to be there for him.

Pete stirred and she looked up.

"You're still here, then?" he asked.

Jenny smiled. "It's *my* room."

Pete closed his eyes again and Jenny quickly shoved her diary under the bookcase. "Dinner will be ready any minute," she told him. "Do you think you'll be up to having a bath afterwards?"

Pete sniffed at his armpit and let his head fall back on the pillow. "Sorry."

When the water was ready, Jenny helped Pete to the bathroom.

"Do you need some help getting... changed?" She couldn't bring herself to say 'undressed'.

"No!"

Relieved, she passed him a large towel and tried hard not to smile at his obvious discomfort.

"Last night..." he started as she was about to leave.

"When we found you?"

His mouth struggled to form the words. "I woke up... with no clothes on. Did you...?"

Jenny stifled a grin. She nodded.

"Oh."

"Your brother helped me," she added, to give him the comfort of doubt. He nodded and she left him in there with at last a hint of pink in his cheeks.

Jenny went back to her room and tidied up. She checked that nothing incriminating was out on display and then made sure she had everything she needed to be ready for work in the morning. She tried to read, but her mind was distracted. What had gone on in his childhood that was so bad they wouldn't speak of it? That the two boys had to hide away from? And was that the reason for his unpredictable behaviour? But then Rachel had said he used to be different, before the crash. The crash that involved Adam's first wife. So much was going on below the surface with this man and she was determined to try and help him, if he would let her. And then her mind was back to Kate and the stresses of the past few days spilled over and she desperately missed the company of the woman who had been her friend.

Pete hobbled back from the bathroom and found Jenny sitting with a book in her lap and tears fresh on her cheeks. She looked up and quickly wiped her hand across her face. "Better?" she asked with the best attempt at fake cheer he had ever seen.

He looked at her. "Definitely. Thanks." God, he was useless with crying women. He really hoped she wasn't going to break down on him, but he felt obliged to ask. "Everything okay?"

Jenny put on a big smile, but her grey eyes were no longer shining. They were dipped to the side. "Fine," she said.

"My clothes?" he asked, relieved he had been spared that fate.

"They're in the wash. James leant you some pyjamas to be getting on with, though." She pulled out some cotton bottoms and passed them over. "Go on. I won't look." She put a hand across her eyes.

After a few moments, he was finished. "You can look," he said and Jenny let her hand fall away. Pete was not impressed. His brother was a good four inches shorter than him and it showed. "May I?" he asked pointing to the bed, and with relief he sat back down and rested his foot up. He could hear her trying hard not to giggle and shot her a dark look, causing her to lose control and erupt into laughter.

"I could go to your place tomorrow and get you some things, if you like?" she said, obviously trying hard to be serious again, but failing.

"I can go there myself," he told her petulantly.

"That remains to be seen."

This woman was going to be the death of him. Why didn't she seize any opportunity to get rid? Was she a glutton for punishment? She certainly didn't seem to have any interest in him outside her obviously misguided sense of duty. She was treating him like a damn child. And if she *had*, it was the weirdest way of trying to win him over he had ever seen.

"I could get you some books too, if you like. Your brother says you've got some big exams in a few weeks."

"Oh, he did, did he? Well, he should have kept his nose out of it." That's all he needed, another knife for her to twist in his back.

"But if they're important, you don't want to miss out and fail. And you'd better ring the hospital and let them know you're in the land of the living. And you should also try to—"

"I'm fine!"

"But I was just—"

"Leave it, Jen." Oh, he knew he was being horrid to her, but he couldn't face being railroaded into anything he wasn't ready for. He saw her chin lift almost imperceptibly as she walked out of the room, but he didn't have long to ponder any thoughts of guilt before she was back, holding out some tablets.

"You need to take these."

She was sore at him, he could tell. He'd upset enough women in his time to know what sore looked like. He would apologise... later.

"I'm going downstairs to talk to Heather and Chloe. Try and get some rest. Would you like me to put on some music?" She showed him the half dozen CDs she owned.

"Is that it?" he asked, dumbfounded.

Jenny nodded. "I like what I like."

Pete looked at the selection of CDs in horror. They didn't look like anything *he* would be into. "No thanks," he said.

By the time Jenny returned, Pete was dead to the world. She pulled the covers up over his body, her stomach clenching as it slipped up across his toned, lean abdomen. She noticed a scar on his right-hand side that looked old and mostly hidden under his arm and she hovered above him, watching him quietly breathing. His mouth twitched and it occurred to her what she wouldn't give to be kissed by those lips... on another day... after the storm. But she couldn't let him see that. Risk seeing him reject her? No. As good as the thoughts might be, she had to hide her heart from view.

Heather knocked gently and Jenny blushed at being caught harbouring lustful thoughts. She met her at the door. Heather peered in and looked mischievously shocked by the half-naked man in her housemate's bed.

"Your mattress," she whispered and passed through the inflatable for Jenny to make her bed on. Heather's eyebrows jiggled in fun at the thought of what Jenny might get up to overnight, but she was instantly subdued with a reproachful look and so she just smiled and scuttled away.

It was bizarre, Jenny thought, to feel uncomfortable getting changed and sleeping in your own bedroom. Pete was fast asleep, she could hear him gently snoring. He wouldn't notice if he remained like that, but he *could* wake up at any minute. She slipped outside to the bathroom to change into her nightshirt and brush her teeth and then, ever so quietly, crept back inside her room, shut the door and climbed into her makeshift bed.

Jenny thought about the thrill of knowing he had been naked only a few feet away from her when he had changed to get ready for bed. She had covered her eyes, at least mostly, but her gaze had fallen across his feet. They had captured her imagination, and when the towel had dropped to the floor around them she was convinced she must have blushed.

Jenny was awoken in the early hours of the morning by someone moving around her room. She flicked on the nightlight and caught Pete, hanging out of the bed, head down in his backpack.

"What are you doing?" she asked, as her eyes adjusted to the light.

"Sorry. Go back to sleep. I just needed some more painkillers."

She wriggled out of her sleeping bag and leant past him to reach them off a shelf. "Here."

"Thanks." He swallowed a couple and they shuffled back into their beds.

"You might as well take two of these while you're at it." She handed him the antibiotics. "Did the pain wake you up?" she asked and he grunted that it had. "Should I get you some ice?" She reached over and felt his forehead, but he pulled away.

"No, go back to sleep."

Jenny felt uneasy letting herself rest while leaving him in pain, so she propped herself up on one elbow and looked at him. "How did you get the scar on your side? It's pretty impressive," she asked.

"Direct, aren't you?"

"Will it get me anywhere?"

He seemed to think about that. "I've had it for ages. Since I was a kid."

"What from?"

"From not minding my own business."

That would be a 'no', then. Maybe she should try to distract him while the painkillers kicked in. She might learn something, she thought. "Tell me about the place you used to live, Pete," she said, undeterred.

"Why?"

"It looked like a nice place to grow up."

Pete was studying the side of his finger.

"Just you and your brother, was it?"

Still nothing from him.

"I hear your mum's a bit of a brainbox. Oxford, eh?"

"What are you fishing for, Jen?" he asked.

"Nothing," she lied. "It's just that I met your brother and saw your old house... I guess I'm just trying to piece it all together. You must have had two very clever parents to produce you two: a doctor and an engineer. What did your dad do?"

"There's more to being clever than letters after your name," he snapped.

She had hit a nerve. Determined to keep calm, she tried to veer away from his father. "I was really just thinking what a confident and sensible mother you must have had."

He turned away to face the wall. "The only sensible thing my mother ever did was learn when to keep her mouth shut. Something you'd do well to grasp before you saddle some poor sod, becoming a mother too."

Jenny's heart tore wide open; she was bleeding inside. She rolled over away from him and clicked off the light.

Pete awoke with the day and Jenny was gone. A note sat beside him on a breakfast tray. 'On an early. Back later. Try and get some rest.' Two white tablets lay on the tray next to a glass of water, along with the bottle of antibiotics. There was a jug of milk and some Weetabix and a feeling of emptiness.

He knew she had been crying in the night. He had recognised the change in her breathing. He'd upset her. What had the poor girl done to deserve this? To deserve him? She was only trying to help, he knew that, but did he actually *want* to be helped? Nobody had thought to ask him that.

Pete wolfed down his breakfast, took his pills and looked around the room. His clothes were in a pile on the side, clean and folded and waiting for him. There was nothing to do, so he lay there and wallowed in self-loathing.

After a while there was a gentle knock at the door. A girl's face peeped around. "Hi, I'm Chloe. Can I get you anything? Jenny asked me to make sure you were okay."

"Could you pass me my clothes, please," he asked. The girl handed them over. "Are you my guard, to make sure I don't wander off?"

"Something like that," she giggled.

"I'll be fine, thanks."

Chloe smiled. "Give me a holler if you need anything," and she disappeared again.

Pete managed to wiggle into his jeans and pulled on his t-shirt. His ankle was still swollen, so he left off his socks, but he was feeling a bit better in himself. He picked up the pillows and rested back against the bedhead. He looked around the room.

A small voice inside his head dared him to peek inside a drawer. He fought it, though his curiosity almost got the better of him. Jenny Wren's bedroom. She was an odd one, with her sensual figure and those seductive grey eyes. He had never seen eyes like those before. Like silver paper on faded denim. He was going to have to concentrate hard to behave around her. He needed to keep his head. He couldn't risk falling under the spell that she

73

cast. She was dangerous and he knew it.

But last night. When she had leaned over him in just a night-shirt, her legs quite bare next to his skin. His blood had pumped harder being within a breath of that. But then she had opened her mouth and started probing with questions. Answers he was not willing to give. Damn, the woman hadn't let it drop. She had driven him to snap at her and left him brooding on guilt. He would be better off away from there. For *her* sake as well as for his.

He looked down at the books beside her bed and picked up the one on the top to flick through. Lorna Doone. It looked like a girls' book, but it was a classic. It might not be too bad. He pulled it up onto his lap and it fell open about halfway through and in it was a picture with a number written on the back. He turned it over and it was... him. At first his mind drew a blank. Jenny had a picture of him in her book? She hadn't seemed attracted to him. Quite the opposite, in fact. Then, as his mind searched for some way to rationalise it, he realised it was a picture taken in his brother's back garden. Jim must have given it to her... But why? Maybe she *did* fancy him? But then whose was the number?

Pete wiggled his foot. It wasn't quite as swollen as before, but it still hurt to move. His throat was a little better, not half so painful now, but to his disgust, he still felt incredibly weak. One more night, he thought. Tomorrow he would get himself off home and face the music, alone.

Jenny returned after lunch and came straight up to see him. "How is the wounded warrior, then?" she asked.

"Bored," he said.

"Obviously getting better, then. How about the ankle?"

"Hurting."

"Your throat?"

He felt his neck and screwed up his face. "So-so."

"Am I going to get anything more than one-word answers today?" she asked and his body responded. He let his gaze travel down the length of her and then slowly back up. His forbidden fruit he had lusted after for so long. She was stronger now. Could he dare to try it? Maybe, if he could shut her up for long enough. He beckoned her in closer with his hand. And she sat down on the side of the bed. Should he be doing this? His brain wasn't happy, so he turned it to mute. He took hold of her hand and started stroking the back with the pad of his thumb. She looked into his eyes, a world of uncertainty watching him.

"Thank you... for finding me," he murmured and he let his fingertips play gently with the soft delicate skin of her forearm and hand. He could see fire in her eyes, as they widened before him. Her breathing quickened and her cheeks flushed. He hadn't lost it. He leaned in, pulling her gently to him and—

"I talked to Anna from occy health today," she blurted out, pulling back out of his reach and standing up, away.

Damn! Disappointment and sudden relief swept over him. Then it dawned on him. Wait a minute. What had she said? Pete couldn't believe it. Bloody meddling woman! "What did you go and do that for?" he snapped. "*I'll* ring the hospital when I'm God-damn good and ready! I don't need you apologising for me." He tried to stand up, but his weakened response was not having the dominating effect he had reached for and he crumpled back down, swearing. He let out a loud huff of discontent. The tension eased, but he wasn't happy. "Go on, then. What did you tell them?"

"I just asked if 'hypothetically' I had a person in my care who had been missing for a while from work, how I should go about helping them back? 'Hypothetically.'" She was looking straight at him now, cautious, but daring him to disapprove.

He sighed. "Just that?"

"No. We discussed things, but it was all 'hypothetical'. I didn't mention your name once."

Like she'd actually have to. Pete doubted there were many other people who worked at St Steven's who had gone AWOL from work in the past few weeks.

So the game was up. Half the hospital would know by morning. He rested back against the pillows. "So... What did they say?"

"You have to ring them, Pete. And you have to be back in work on Monday. It's been more than two weeks. Any longer and you'll be out on your ear."

He considered this. "Might not be such a bad thing."

Jenny's brow creased. "You *are* kidding me? After all the work and years you've put in? You have to get back in there and finish it, Pete. You have to get this exam done and complete the course. For heaven's sake, you're nearly there. You can't throw it all away over... What the hell *is* this over, Pete? Because, for the life of me, I still don't know. You won't speak to me. You won't share. You won't tell me anything. You've been given so much in this life. Why do you have to be so ungrateful?"

Been given so much? What had he been given? He had had to fight for everything he had. Fight and work, and damn hard too. "You may have had a wonderful childhood and cruised on through till now, Jen, but I'm damn sure I didn't. What do you want from me? Do you want me to spill my guts to you so you can feel like you've done your bit? So you can tick me off your list of lost causes? I've got nothing and no one and that's all there's ever been!" He took a deep breath and stared at the wall, wishing to God she'd just walk away. Just walk off and complain to her friends about the miserable excuse for a man taking root in her bedroom. But she didn't. She just stood there and looked at him.

He could see her frame was tense. It might even be shaking. Her eyes were so unreadable; he never knew what was going on inside her head. As for having a crack at her? Hadn't that just been a peach of an idea? He swore again, under his breath, and looked back at her.

His gaze sunk to the bed. She should run away, far, far away from him. He didn't deserve her care, or affection. She should kick him out on his ear for being inexcusably ungrateful, but instead, she quietly walked over and sat down next to him and took hold of his hand. It was a simple, innocent connection, but in that moment, Pete held his breath and felt her warm, loving touch mending him. And all at once he was crying. Tears were flooding down his face and his walls were caving in. He was so tired, so empty and so terribly alone. And she pulled his body against her and held him.

Chapter 7

Jenny knew it had been a breakthrough for Pete to sob on her
shoulder like that. They hadn't spoken much more that afternoon,
but Jenny stayed with him, trying to cheer him up and waiting till
he seemed more comfortable and then she helped him down the
stairs for the evening meal. They had watched TV with Heather in
the evening and it had all felt very easy. Pete had been a different
man: genial and relaxed. She liked it. Too much, in fact. She
had to remind herself to be careful. It was important for her to
keep her head when she was around him. If he had the slightest
idea of the way she wanted him, he'd have her weak, in his power
and ticked off his list in a heartbeat. She needed to stay focused.
She needed to remember why she was doing this. She was there
to help him get back on his feet, to get through his exams and
become a consultant. Being knocked off *hers* was not part of
the plan. If she ended up just another notch on his bedpost, she
wouldn't be any use to either of them.

All thoughts of how good he had felt in her arms, how good
he had smelled, had to be put to the back of her mind now. Only
her diary would know about those sorts of things. It could be her
escape. In the real world, she was going to have to be the bossy,
disapproving nurse friend she had to be, because that was who he
needed right now. She had a few precious minutes while he got

through the bathroom to unburden her soul, so she grabbed them.

He's still here, with me, sleeping in my bed, only inches away from me, she wrote. I can sense him next to me in the darkness and am resisting the urge to touch.

He tried to make a pass at me today, when I got back from work. It was far too close. All I could see were his soft, golden eyes and his mischievous lips. His pale pink, tender lips. Yes, this is going to be hard, but I won't give in. I can't.

Pete walked back in and she let her eyes slip from her hastily opened book to glance at his bare feet. The same feet she'd seen stepping into his brother's pyjama bottoms last night after his towel had dropped to the floor around them. She felt her cheeks flush and slipped her diary back under her pillow. She looked up.

Pete sat down on the bed. "What am I doing here?" he asked. His voice was soft and his face looked weary.

Jenny got up from where she was sitting, on the inflatable bed, and sat down next to him. She put her hand over his. "You're letting someone take care of you, just for a while."

He looked at her, his eyes searching hers for answers. "Why?"

"Because you need to."

His gaze fixed firmly on their hands, held together. "But why you, Jen?"

What did he want her to say? Was he unhappy it was she who'd come to find him? She could hardly tell him the truth, that nobody else cared enough and that she had needed this almost as much as he had. So she told him half of it. "Because I thought you probably needed someone and I was the only one who seemed to have the time to find you. I wanted to. Besides, it's about time I returned the favour." She looked at him then and watched as his eyes slowly understood.

He nodded.

"How's your ankle?"

He wiggled it. "Getting better."

"And how are you?" she asked. Her heart was beating quicker

now, the familiar nature of their conversation and his proximity both taking their toll.

He took a deep breath and let it out slowly. "Don't get too close to me, Jen. I'm bad news." Then he tried half-heartedly to lighten the mood. "Look, I've already stolen your bed and you have to work in the morning."

"You haven't stolen anything," she said. "I put you there."

"But I'll take the sleeping bag tonight, anyway. And I'll get out of your hair in the morning."

Jenny looked into his eyes, those warm whirls of golden hay shining in the sun, and fought the urge to kiss him. He was crushed and defeated, but had still spared a thought for her. "If that's what you want." Tomorrow she would try and get him to return to his studies, but tonight she would let him just be.

Snuggling up inside her bed, Jenny was conscious of the scent of him lingering around her. Pete had been lying there; his body had touched those sheets. She turned her face to the wall and quietly breathed him in. In the black of the night, she rolled her eyes and wondered how she was ever going to get to sleep. But after a while she could hear Pete's breathing drop to a steady rhythm on the floor and she let herself relax and fade away.

She was awoken a few hours later by something thrashing and moaning below her. Her heart raced in panic. It was dark; she couldn't see. Then she remembered: Pete! With a tweak of the curtains, moonlight drifted in and she made out his restless shape on the bed on the floor. He was thrashing about and groaning, still asleep, but obviously distressed. Jenny called to him, softly. "Pete. Pete. Wake up, Pete," but it did nothing to penetrate his desperate world. He calmed a little and she waited, propped up, to see if he would settle. Suddenly he jumped and started to shake, moaning louder and more terrified. She pulled back a curtain to let in some light, slipped quickly out of bed and crouched down beside him.

"Pete." She shook him gently. "Peter. Wake up. Wake up."

And then he opened his eyes and for a long moment they both held their breath while he stared at her, first tortured and then confused. His body was glistening in the light of the moon and she could feel him shaking under her touch. "It's me, Jenny. You were having a nightmare." She let go of his arms and, almost afraid, sat back on the bed. But Pete launched himself forward, grabbing onto her, his fingers digging in to her lower back, his face buried in her lap as ragged breathing tore through his chest.

At first Jenny was startled by the power of his despair; she found herself hesitantly soothing her hand down his back to try and calm him. But with her own senses heightened, she felt the hot caress of his breath seeping through her nightshirt and coiling around her thighs. The feel of his warm, muscular body clinging to her own in such an intimate way was intoxicating. But it was not her *body* he needed, it was support and comfort, and never had this been harder for her to remember.

When at last his breathing settled, Pete lifted his face from her lap and apologised. She sat back against the head of her bed, lifted her duvet and patted the space beside her. Pete looked at her for a moment and then slowly climbed in. She held out a hand and he took it. "Talk to me," she said.

There was a long pause, where he must have been considering if he could speak to her and what he could say, but she waited and said nothing, giving him space to collect his thoughts.

"It was her," he said.

"Ali?"

He looked at her.

"James told me about the crash."

He seemed resigned to the news.

"It replays in my head. Always the same. I get it more often when I'm stressed, but it *can* come completely out of the blue."

"Tell me about it."

Pete looked at her. He seemed to be assessing her worth, whether he was able to trust her or not, but in the end he settled,

81

smoothed the back of her hand with his, and spoke.

"I see her. Every time it's the same. I wake up in the car wreck and all I can smell is the blood. I can feel it trickling down my face and she's just standing there, in front of me, beyond the bonnet of the car, calling my name. My eyes are closed, but I know she's there. "Wake up, Pete, wake up," she's saying. And then I open my eyes and…" His voice started to falter. "I see her, and she's smiling, and for that split second I'm so grateful that she's okay and I'm the one who's injured and then the sirens blaze out, and for some reason I look round… and she's right there, strapped into the seat beside me… dead." He swallowed. "She's dead." His voice trailed away as Jenny pulled his hand to her lips and kissed it.

What could she say to ease the burden of this poor man? What words could she speak to save him? None. So she rested their hands down on the bed between them and turned to look at him. "It wasn't your fault," she whispered and the pain in his eyes left a scar in her heart. "It wasn't your fault."

His brow crinkled. "She was my responsibility."

"But it wasn't your fault."

He shook his head. "You don't understand. I made her go."

"What do you mean, you made her go? She was a grown woman."

"She wasn't going to go to the party. I was the one who persuaded her."

"Do you think she would blame you for that?"

"I know Adam did."

"Adam was her husband. He was too close to see things rationally. How did it happen?" Jenny knew it was dangerous to ask him, but to play it through might help him to see.

"A drunken teenager ran a red light. Slapped straight into the side of me. Of us."

"Well, then. It *wasn't* your fault."

Pete met her gaze then and the sadness of the years flowed through him. "I was responsible," he said.

They sat together, hand in hand, for a while, until Pete rallied his spirits. He patted the back of her hand. "You'd better get some rest," he said. "You've got to be up in a few hours," and he made to slip out of her bed and back onto the floor. But she held onto his hand and, leaning her head against his shoulder, she silently urged him to stay. Not to satisfy any carnal desire, but for the comfort, the comfort of knowing he wasn't alone when he slipped back into sleep.

The following morning Pete woke up around ten. Jenny was long gone, stealing away with the dawn, silent and gentle. What had happened there between them last night? He had lain there for hours, holding her in his arms, afraid that if he closed his eyes she would disappear. He had felt her limbs curling up within the protective arc of his body as they'd slid further and further under the covers and she'd dropped off to sleep.

At first the urge to touch her, to explore, had quite overwhelmed him: the smell of her skin, the touch of her hair against his cheek. If it had been anyone else, he would have thought no more of it, but as the hour had moved past, he had felt a new emotion creeping over him, something long ago forgotten. Like it was *his* job to protect her, to watch over her as she slept, and he had done it, willingly.

Why was she being so kind to him? She seemed to feel some sense of duty towards him. He didn't know why. He had been acting on instinct when he'd pulled her boyfriend off her that day. Chivalry wasn't in him. She was a fool if she thought it was. He'd run as quickly as he could after that and not looked back. Too dangerous by daylight even, although often he had been tempted. Whatever her reasons, he certainly hadn't earned this.

Jenny had shown warmth and acceptance, even affection for him. It wasn't lust, not as *he* knew it, not on her part, at least, but it wasn't love either. *Love* he had known once. Love was a consuming fire. It held you in its grasp and ripped you apart. It

83

was life and death, breath and bone, and he would never know love like that again. Jen appeared to be everything he wanted, everything he needed deep down, but she didn't see him like that, and to love without being loved in return was agony. He couldn't go back there again. He would widen the gap, move back to his flat and try to set her free from him once more.

He tidied the room, so that when she got back, it would be just as she'd left it. He deflated the bed and rolled up the sleeping bag. He picked up her pillow and... What was that? He thought he had felt something while he'd tried to get to sleep in the night. He picked it up and looked at it. It was a diary. Jenny's diary. He tried to put it back, but something stopped him letting go. He knew he shouldn't look, but quite without sanction, his hands opened to the first page and his eyes began to read.

Temptation pulled him in, until the word "Michael" blinded him like a mirror to the sun. Jenny had a boyfriend, and suddenly the book snapped shut. Of course she had. She was stunning. How self-centred and stupid had he been? And he slipped it back under her pillow.

Pete looked around. He was grateful for everything she had done for him, for finding him and caring for him and listening to his woes, but this was where it had to end. She would strip him bare if he let her and he wasn't ready for that. Not emotionally. It was time to go back and stand on his own two feet. He borrowed a phone he found lying about in the living room, rang for a taxi and picked up his bag. Then he hobbled out to the pavement, where his taxi was waiting and went, before anyone could notice he was gone.

The outside world was busy as he cruised through the streets back to his flat. He looked at his watch. It was Saturday. Time had meant nothing to him as he had tried to run from his past, but here was life again, still there waiting for him, as if the last couple of weeks had never happened.

A few hours and Jen would be home and grateful that he was

out of her hair. She could go back to her boyfriend and forget about him and he wondered if this 'Michael' realised what a lucky guy he was and hoped that the man, whoever he was, was good enough to deserve her.

The taxi pulled up outside his building and reality flooded in. He was back to his empty life, with work and women and drink. He put his key in the lock and walked in. No feeling of home hit him, no relief to be back, on the contrary, in fact. He was back where he had started.

Work and women and drink.

Work? Well that horse had bolted. Women? He tried to summon the enthusiasm, but that sensation was numb, so drink it was. He dropped his bag on the floor, poured himself a large bourbon from the shelf in the kitchen and settled back onto the settee.

He was woken a while later by hammering on his front door. It wouldn't let up. He called out for them to stop, but whoever it was, was persistent. Clawing back to reality, he called out to them again. "All right. All right. I'm coming," and he hauled his sorry frame across the room.

As he turned the key, Jenny burst in and in the space of a second, her expression changed from concern to anger. "So this is what you're up to. I come home from the shift from hell and find you gone. No note, no goodbye, no 'see you around and thanks for everything', just gone. So I hightail it over here to make sure you're okay and what do I find? You're straight back to the way you were before, hell bent on destruction and already halfway to pickling yourself." She was fuming and even more attractive like that. He smiled, what he thought was a charming, 'don't you really want to sleep with me?' kind of smile and touched her cheek. She pulled back and went to slap his hand away, but he caught her by the wrist and pulled her against him. She fought to free herself, surprising him with her strength.

"Get off me, you oaf. You're drunk and you stink of booze!"

She kicked him in the shin, broke loose and immediately fled to the kitchen. Reeling, Pete rubbed at his leg and heard an ominous glugging sound. She wouldn't!? He rounded the corner to find her opening the final bottle of spirits.

"Stop!" He held up both hands, concern etching his face. "That bottle's very expensive. It cost—"

She unscrewed the cap and started to pour. He lunged at her, but she held him off just long enough to empty it. He made a grab and the bottle flew out of her hands, sending the final drops of amber liquid trickling down his wall, the glass smashing loudly on the stone-tiled floor and he looked at her in disgust. "What the hell did you do that for?"

"To stop you trying to kill yourself. What sort of friend would I be if I let you get drunk every time you wanted to run away from your problems?"

She had called herself his 'friend'. For a moment he was stunned, then the realisation of what she was doing kicked back in and her meddling lit his ire. The last thing he needed was friends like that. "What the hell do you know about my problems?" he shot at her.

"I know you're beating yourself up over something that wasn't your fault. I know that you're throwing your life away because you're too afraid to try, and I know that you're too proud, or too stubborn, to let anyone help you."

She stood there, brazen as the day, defying him to deny it. So he decided to see how she liked having *her* life put under the microscope. "And you're the person to help me out here because…? Who the hell do you think you are? God's gift to mankind? You must be what? Nearly 30? You're not unattractive and yet you're still single. I could ask the question, what's the matter with you? Unable to keep a boyfriend for more than a quick shag? Or maybe you just enjoy being a punch bag?!"

What was this? Had he hit his mark? Jen's face paled. Her eyes were shining with unshed tears and her face told him he had gone too far. She grabbed her keys from the side and hurried for the door. But the glass crunching beneath her feet slowed her escape, giving Pete just enough time to realise his mistake.

"I'm sorry, Jen."

She carefully crunched around him. A piece of glass lodged in her brown-leather boot and she cursed under her breath and reached to pull it out. She cut herself and swore. Tears had started dripping down her face. Moving back to the sink, she ran the tap and Pete just stood there, not knowing what to do. Then he woke up from his angry haze and was filled with remorse.

He walked over to stand next to her. "Let me see."

Jenny pulled her finger away from him. "It's fine."

"Let me see," he said again more firmly.

Jenny held up her finger. A slice down the side had left a trail of blood weeping into the sink. He grabbed a clean tea towel out of a drawer and wrapped it around, raising her hand above her heart. He held onto it. "Forget all this. I'll clean it up later. Come with me," and he walked her back out to the living room. "Sit down and hold this up."

A couple of minutes later he was back with a box of tissues, a plaster and a glass of icy water. "Here." He put them down in front of her and took over holding her hand. He sat there, his body angled toward hers, his good leg tucked underneath him on the settee. "Talk to me," he said.

Jenny's expression told him she knew what he was doing, but at least she tried to smile. It was short-lived, however. She was very quiet and it wasn't something he was comfortable with. "What is it, Jenny Wren? What bit of my hideous tirade upset you the most? Please, tell me. If you tell me, I won't make you go back out and buy me another bottle of that fine malt you destroyed." She shot him a look that dared him to try. "Please, Jen. I know I can be a callous bastard. I didn't mean any of that. I was just lashing out. Was it about still being single?"

She pulled on her hand for release and he carefully unwound it and let it go. "Not too bad," he said and he put on the plaster.

Jenny sat there, cradling her injured finger, curled up with her knees facing him and her hands held tight. "The punching… That was only ever the one guy. I was stupid. Weak. You were right."

Pete didn't know what to say, so he said nothing.

"I was 17 when I left home," she continued. "I fell out with my parents. I'd been in love, you see, with a lad from the village. We were going to start a life together, but our parents got together and the next thing I knew he was gone. Off to London, to make a name for himself. He's a lawyer now. I looked him up."

"What happened?" he asked.

She shrugged. "I don't know. But I never heard from him after that. He didn't say goodbye, didn't write a letter, just… left."

Pete realised now why she might have reacted so badly to him walking out.

"I hated my parents for pushing him away. I couldn't eat, didn't sleep. We rowed all the time and then, just when everything seemed to be settling down, they arranged for me to go and live with my aunt for a bit and I never went back."

"Not ever?"

"It was just easier that way."

"And you have no idea why the guy didn't try to contact you later on?"

Jenny shook her head.

"Well, he didn't deserve you then."

At this she looked up and Pete looked into her eyes. Moon pits, deep and silent, their mysteries were hidden in the dark recesses of the night. And, like the first rays of sunshine on the spring lawn, he felt the frost on his heart melting.

"What about your parents? Have they never tried to get you to go back again?" he asked.

"They tried," she said. "But… It's not easy to explain. It was like I felt let down, but not let go. They were smothering me."

"Not even at Christmas or birthdays?"

Jenny shook her head.

"Have you got any brothers or sisters?"

"One. A sister. She's eight years younger than me."

"Do you see her?"

"No. I do sometimes think it would be nice to, though. She must be what? Twenty-three now." She took a sip of her drink.

"I'm sorry," he said then.

"It doesn't matter."

"I wouldn't have survived without my brother. I know I said the other night that I have no one, but I do have him. Why didn't you keep in touch with her?"

"I guess I just wanted to leave it all behind. Close the door."

Pete wondered about what she wasn't letting on. Her eyes seemed to be avoiding his, like she was afraid of what he might see. He would have to get her to think about her family. She needed them, whatever she thought now. "You know, if the guy had been half the man you deserved, he would have fought for you," he said.

Jenny looked up at him, her eyes reflecting the sad lonely place that he knew. "Yeah, well, I don't think I'm the fighting type," she told him.

A moment passed, when Pete wanted nothing more than to pull her into his arms and show her how much a man could be, how much she was worth, but of course, *he* was not. And he pulled himself together.

She sniffed and turned to face him. "No one's come close since." She let her body relax. "Have *you* ever been in love?" she asked him.

"Me? No."

"What, never?"

He shook his head. "No."

She smiled at him. "But I bet you've said it a thousand times, to get women into bed."

He shook his head. "I'm not a deceiver, Jen. I never *promise* anything." He settled back beside her, a sweetly smug grin quirking

89

up the corners of his mouth. "I don't normally have to."

She chuckled. "Such modesty." And then her face fell. "No love, no promises? Your life's almost sadder than mine," and she looked at him, making Pete feel for the first time in many years that he might actually be missing out on something. And in that moment he was afraid that he had let her get too far under his skin. He felt awkward in her spotlight and ashamed of what he had become. Not good enough for the likes of her any more, he was resigned to the women who just wanted fun. There was no tenderness in that, nothing that would unsettle him and that was where he had been comfortable, as long as he didn't think too much.

"So, how are we going to get you back on the horse?" she asked him.

"Excuse me?" For a moment he thought she had been able to read his mind, but her expression was one of innocence.

"You have an exam to sit and you need to get cracking. We've got almost a month to get you up to the mark, so we'd better get going."

Pete shook his head. "Oh, no. There's no 'we' about *that*. Anyway, four weeks is not nearly enough time. I should have started ages ago."

"Then we need to get a move on. I'll be round every couple of days to test you on what you've learned. You write out a schedule and stay off the booze. Stop swanning around with all those hot women and get your head down. I believe in you, Peter Florin. You wouldn't have got this far unless you could make it."

"I'd be better off resitting another time," he told her.

"Pull your finger out and just try. That's all I ask. For me?"

Pete sighed. What was it about this woman that refused to let him go? "All right, then. I'll try. But don't hold your breath. And if I'm not allowed any hot women or drink, I'm going to have to find another vice to sink my teeth into." And he watched as her face took on a curious expression.

Chapter 8

Sunday, Jenny had the day off and she was a woman on a mission. She spent the morning searching the net for tempting recipes and then bought what she needed and began to bake. She was going to have to put in a few miles to make up for all the tasting she had wangled in the making of the treats, so while they were all cooling on the rack, she went on her much-anticipated run.

She tried to put out of her mind, while she was running, the direction in which this was taking her. She counted her steps: one, two, three, four, one, two, three, four. What was she doing? She was doing a good thing. She was helping Pete back on track and dodging heartache in the process. Well, at least that was the idea.

She collapsed in the front door at ten to three, showered, packed up the baking and walked the three miles to Pete's front door.

She knocked, unsure now if he was even in. She should have checked, but how could she? She needed to get his phone number. She knocked again and the door opened.

A rather surprised-looking Dr Florin stood before her in bare feet, jeans and a t-shirt and Jenny felt her insides quiver. "You needed a vice," she said.

Pete looked mischievously at her until she cottoned on to his train of thought.

"Not that!" She rolled her eyes. "I've been baking. Can I

come in?"

Jenny walked into the flat and put the bag down on the kitchen counter. "Chocolate-chip cookies, chocolate brownie and raisin flapjack," she announced, pulling cartoon paper plates loaded with biscuits out of her backpack. They were wrapped up tightly, in several layers of cling film, but they didn't seem to have appreciated the journey. "Sorry if they're a bit broken. They've been jiggling up and down on my back for half an hour."

At that, Pete looked like he was about to burst a blood vessel. "I walked here," she clarified and he looked suitably impressed. She wrestled off the cling film. "Ta-dah."

He raised an eyebrow. "Blimey."

"So, what do you fancy?"

Again with the cheeky smile.

"Of the biscuits!"

Pete walked over and looked. "All of them," he said.

"Good. Well. They're not free."

He frowned.

"You have to earn them. How much work have you done since yesterday?"

Pete explained to a very surprised Jenny all that he had achieved in the past 24 hours since she'd last seen him. She was impressed. "Well, okay, you can have one, then."

"One?"

"Okay, two."

"Grief, you're a hard task master. I thought I'd done really well. Especially considering I've been battling the remains of tonsillitis."

He pulled a brave face, but his boyish charm wasn't fooling her. She knew he was used to it working with women, but she was still a little sore from his attack on her the day before. She smiled and walked off into the kitchen and poured them both a drink of juice.

"Make yourself at home," he said, grinning.

"Thank you. I will."

The two sat down with a drink and some biscuits and chatted about the small things: their days, her running, and his debatable ability to last on this one vice.

"So who taught you to bake like this," he asked finishing off the last few crumbs in his hand. "Was it your auntie?"

"No. I don't think so. Probably Mabel."

"Who's Mabel?"

"Our cook back home."

"You had a cook? How rich were you?"

"Me? Not very. My parents...?" She shrugged. "They're quite well off, yeah. Got a house up near Kendal."

"And you really don't have *anything* to do with them any more?"

Jenny didn't want to go there again. How he had so easily got her to open up to him the other day was a miracle. He made her feel as if she could trust him, like an old friend. If only she could trust him with her heart. She tucked her feet up onto the settee next to her and tried to divert the conversation.

"Your mum sounds pretty cool." Jenny saw the expression on Pete's face darken. "An Oxford don?"

"A lecturer. Yeah, she's great. I haven't seen her as often as I should have these last few years."

"Is that your way of trying to protect her?"

Pete looked at her. "Something like that."

"Just think how proud she will be when you pass the last exam."

"Is that your subtle way of putting the thumb screws on me? No pressure then, huh? I've just got to do it for you *and* my mum, or you'll *both* be disappointed? I guess I'd better get back to it."

She smiled. "Unless you want to talk about yourself some more?"

"Right. To work."

Jenny grinned at him. "Would you like me to test you on anything?"

"Not just yet. Give me a couple more days."

Jenny decided to leave then and let him get on with his work, reminding him not to eat the whole tray of cookies in one go and she walked home. She felt positive now. He might not be her lover, probably a good thing as it happened, but he seemed to be comfortable as her friend. And that was what she wanted… wasn't it?

She reflected on how much she had told him about her childhood. More than she had told anyone else, ever. But give and take might be a way to get him to open up. She felt guilty that she hadn't told him the complete truth about herself, but it was enough. He didn't need to know the real reason her life had fallen apart so dramatically back then, but having opened up to her, surely he had earned a little.

Pete returned to work the following week. He made peace with his consultant after a stern talking to; he was on his final warning now. He took a ward round, getting up to speed with the cases on ITU and then headed over to pain clinic as soon as he was through.

As he had promised, he was at occupational health at midday and awkwardly checked in. The doctor saw him, Pete giving up enough information to account for his disappearance, yet keeping as much to himself as he could. He was examined and referred for counselling, and an appointment was made for six weeks' time.

Free again, he hurried back into the canteen to grab a quick bite before his afternoon list. He spotted Jenny on her way into work as he made his way up to theatre. She was walking with two other nurses. He smiled and said hello, and the nurses she was walking with beamed back, but Jenny's face was enigmatic. What was with her? He thought she'd be pleased to see him back on form, returning to his responsibilities in the hospital again, but something in those grey eyes wasn't right. He puzzled on this until he started his list and then again when things were quiet.

That evening he hit the books. Six weeks to counselling. Like he was ever going to make it to that! He wondered if Jenny was going to come round that evening, so he could ask her what was bothering her. But she didn't show.

He ate her delicious flapjacks, but hadn't the heart to tell her he didn't like chocolate. And he *would* study hard, but for whom? If he was honest, it might have been vanity, but it was for her. He didn't want to let himself down in front of Jenny. He wanted her to be proud of him. So, in fact, it was for *him*, wasn't it? He was getting used to the girl. The way she had started coming round, the way she seemed to actually care, was growing on him. She was… intriguing. Was he starting to care about her?

Pete worked till half-eleven at night and was quite pleased with how much he had covered. Having tried and failed the exam once before, under similar circumstances, he had a good idea of what was involved and he had been through the mill of weeks of revision once already. It was a good job he had. Four weeks to go. It wasn't a huge amount of time to get himself ready.

He climbed into bed with his mind still whirling and remembered what it felt like to go to sleep without the company of alcohol or a guilty conscience.

The next day he was looking for Jenny at work. He didn't know what shift she was working, but he wanted to see her, to tell her how much work he had done. To show her he was being good. He wanted to see those grey eyes change colour when she laughed, to see the twinkle in her eyes when she was being cheeky and to feel her presence in his life, making him strong.

And as if some spirit had heard him, that evening, after he returned home, she was waiting for him on his doorstep.

"You didn't walk all the way over here again, did you?" he asked, seeing her in tight sportswear and looking flushed.

"No, I ran."

"You ran?"

"I wanted to check on you, but I wanted to go for a run too. So I ran here." Pete invited her in and she rested her rucksack on the ground. "I brought along a book in case you weren't quite ready."

"Ready for what?"

"To be tested."

He laughed. "Give me a chance; I've only just got in. Why don't I run you a shower and while you get freshened up, I can grab us something to eat and then you can grill me to your heart's content."

"Sounds like a plan."

Pete turned on the shower and found a clean towel in his cupboard. She confessed to having packed a spare top and deodorant in her bag in case she was unapproachable, but this would keep her occupied and off his back while he worked out what he wanted to do.

He searched through his kitchen for something to make, but ended up ringing for a pizza. He changed into casual clothes, some dark-grey jogger bottoms and a t-shirt and then hunted around for something to drink. There was nothing. Not one measly beer. She really had gone all out on reforming him. Well, then, it was her own fault if she had to drink milk.

He could hear the shower running and tried not to picture a beautiful woman in his bathroom. A beautiful *naked* woman. A beautiful *wet*, naked woman soaping herself down... He took a deep breath. *He* was going to need that shower at this rate. Time to study.

Pete ticked off the slots on his timetable. So far he had managed to cover almost half the pregnancy-related topics. He wasn't confident on diseases and emergencies in obstetrics. Maybe Jenny could test him on those?

Jenny emerged from the bathroom and Pete almost lost the power of speech. Fresh, clean, athletic, Jenny Wren was in his flat, damp-haired and bright-eyed, wanting to be with him. Of course, she didn't want to *be* with him, she just wanted to *help* him, and that was different. For her. He took a deep breath.

"I'm struggling a bit with obstetrics," he managed, and then hearing his voice, he cleared his throat and tried again. "Is that going to be all right for you?"

"Of course. Anything you like. Where shall we begin?"

96

The two of them sat down on the settee and he handed over his revision notes and textbooks and they settled down to work. Ten minutes later the pizza arrived. Pete answered the door and brought it back in. "Haven't had a chance to get any shopping yet," he said in his defence. But he opened it up and the smell wafting across at them was so good and Jenny tucked in. "Meat feast with extra cheese."

Jenny moaned with pleasure at her first bite and Pete was transfixed. He tried to eat, distracted by how turned on he was feeling.

She licked her lips and then her fingers. "You're forgiven," she said. God help him, but he didn't want to be. He wanted to do all kinds of depraved things with her. Finger food had been such a bad idea. He tried to remember that the girl had a boyfriend and concentrated on the pizza packaging: corrugated card with three colours of printing, and somehow he got through.

After she had wolfed down two big slices, Jenny's pace slowed a little, allowing for conversation. "So, how did it go, back at work yesterday?" she asked, picking out another slice from the enormous gooey pizza.

"As well as can be expected," he told her, watching the cheese strands playing tug of war with her lips. "Had to take an earful about responsibility from Dr Lambert, but he's not that bad. It could have been a lot worse. It probably should have been." He wanted to kiss those lips. He wanted to lick every bit of her and finish at her mouth.

"What about occy health?"

Pete paused mid-chew and looked at her. Occy health? That was going to help his will power. "They've booked me in for counselling in six weeks' time."

"Six weeks? Is that the earliest they could do?"

"Apparently."

"Not that it matters. If they think I'm going to go along and spill my guts to a complete stranger, they can think again."

"But won't you have to?"

"My rotation finishes in about six weeks – fingers crossed – I only have to stall them for a couple of days and I'll be away." Jenny seemed unimpressed. "Would *you* go and tell some head-tilting, psycho-babbler about your private stuff?"

Jenny frowned. "They're qualified counsellors."

"But they don't know me."

"You need to talk to someone, Pete. It's important."

"I'm talking to you, aren't I? Unless you'd rather I didn't?" It was true, he was. How had that happened?

"No. Of course. It's fine if you'd rather, although I can't claim to be anything like as good as a professional."

"But I can speak to you. And… I like you. I might go as far as to say I even *trust* you."

Jenny's eyes met his and he felt something quiet pass between them. "Do you trust me enough to tell me something about your dad yet?"

Hell. What had he started? It was time to bail out. He didn't mean he wanted to actually *talk*. Not *actually* talk. He just meant *theoretically*. "Perhaps. One day."

She was still looking at him.

"Why my dad?"

"Because you never speak about him. Because I know a little about your mum and I've met your lovely brother. And although you hide it well, I know there is something troubling you in your past. Something you had to learn to hide from as a child."

"Or we can talk about emergencies in labour?"

"We can talk about whatever you want, but sometime you'll have to let it all out and get over it, in order to move on."

"Get over it? Like a dose of the flu?" She had no idea. He shook his head in disgust and suddenly his temper was rising. "You think saying a few words can get you over years of watching your mother being beaten? Years of listening to her crying? You think that just because I tell someone that my dad was a filthy drunk, who picked on my mother because she was more successful than him, that I'm going to suddenly feel much better about things? Words won't block out memories, Jen. They won't take away the pain of the first time he hit me. He was a bully and a thug and I'm glad he's gone. I hate him. I loathe him, with every ounce of breath left in me."

She was quiet, then. Pete took a deep breath and forced it down inside. "Are you happy now? Because *I* certainly don't feel any better. Do you?"

Jenny reached out with her hand and he flinched away from her touch. She slid closer and he glared at her. What was wrong with this girl? Did she have a death wish? Or was she just determined to be miserable? Why didn't she just leave him to tear himself apart on his own? Most other girls did.

Slowly, Jenny slid her arms around him and he melted into her, exhausted and shaking. His face buried in her warm neck as she eased the tension away from him with her stoical soft acceptance. What had this woman done to him that he came so easily undone?

They stayed that way for a long time, just holding on in the moment, releasing the bitter bile that flowed through his veins. And then Pete pulled away and he looked at her and all pretence was lost. He could speak to this woman and she never seemed to judge him, not on the important stuff anyway. She accepted him, all the bad that swirled around within him; she was washing it away. She sat back, then, saying nothing and without even realising it he was suddenly unburdening himself to her, all his past and all of his woes.

"My first memories of it are from when I was seven. Mum had just got a new job and it paid far better than his. That was the first time I remember the shouting. Jimmy must have been about three at the time. I remember us cowering in the playhouse in my bedroom, quiet as mice, afraid of what was going on downstairs. I wasn't aware of any violence then, but a month or two later I noticed a purple bruise on my mother's wrist when I knocked into it. I remember being upset because I thought I had done that to

99

her, but she told me it had happened the day before."

"He started drinking not long after that. He would come in later and the rows became more frequent. About a year or so after it started, my mum was ill and he told me I had to sort Jimmy out myself and get us both to school. So I did as I was told; I was only a child. But when I got home that afternoon, I went in to see her and... she was..."

Jenny reached over and took hold of his hand. "Was she badly injured?"

"She was purple, Jen." He shook his head as unshed tears threatened to spill over at the memory. "Her face was swollen and had been bleeding and she had bruises on her arms and neck, everywhere I could see."

Tears glistened in Jenny's eyes. "Oh, Pete," she whispered and her pity made him try harder to be strong.

"I knew who had done it, although she tried to make out it wasn't as bad as it was. And when he got home I launched at him, kicking and screaming. That was the first time he laid a hand on me. He picked me up by the arm, twisted it and shoved me hard against the wall. "Never forget who's in charge in this house," he told me and as he let go of my arm, he slapped me hard across the ear and I fell to the floor.

"Jimmy was so tiny. He didn't speak for a month after that. He started wetting the bed and I had to sort him out in case Dad got to hear of it and did the same thing to him.

"It was shortly after that Mum took me aside and told me to find a safe place to go. She told me to find a place away from everyone, where we could build a little den, and if she ever thought it safer, she would give me the signal and I would take us off and hide there until it was safe to come back." His face started to crumple. "I knew what he was doing to her. I wanted to stay and protect her, but I was scared. I was so scared of him, Jen. And someone had to protect Jimmy. I would never have let him hurt Jimmy."

"And you kept him safe," she told him.

He nodded. "Yes."

"Then you did what she wanted. You kept the two of you safe. You should be proud of yourself, taking on that huge responsibility at such a young age." She squeezed his hand and coaxed his gaze to look at her. "You were a good brother, Pete."

Pete let his eyes fall away again. "But a rubbish son."

Jenny lifted his chin with her fingers. "You were a good son too. It might not have felt like it at the time, but you couldn't have changed anything. You were only young yourself."

He looked into her hazel-tinged grey eyes and wished he had more to offer her. She was his remedy, his balm against the scars of life. And he wished he had it in him to be worthy of her, that she could learn to love him and be loved in return.

Not long after that, they returned to work and studied hard until well after ten, when Jenny admitted she'd better go home. He drove her back to her house as he was unhappy with her walking alone at that time of night.

Outside her house he pulled up and she turned to him. "Thank you for this evening," she said and for the life of him, Pete couldn't think why.

"No, thank you," he told her and a minute lingered in the air between them when he didn't know what to do. The possibility of something more happening between them sparked in his mind. It haunted him, dangling something he was afraid to want just out of reach. But she was taken, and it was too big a risk. Then she slipped off her seat belt and got out of the car, and the moment had passed.

"Get some proper food in before next time," she told him. "Man cannot live on pizza alone."

He smiled and called back to her, "Oh, yes he can," and switching the engine back on, he pulled away.

Jenny couldn't explain why, but for the next few days, life seemed to tick along just a little lighter. Nothing felt quite as much trouble, and by the weekend, when she had some free time, she was eager to get back over to Pete's to see how he was getting on. Once again she searched about for recipes and then baked her heart into everything she made.

She turned up on Saturday afternoon. The day had been nice and she had taken her time walking the route to his building, enjoying the cool breeze and the smell of freshly cut grass. The sun's dazzling rays beat down on her face until she arrived at Pete's flat to find he wasn't home.

She cursed herself and, feeling incredibly foolish, walked the three miles back home. She still hadn't plucked up the courage to ask him for his number. If she had, she could have called and made sure he was in. But where was he? Was he out somewhere drinking? Was he dead in a ditch? Anything could have happened to him.

By the time she got home, Jenny didn't feel like going for a run. She packed the goodies into an old tin and hid them in her room, putting on some music. Patsy or Nina? Either would be suitable. Patsy for when she needed a little consoling, but Nina if she was really brooding. Nina, she thought. She lay on her bed and felt the time hang heavily upon her. Was she being a fool? He had warned her not to get too attached to him. Had she got closer than she'd planned to? Who was she kidding? She knew full well when she set out on this journey that *that* had happened a long time ago. She screwed her eyes up tight, trying for a second to block the feelings out and then pulled out her diary.

I went to him today and he wasn't there. I miss him. I miss the way we are when we're together, the way we're starting to connect. He trusts me; he said so. We can sit on the settee together and be relaxed. We can laugh. We can cry. We can... love. I'm not saying I'm in love with him. I don't trust him as yet. I'm afraid that he could use me to get over all of this and then return to his women and frivolous ways. This is no fairy tale. This is life. But I miss him all the same.

She heard the letterbox clack and the post slap down on the mat, and walked back downstairs to retrieve it. There was only one for her, so she left the rest on the side by the front door and took hers back up to her room.

It was a letter from her auntie, which was odd, because she normally rang, so she opened it with some care and a good deal of suspicion.

Chapter 9

Dear Jenny,

I know you will need time to think about this, so I have put my thoughts down in a letter. This way you can read them again and again, as often as you need, to make up your mind.

I have heard from your mother, and Time For Life magazine is doing an article on your father in a couple of weeks and they are asking to do a photo shoot at the house. Understandably they would really like you to be there. Now I know your first thoughts will be to tell them to go to hell, but just think about it, sweetheart, just think about it, for me. They are your family and they love you and they miss you every day. Haven't you made them suffer long enough? You know I love you and you will ALWAYS have a home with me, but they're your flesh and blood, Jen. And that's important. Your uncle's father died before he ever had the chance to make it right between the two of them and I know that haunted him till the end of his days. Don't live in the past, my girl, look to the future. Give them a chance and just try.

The photo shoot is midday on Wed 21st August, at their

*house. I hope you decide to go. If you want to talk to me,
please give me a ring. I always love to hear from you. I'm
here if you need me.*

I love you.

Auntie May

Jenny put the letter down. Her aunt had been right; her first
response had been to block them out. And that was exactly what
she intended to do. Images of home flitted through her brain.
Too painful.

She spent the rest of the afternoon and evening vegging out in
front of the TV. She'd refused to go out with Chloe, giving the
excuse of a headache, and sat and stared at the screen, completely
failing to cheer up.

She was brooding; she knew she was. She was wallowing in
self-pity and she didn't care. After all her effort, Pete hadn't even
been home and then with the letter stirring old memories...

Flicking through the channels, she resolved that first thing in
the morning she was going to walk round to Pete's, get his phone
number and take him his cakes, and then she would think about
booking a holiday. That would cheer her up.

Jenny didn't sleep well that night. She tossed and turned,
but finally the morning came and she was up with the lark and
raring to go.

She arrived outside Pete's door and looked at her watch. Just
gone half-nine. He didn't strike her as the type of guy to be at
church on a Sunday morning. She knocked. After knocking a
second time, she was just about to leave when the door cracked
open and a bleary face peered out.

"Jen? What's the matter? Are you all right?"

God, she had woken him up! Keep it light, she thought, don't
scare him off with the third degree. "Provisions." She smiled and

held up the bag. Way to look casual, Jen.

Pete looked at his watch. "It's nine-thirty on a Sunday morning!"

"I made muffins." Her voice was weaker. She was too early. She had dragged the poor guy out of bed. What on earth was she meant to do now? She passed them across, suddenly embarrassed at her intrusion. "I'm sorry. I'm a bit of an early bird, I guess. I'll leave them with you. I'll just go and…" She started to back away down the stairs.

"No, Jen. Stay. Please. I just wasn't expecting a visitor so early. I—"

"I didn't have your number."

His eyes brightened. "Come inside. The least I can do is offer you a cup of tea. I bet you walked all the way over here again, didn't you?"

"I like walking." He had opened the door wider now and he was wearing only his pyjama bottoms. His toned upper body was… distracting. She had to try and ignore it. Look at his eyes, she thought.

Pete ushered her inside and she perched against the breakfast bar, a safe distance away from him while he made some tea.

"How are things, then?" he asked.

"Oh, hunky dory." Eyes up, girl, or you're never going to get through this.

"Only you seem a bit… odd."

He passed her over a cup of tea, looking at her and then wandered into the living room to sit down. He was within inches of her now, all bed-head and ruffled, his naked chest and abdomen crying out to be kissed. She took a deep breath and tried to steady her nerves. "I came over yesterday, but you weren't in." Her tone sounded disapproving and she was embarrassed by her lack of cool.

Pete smiled. "I was doing as I was told," he said. "Getting some food in."

"Oh." So much for her overactive imagination. Of course he was. He had to eat, didn't he? "So how's it going?"

106

"You mean the studying? Okay, actually. I may need your help again in a day or so, when I've finished with ENT, but... good, yeah. You seem to be good for me, Jenny Wren."

"My surname isn't actually Wren. You *do* know that, don't you?"

"Yeah, I know," he said.

She nodded. There was a silence and then, out of nowhere, it all came tumbling out. "My parents have asked me to go home for the day for a photo shoot."

Pete looked surprised. So was she. Why was she telling him this?

"A photo shoot? Do you think you may have underplayed their status just a little when you told me about your parents the other day?"

Jenny rolled her eyes.

"So... Are you going to go?"

"God, no!"

"So what's the problem, then?"

"I don't know. It just... I guess it brought it all up again. That's all."

"It sounds like it still upsets you."

Jenny couldn't begin to explain it.

"How many years has it been, Jen?"

Jenny didn't have to think. "Fourteen."

"Fourteen years? You haven't spoken to your family in fourteen years? No wonder it still upsets you. I can't imagine not seeing Jim for six months, let alone 14 *years*. Don't you want to make it right between you?"

No. No, no, no, she thought. That wasn't entirely true. Part of her wanted to. She wanted to see her sister. But it was just *them* and... "I'm afraid if I go, it'll stir it all up again and... Maybe I should just let sleeping dogs lie?"

Pete looked at her for a minute. "Seems to me like it's already stirred up. Look at you. I've never seen you in such a state. What happened to my bossy, overbearing nurse?"

Jenny gave him a look, but then smiled sadly.

"And you really haven't seen them, or spoken to them since you were 17?" he asked.

She shook her head. When she heard it out loud, it sounded ridiculous.

"And they've not sent you any birthday cards or presents?"

"Well, yes, but—"

"Didn't they pay your way through nursing training?"

"No, I think my aunt did that."

"You think?"

"I don't know. I assumed it was her. She wrote the cheques."

He sat still, looking at her for a minute. "If it was me sitting here telling you this, what would you be saying to me?"

Jenny squirmed. She knew full well what she'd be saying, but this was different. "But it's not the same thing. I'm not asking you to face your dad… although…"

Pete looked horrified. "Don't even go there."

She shrugged. "It was too hard, living there. I'm not sure I can ever return." It was just different.

He stroked her cheek in a show of affection that stirred the corners of her ailing heart. "Think about it, Jen. In the words of a very wise person. You've got to let it go. Face up to your past or you'll never be free to move on."

She took a deep breath and let it out. "And have you… let it go?" She was hopeful that he had. He seemed to be much better than last week. But his eyes clouded over.

"I'm trying," he said and he was serious, and she felt it.

They were silent for a moment after that, Jenny almost felt proud of his fight to reclaim his life.

"How did you find out about the shoot?" he asked at last.

"Auntie May wrote to me about it."

"And what did *she* have to say on the matter?"

"She thinks I should go."

He squeezed her hand and then got up and fetched his mobile. "Tap your number into that," he told her and she typed in her number and passed it back. Pete sent her a text. "Now you've got my number too, so if you do decide to go, you'll always have a friendly voice at the end of the phone if you need one."

Jenny checked her phone and put it away in her pocket. "Thank you," she said.

"Now let's go and investigate those cakes you've brought me. Anyone would think you're trying to fatten me up."

Oh no. Why did he have to go and say a thing like that? Now she was forced to look at his naked body and appraise it. She pasted on a smile. Look at the eyes, Jen, not his abdomen. Look at his eyes. "I'd better go. You're not going to get any work done while I'm here."

"Ain't that the truth," he said in a velvety, low voice that melted her insides and Jenny glanced away, suddenly unsure of his meaning.

After Jenny had gone, Pete hit the shower and turned it to cool. He had to get the thoughts about her out of his mind. Jen obviously had just as much as him to deal with. Maybe that was why they had found themselves together. But she had a boyfriend and good luck to her. He was not a sensible option for a girl like her, anyway. He was damaged goods and that was all he would ever be. Work he could get a handle on. Immersing himself in that had been a tonic, but apart from when he was with her, he was still the turbulent soul he had always been and that was dangerous.

He pulled on some clothes and looked at the pile of cakes she had brought him. It was time to pay a visit to the local gym. See if it remembered him.

Pete arranged to meet his mate, Neil, a night porter at St Steven's, inside the weights room, where they did half an hour of training before going for a swim.

"So are you going to come back to the ring?" Neil asked him when they were standing in line to do some diving. "We've missed you."

"Perhaps."

"I told Rich you were back in the neighbourhood. He's been expecting you."

"Okay, I'll try and find time to get myself down there. I've got a lot on at the minute, though; exams coming up, but it might do me some good."

He showered in the changing room and walked out to the main door, where Neil was popping a packet of crisps out of a vending machine. "Tell Rich I'll give him a call," he said. "Same time next week? Actually, no, I can't, I'm on call next weekend. I'll have to give you a ring. Might have to be one evening this week."

"Just let me know," Neil said.

Pete drove back to his flat and skipped up the steps. He felt invigorated, ready to face the day. It was time to get down to some serious work. He didn't want to look like an idiot, not knowing his stuff the next time Jenny came round to play. Hmm, 'play' he thought. Jenny was not the kind of girl for 'playing' with. She was good, kind and worth the wait to know. She was not for him, though, not unless he was totally stupid, because knowing him, he would only mess the whole 'friends' thing up and then he would be nothing to her and he wasn't sure he could take that.

As he set out his books to start reading, Pete thought about her and her family. There had to be something more to it, surely? Something she wasn't telling him? Whatever it was, he hoped she took her own advice and started to face her demons. She was an angel when she relaxed. Yes, Jenny was a keeper, but sadly not for him.

Monday morning, Jenny was on a late, that meant a nice long lie-in and a big brunch before getting ready to go to work. She wouldn't be able to spend any time with Pete that day, but she might see him. Maybe they would bump into each other in the corridor. They might have time for a quick chat. A smile, even,

110

would be okay.

Jenny was ruminating about the thought of seeing her parents. She had thought a great deal about her sister since mentioning her to Pete. Lizzy had been only nine when she'd left, she would be 23 by now. What had become of her? She had been an irritating little sister back then, but she could be a friend now. The thought of rediscovering her sister began to take root in her heart and was waging war with her anger at her parents. It was because of them that she hadn't seen her sister for so long. Could she put up with the one in order to accomplish the other? Could she go back there? This was something she was going to have to think about.

For now, though, she had to push it to the back of her mind; she had work to do. Maybe something magical would happen to make the decision for her.

Pete had only three weeks left to get himself ready to pass the exam, so she would have to be on to him, to make sure he pushed himself, continually watching for mood swings and any weakening. It occurred to her to think about what was going to happen when it was all over. He would no longer need her. Would he still value their friendship? And, more importantly, where would he go?

Her day was busy and the work taxing at times. She had a 101 things to be doing and only one pair of hands to do them with. A great influx of emergencies overnight was hampering the bed situation for the routines that day. Then ITU called and said they had a nurse go off sick and could they possibly send one of their nurses down to collect the patient to be transferred up? Jenny drew the short straw and was swiftly assigned the task.

She buzzed to be let on to ITU and the nurse in charge of the case met her. It was a man who'd had an aortic aneurysm operated on and had needed a few days of their support, but he was fit to go to a normal surgical ward now and she was brought rapidly up to date on his treatment. A porter arrived to assist with the transfer and they slowly made their way along the corridor, chatting to the patient as they went.

Waiting for the lift to arrive, another trolley pulled up with a little girl looking pale and ill. She was clutching a pink fluffy unicorn to her chest and Jenny realised, just from looking at her, that she wasn't going to get better any time soon. She felt compelled to try and make the girl happy, at least a smile to brighten her day. "He's beautiful! What's his name?" she asked, pointing to the toy.

The nurse travelling with her told her it was a 'she' and her name was Penelope.

"Penelope? What a pretty name for a unicorn," Jenny said. "Is she keeping you company while you're in here?"

The girl nodded, her eyes wide, taking it all in.

"I bet she gives good cuddles. Oh, excuse me." Jenny leaned in closer. "Penelope says you give good cuddles too. Is that true?"

The little girl smiled and squeezed her toy against her. And then the far door opened.

"Goodbye, Penelope, take care of her, won't you?" she said and the little girl was wheeled inside the lift and the doors closed around them.

A minute later, the lift returned and just as the doors were closing behind them, Fiona, from physio, hopped in. She said hello and they stood in silence waiting for the lift to ascend. At the second floor, the lift opened and all four of them made their way out: the porter pushing the patient and Jenny and Fiona following behind.

As they stopped by the door to the ward, Fiona passed behind Jenny to get out of their way. "Oh, I forgot to ask, how's it going with you and Mike, Jen?" she said.

Jenny turned around to look at her. "Oh, that was over ages ago. It was only a couple of weeks at the beginning of the year. Complete disaster." Then she smiled. "Keep up, will you." She turned back and, waiting to come out, with the door held wide open for them, was Dr Florin. Jenny felt her cheeks flare. He was looking at her and he wasn't smiling. Time to bluff it out.

"Thank you," she said and they pushed the patient down onto

the ward and parked him up in his room. Damn! She didn't know why, but she felt uncomfortable with Pete having overheard that. There was no question he must have heard it, but why was he so disapproving? Finding no answers, she got on with settling the patient on to the ward and then headed back to the nurses' station to sort out the paperwork.

Pete got home, hung up his jacket and leaned his forehead against the wall. That was so inconvenient. He knew it was wrong to have read even a snippet of Jen's diary, but it had made him more sensible, thinking she had a boyfriend. It had been January 1st he had looked at. Jenny had been so excited about going out with him. But it had obviously just been a flash in the pan. She wasn't attached, well not to him anyway. She was – potentially - free. God, that made things so much more complicated. He wanted her, that was a given, but thinking he couldn't have her... shouldn't have her, had made him toe the line. Now that line had snapped.

He supposed he should really do the honourable thing and pull away. He didn't want a relationship and she was too tempting to be around now she was free. But she was stubborn. He could also find himself a girlfriend, but he didn't *want* a girlfriend, that wasn't his thing. And she had been so good to him too, had been all along, even when he had been wretched. Could he manage to keep his hands off her and be a gentleman? It had to be in him. Somewhere. He remembered. He *really* needed a drink.

Pete searched around his flat. Bloody woman! He must remember to get some alcohol the next time he went to town. He looked under his counter, to an array of baked goods growing old in their tin. He wanted to see her and knew only one way; he'd better get through some more of his work and give her something to test him on.

It was a long time waiting for Friday night, when Jenny was free to come and see him again. He rushed in from work, showered, changed and brushed his teeth, and then with every attempt to

113

appear nonchalant, waited for her to arrive.

At six o'clock she knocked. Pete called out. He had left the door on the latch so that he could look studious and focused when she arrived, but his heart rate kicked up a notch at the sound of her voice calling out as she closed the front door and walked in.

"Hello. Where are you?"

Suddenly the plan seemed ridiculous. His desk was in his bedroom. Not a great place to summon her if he was trying to be good. He hadn't done 'good' in a long while. He was rusty. He shot up and skipped out into the living room. "Hi. I was just doing some studying."

"Of course. What is it at the moment?"

"Maxillofacial."

"Ooh, tricky?"

"It's not too bad, actually. Would you like a drink?" He was on edge, he could feel it. He was turning into a blabbering fool. What was it this woman did to him? Was it that she was hot but not interested? Was it that she was too good for him? The forbidden fruit to claim and conquer? Whatever it was, she was doing it well. It was doing his head in. He breathed deeply.

"Are you all right?" she asked. "You seem... uneasy. I haven't come at a tricky time, have I? You did say six."

It was always a tricky time seeing her, for him anyway. "No, you're absolutely fine. I'm fine. Let's get you a drink and we can sit down."

They took their drinks over to the settee. "How was your week?" he asked.

"Busy. There's a bug going round. Staff off everywhere. How was it in theatre?"

Pete was watching the words forming on her lips. Her neck as it arched down towards her collar bone. The hollow just above. His eyes drank in the sight of her and then slid on up to the lobe of her ear and the sexy diamond earring at the top. Her skin was tanned and aching to be kissed. He swallowed. Hard.

114

"Pete? Are you sure you're okay? Have you had another nightmare or something?"

She was talking to him. He had to snap out of it before he embarrassed himself. A surreptitious pinch to his thigh and his eyes met with hers. "Theatre? Yes. Okay."

"I think you might have been overdoing it. Are you sure you're up to me testing you?" she asked him. She looked concerned.

He swallowed again. "Yes. Absolutely." Mentally, he slapped himself. "I'll go and get my things." Pete walked back into his bedroom and silently screamed. "You stupid idiot!" he whispered and sucked in a deep breath. "You can do this. She's just here to get you through your exams, that's all. As soon as you get this over and done with she'll be satisfied and you won't have to see her again," and he slapped himself a few times about the face and then reached for his books.

"Are you all right in there?" she called out as he emerged from the bedroom with a sunny smile in place. "Only it sounded like you dropped some papers, or something."

"No." He put the work down on the living-room table. "Here we are." He handed over the study notes and pointed out which bits he needed testing on.

"How are you doing for biscuits?" she asked him.

"Almost gone," he said and rested back against the side of the settee, ready to pay attention.

About an hour later they were discussing the ins and outs of the laryngoscopy and bronchoscopy when Jenny's stomach started to rumble. "Haven't you eaten?" he asked her.

"No. But I'm all right. Don't worry."

Her stomach rumbled again. "No, you're not. How stupid of me. I'll order us some pizza."

"Do you ever live on anything else?" she teased.

"Would you like something different?"

"No. Pizza is fine. You're very jumpy, Pete. Do you think you'd better take a night off?"

115

Would that mean she would go back home or the dangerous temptation of losing his focus? Neither was good. He valued her friendship and couldn't screw it up. "No."

"But you're working this weekend, aren't you?"

It made no difference. If he didn't work tonight she would either walk away, or they would have to spend an evening together for real. "I'm good. I'll get an early night. I'll just ring for that pizza. Same as last time?"

Jenny nodded. "Okay, yeah." She licked her lips and his head almost exploded.

Hydrogen, Helium, Lithium, Beryllium, Boron, Carbon, Nitrogen, Oxygen. He could get through this. He breathed out and dialled the number.

When he sat down again, he chose a seat across from her in an armchair. She looked quizzically at him. "Where were we?"

They carried on working until the arrival of the pizza 20 minutes later, when Pete lost all control of his thoughts. Watching Jenny gorge herself only a few feet away from him was about as erotic as it could get. She might as well be stretched out naked in front of him, rubbing baby oil into her soft, heaving breasts the way his hormones were raging that night and Jenny seemed to be entirely oblivious to the situation. And thank God for that! If she had shown *any* sign of having the same thoughts going through her mind as he had through his, he would have had her stripped naked and under him in seconds.

In the end he called it a night and, barely able to breathe the entire way home, he dropped her at her house and he could swear there was a moment's hesitation as she went to get out of the car. She hovered, but then she was gone, and his heart flipped out watching her walk up the tiny path to her front door. She waved goodbye and he waited till she was inside, before slumping over the steering wheel and then driving back to his flat to dunk his head in a bowl of ice-cold water and drag himself off to bed.

Jenny closed the door behind her and sank back against it. What was she thinking? It had all started as a chance to help him, to pay him back for what he had done for her; now she was besotted with the guy. The proximity of him took her breath away. She had been grateful, if a little puzzled, when he'd moved a space away from her. He smelled so good and her mind was playing all sorts of tantalising tricks on her, heightening her senses and ramping up her pulse rate.

But he had been on edge, she was convinced of it. Perhaps he was backing off, fed up of her checking on him. Or maybe he could sense her attraction and was pulling away. Was she making matters worse, going round there and interrupting all the time? At least he seemed to be enjoying her baking.

She swallowed what was left of the saliva in her mouth. He was on call this weekend, anyway, so they would have some time apart from each other to see if that helped them both; him to have a break from her and her to tamp down her feelings for him.

Heather walked into the room. "You all right? You look a bit flushed. Been running again?"

Jenny was wearing jeans and a t-shirt with sandals. It amazed her how someone so unobservant could end up in their profession. "Yes," she said.

Five minutes later, Flis came crashing through the door. She flounced across to the settee and flumped down. "I'm back. I'm back. The wanderer returns. Oh, I'm exhausted. You won't believe the things I've been up to these last two weeks," and she proceeded to regale them about the many places she had visited and people she had met whilst she was getting loved-up in London. It took a while, but Jenny was grateful for the diversion.

"So, anything interesting happen around here while I've been away?" she asked when she had finished telling them everything about herself.

Jenny had warned Chloe about Flis's entanglement with Pete on the day that he had left their house, but panic gripped her as

117

she suddenly realised she had forgotten to mention it to Heather.

"No, all quiet here. So how are you and lover boy, then?" Jenny said, trying to switch the attention straight back to Flis.

But Heather was excited. "Well, apart from the whole Dr Florin thing."

Chapter 10

Jenny wanted the ground to swallow her up. Flis turned and looked at Heather.

"What?"

"He went missing, didn't you know? Jenny went off on a crusade, found him and brought him back here. He was looking pretty rough for a couple of days. But he's all right now, isn't he, Jen?"

Flis looked straight at Jenny and her face looked as though it couldn't decide whether to be perplexed or furious.

Jenny took a deep breath and played it down as much as she could, but Heather, bless her cotton socks, just kept dropping her further in it.

"Still, she's been keeping the house smelling lovely with all the baking she's been doing for him."

Jenny could swear there was fire coming out of Flis' eyeballs now. She wasn't looking directly at her, but she could feel the heat from them. Jenny focused her attention on a stubborn pizza mark on the edge of her t-shirt.

"How could you?" Flis said at last. "You know what that man put me through and you go and throw yourself at him. I don't know whether to feel sorry for you or betrayed."

Although in her mind she had done plenty, the reality was

quite different and Jenny felt she had to defend herself against the attack. "It's not what you think, Flis. Nothing's happening between us. I'm just helping him out."

Flis snorted. She obviously did not believe *that* for a second.

"Honestly. He doesn't think of me in that way. He never has," and that was the point. It was true and it hurt. "He's more of a big brother to me, and he was having a hard time—"

"The poor dear!"

"—and I… I was the only one who had any time to reach out to him."

"You're breaking my heart."

Jenny was getting frustrated. Why the hell did she have to justify herself to Flis anyway? "Nothing's happened!" She made an effort to calm her voice. "Besides, why do *you* care so much? I thought you were all hunky-dory with lover boy?"

Flis sagged back, her smile trying to reclaim its position on her face. "I just worry about you, Jen. Don't let him use you, will you?"

Was that true? Jenny wasn't convinced, but she would take the peace that it offered. "I won't," she said, but she was not at all sure she would say no if he tried to claim his one night with her too. She knew full well he would break her heart if she let him, so she needed to keep a safe distance. She looked earnestly at her friend. "I won't," she assured her.

Jenny stopped writing in her diary from that point on, afraid her confessions would burst her fragile bubble of hope. She didn't want to confront her growing feelings for this man and most certainly didn't want to consider his. Time to put her head in the sand and let life drift on by and hopefully things would be clearer after he'd passed his exams.

But Pete wasn't the only thing she was blocking out of late. Her trip home was also weighing on her mind. She would have to make a decision soon, but what was she to do? Pete and her aunt seemed convinced she should go. But going back…? She took a deep breath. Could she actually face that? Her room. Her parents. The tiny grave on the hill? Face up to your fears, that's what he had said. It had been troubling her more of late. It had started with Kate and Selena, but the things Pete had said about Lizzy had made her think too. Yes, he was right, she had to go; she couldn't block it out any longer.

Jenny retrieved the letter from the wastepaper basket in the corner of her room and checked her rota. Wednesday 21st? She *was* free that day. She was even on a late the next day in case she was back late at night. She flipped open her laptop and checked for train times. Yes. It was doable.

She had not been back to see Clara since she'd left. She had done her best to pretend it was all some bad dream, but it had crept back in, slowly, quietly, pulling her down and whispering to her heart. It was calling to her now, stronger than ever. She *had* to go, for Clara.

The next day Jenny rang her aunt to tell her to let her family know she was coming. She booked train tickets and rechecked her rota. Yes she could do this and she would be okay. She had nothing to be sorry for, except to Clara, for not holding on tightly enough to her fragile life. It was time to go back and see her. It was long past time.

The weekend went by very slowly. Pete was in work and his distance from her felt all the more difficult when she was free.

She cleaned a little, shopped and saw her friends. She visited her aunt, who was pleased to hear she was going, but her mind kept coming back to think about Pete. She tried to write, to take her mind off everything hurtling in on her, but she was missing him. She knew she was going to get burned now. It was inevitable. But she yearned to see him more than ever. Reason had taken a holiday and it wasn't coming back any time soon. She tried to remind herself that this wasn't going to end well for her, that she wasn't his type, but it made little difference, she wanted to be. No. She wanted him to be hers.

By Monday evening she was desperate to see him again. She

rang him the moment she thought he would be out of work, to see if he needed any help with his revision, but he said he had been so busy over the weekend that he was completely whacked out and was just going to hit the sack, so Jenny wished him a good night's sleep, closed her phone up and burst into tears.

What was wrong with her? At what point had she turned into an emotional wreck? She was a strong woman, able to withstand a hurricane and move on with her life, or at least she thought she was. She needed to get a grip. It was probably everything else coming back to her again. One more night and she would have other things to concentrate on. Wednesday morning she was going to take the 7.50 to Birmingham New Street and then the 9.33 to Oxenholme. She would catch a cab from there. She should get there around midday and, if she played her cards right, she would be home again for tea.

On Tuesday morning, Jenny was in work. She threw herself into her tasks, immersing herself in other people's lives in an attempt to block out her own. Pete walked on to the ward to check on his patients before the morning list. She smiled and waved hello as Amanda took him around the ward and she watched him from a distance. He was a lovely, gentle man. She could see the warmth in his patients' eyes; they felt safe with him. He exuded confidence and showed nothing but kindness, if only he could stop being such a player. He hadn't been, once upon a time; Rachel had said so.

She grabbed a colleague to check some controlled drugs with her and heard footsteps coming up behind them. She turned around and there he was. He smiled and Jenny could feel her cheeks burning.

"I need your help with some cases this evening," he said. "Around six?" She nodded and he walked away and Jenny tried to focus on the pills in her hand.

Getting home just after three, she had three whole hours to kill before Pete got home. Flis was in too. How could she get past her? She didn't want to run to Pete's that night; she would turn up hot and sweaty and have to shower again. *Not* advisable with her hormones raging like this. She realised she hadn't done any baking and he said not long back that he had almost run out. Quickly she set to work, using whatever she had in the house to be able to take something with her. Shortbread would have to do; she had enough for that.

Heather came down as she was lifting it out of the oven. "Mmm, that smells nice. Can I have some?"

"Sorry."

"Oh, you off to Pete's again?" she asked.

Flis looked up from where she was sitting in the living room. Her radar ears had overheard. "You're not baking for *him* again, are you? She appeared around the kitchen door. "I thought nothing was going on between the two of you?"

"It isn't, but I'm keeping him supplied with cookies on the understanding that he lays off the booze and hot women."

Flis burst out laughing. "And you think some home-made cookies will stop him wanting to shag anything in a skirt, do you? Why didn't I think of that before?"

Jenny felt suddenly foolish. Who was she kidding? Flis was right, although she could have phrased it more kindly. She looked down at her shortbread lying flat on the tray in front of her. Heather shot Flis a look and rested a hand on Jenny's shoulder.

"I'm sure he's very grateful for everything you're doing for him, Jen. Have you got something to put that in?"

It was a slow walk over there that evening and when she arrived, Jen didn't know what to do. Should she drop the biscuits off and make her excuses, or help him with his studies, torturing herself even more, but doing what she said she would do? She knocked on the door.

A second later the door swung open and Pete was standing there with a smile as wide as the ocean. "Come in. I hope you haven't eaten."

Something was different. The lighting in the flat was subdued and Jenny noticed the table had been laid out for two. Hesitantly, she walked inside.

"I wanted to show you I *can* cook, when the pizza place is shut."

"But it's not shut on a Tuesday," she said, slightly confused.

"I wanted to cook for you, Jen. To say thank you."

Jenny's stomach clenched. Was this a romantic thank you or just a thank you before a goodbye? Or was it just a thank you… with mood lighting, and was that…? "That's Nina Simone!"

Pete smiled. "I got curious. She's not bad, actually."

"Not bad? She's pure gold."

He chuckled. "Take a seat. It should be almost ready. Red wine?"

Jenny looked at him.

"There's just one bottle, I promise. You can check if you like."

"That would be lovely, thank you."

Feeling slightly uncomfortable, Jenny took a seat. A few minutes later, a bowl of spaghetti bolognese and a salad were placed in front of her and garlic bread was put down by her side.

"Garlic bread? No kissing for you tonight, then," Jenny quipped and then instantly realised what she had said and blushed crimson.

"Only with those who've had it too," he told her.

Oh God, oh God, Oh God! Why had he said that? She tried to swallow a mouthful of spaghetti while Pete poured the wine.

"Cheers," he said and they clinked glasses, their eyes holding each other's gaze. And in that moment, Jenny could swear he was looking at her with something far stronger than friendship or lust. She took a swig and it went down the wrong way. She choked and thumped her chest. At least it broke the tension, but it was not something she wanted to repeat.

Throughout the rest of the meal, normal service was gradually resumed, so that by the end, Jenny felt comfortable enough to stay and help out with his studies. They settled into the living room, with Jen on one side and Pete on the other. She asked him questions and he answered, trying to cover everything he needed to know.

At ten, Jenny's phone started to bleep. She picked it out and turned the alarm off. "I've got to be getting home, I'm afraid," she said. "I've got a train to catch in the morning."

Pete looked confused.

"To see my parents."

"You're going, then." He sounded pleased.

"Yes. I decided it was time."

He smiled. "Good. I'm glad. Are you going to be okay?"

You know, she really thought she was. "Yes, I think I am."

She started to gather her things and Pete took his work back into his bedroom. Jenny retrieved her bag from beside the door and Pete walked back in and looked at her.

"Thank you," she said. His eyes ate her up from across the room. Sexual tension crackled between them, a whole world away from the bickering intolerance there had once been. Her nerves were clattering down the length of her limbs. She had to get out of there. She was scared.

Facing a car journey in close proximity, she decided to bail out and with a fleeting smile and an almost whispered goodbye, she made a move for the front door.

Pete spoke up from behind her, confusion rippling his voice. "Jenny?"

"I need to go. Sorry," she called back as she trotted quickly down the first flight of steps. "I'll let you know how it goes." She prayed he wouldn't follow. Her ears were on alert, listening out for any sound from above her, but focusing on getting clear, she kept her eyes forward.

Footsteps came up quickly behind her, catching her at the top of the final flight of stairs. He grabbed her arm and pulled her around, his gaze searching her face for explanation.

"Why are you running away from me, Jen?" His breathing was more laboured than hers. His head crowded in on her as his body slowly pushed her back against the wall. His breath was hot on her neck, causing her to shiver.

"Don't run away from me."

Jenny thought her heart was going to give out, it was thumping so hard inside her chest. She couldn't breathe, she couldn't think, she—

Pete put a finger under her chin, lifting her head to look up at him, but she couldn't. She didn't trust herself. Did he really want her, all of her?

"Look at me, Jen."

She mustn't.

"Look at me." His voice was firm and urgent. His breath was all around her, his seductive masculine scent destroying her resolve. Heat was burning her up as she finally lifted her eyes and they met with his.

"God, I want you," he whispered and his soft lips met hers as the world around her tipped and delicious, forbidden sensations melted her to her bones.

Powerful fingers held her face so gently and then one hand moved to the back of her head, threading through her hair and pulling her to him. The kiss deepened and her hands came to settle on his chest. Hesitant at first, she managed to cling on to the last shred of self-control, until his body pressed in on hers, making her aware of how much he wanted her. Hot, hard muscle wrapped in fabric urged her on and she flattened her palms. She could feel the beating of his heart as it kicked and fought to keep up with him. She let her bag fall to the ground, and, unable to fight it any more, she gave in. She had fought against this for long enough; she was exhausted.

In the blink of an eye he swung her up into his arms, caught her bag in his fingers and carried her back up the stairs to his flat. His eyes were fixed on hers with an intensity she had never known. She was powerless to tear her own gaze away. She was afraid, but she had relinquished all power to the inevitable. This had always been going to happen, she knew that now, and tomorrow she would be happy to pay the price, but tonight, she was his.

Chapter 11

With the taste of her still on his lips, Pete lay back, breathless.
His pulse was still pounding in his veins. He turned his head
and looked at her, his mind reeling. He had never felt such a
connection in his life. He couldn't peel his eyes away from her; her
supple body, the way her eyes shone like the wings of a butterfly
in sunlight. His body was shaking and he was filled with need.
God, how much did he want this woman? Fear like he hadn't felt
in years curled around him at the thought of her power over him.
She might yet reject him. She knew his reputation and his past,
well, some of it. Enough to make her run in the opposite direction if she had any sense. He was staring at her and he couldn't
help himself. She, on the other hand, looked serene. What had
he done? He hadn't just crossed the line. He had pulverised it.
He was in uncharted territory.

She swallowed, and the slow, lazy undulation made him want
her all the more. He was losing control and that terrified him.

"I—" she started.

"Shouldn't have done that?" He put on a smile, trying to ignore
the overwhelming panic that suddenly filled him.

She paused. "I was going to say: had not seen that coming.
You've never wanted me before. What happened?"

What was she saying? He had always wanted her – in his bed

– from the first time he set eyes on her. It was the danger he felt looking into her eyes that had kept him away. Before, when he had known her just a little, he had focused on her weakness as a reason to put him off, but with his return, he had found a stronger woman. She was vital and daunting, and the thought of having a real relationship with her terrified him. He shook his head. "You were off-limits."

Jenny rolled onto her side to face him, her eyes deftly searching his soul. She tucked the sheets up over her, in some small way hoping to cover her modesty. Did she not know he could look at her for eternity?

"Kate had such a go at me after Flis. But then Soph got hitched and it was only you."

Jenny looked at him then, seeming to speculate on his reasons for breaking the pact. Up close her eyes were not grey at all. They were a mixture of blue and light brown, with flecks of green and the light dancing within them lit the touch paper of his heart. He felt guilt and love and need overwhelming him, and he was afraid.

"But now that doesn't matter any more?"

"No, I mean yes, but… I thought… I thought…" Hell, who was he kidding? He would have sold his soul to the Devil that night for just one moment of passion with Jen.

Her eyes were so searching, he couldn't bear it. "Didn't you want it too?" They closed now, and when they reopened they were focused on his body, not his face, so he couldn't read them.

"Pete, I have wanted you ever since the very first day I met you." What?

"I just needed something more than you seemed willing to give." And there it was. He had been right. She was too decent to be toyed with. It was all or nothing with this girl. And that was something he wasn't even sure he was capable of, not any more.

"But you know me now, more than anyone." Doubt suddenly flickered across her eyes, causing a tide of shame inside his heart. "Please don't hurt me."

Pete pulled her against him, to comfort her, but also to prevent her from looking into his eyes.

She took a breath. "I'm not looking forward to tomorrow, it's going to be really hard for me, but perhaps, if I know you'll be here when I get back, with a warm shoulder to cry on, I think it could be something to cling on to if it gets tough out there."

'Cling', the word in itself made him panic. He thought again about her reunion. Something about her split with her parents still didn't add up. Maybe now was the time to ask her. "Why have you stayed away for so long, Jen? You're such a forgiving sort of soul, why haven't you been able to make peace with your family in all this time? What is so bad back there that's keeping you away?"

Jenny rolled onto her back and stared at the ceiling and he didn't know whether to touch her or to give her space. And then she knocked him sideways.

"I haven't told you all of what went on back then. Some of it is very painful for me, even now."

Silence again as he fought to contain his breathing.

"I was pregnant. That was what the whole stink was about. Simon's parents wanted to send him away, to keep his future unhindered and my parents just seemed to go along with it."

"But why? You'd think, if anything, they would have wanted him to step up and marry you."

"But they didn't. I don't know why. Probably a pile of money changed hands. Some deal must have been done. And I guess I was an embarrassment."

Pete shook his head in disbelief. "How old were you again?"

"Seventeen. But that wasn't even the worst of it. I kept her, you see. I had a little girl. Clara." Jenny fiddled with the earring at the top of her ear. "She was beautiful, Pete. Perfect. Such tiny little feet. Except she wasn't... She was just a day old when I lost her. Some long, complicated disorder. After that I couldn't face them. They couldn't face me." She took a deep breath and shrugged. "They sent me to live with my aunt."

Pete pulled her to him, wrapping her in his arms, as if by bringing her heart to rest against his, he could fix everything. But he couldn't and now, more than ever, he realised his mistake. He didn't have it in him to be everything Jenny wanted him to be, what she needed him to be, and because of that he was going to be damned to hell. What could he do? "Will you stay the night?" he asked, not knowing quite what he was hoping for.

"I'd like to…" she said, "but I can't. I have to be up early to catch the train." And so, with an awkward flourish of dressing, he escorted her down to the car and drove her home.

Outside Jenny's house, he pulled up and stopped. More beautiful than ever, she leaned across and touched his lips with her fingers. She pulled his head towards hers and heaven caressed him. Her kisses were something he had dreamed about but never tasted, until now. Whole worlds of possibility rose up around him. She wanted him, and right then, in that car, he wanted to be all that she needed.

"I'll call you tomorrow," she whispered and he nodded, biting his lips. She got out and as she leant down to say goodbye, words failed him, so he smiled and watched as she put her key in the door and went inside, and then he drove off at a pace that got him far enough away as quickly as possible.

Pete parked the car and walked back up to his flat. What had happened to him? It wasn't like him to lose his head over a woman, let alone his heart. Women normally gave whatever he wanted to take. Jenny had been different. He hadn't set out to sleep with her that evening, though God knows he'd wanted to. She had grown on him, like a climbing rose, curling herself around his heart until to remove her felt like losing a limb.

That night Pete was restless. He knew he wasn't a good bet for Jenny. His ability to 'love 'em and leave 'em' was second to none. He was wrong for her. Loose women were fair game; who was

131

he to deny himself what they were so willing to offer? Maybe it would be better for her if he cut and run. She could easily find someone else. Could he actually do this? He thought about it for a while and then rolled over and turned out the light.

Wednesday morning, Jenny was up early. It was with mixed emotions that she left the house. She was feeling determined and stoical, sure that she had to see Clara's grave after so long. She knew it was going to be desperately upsetting, but she needed to go.

Facing up to her parents after all this time was not something she was looking forward to. Fourteen years she had kept them at arm's length and now Pete had stepped in and made her think about the things she had hoped to keep hidden. Through talking with him, she had uncovered herself, but he had been right: sometimes you just have to feel the pain, rip off the plaster and see. Jenny just hoped the bleeding had stopped. But to see her sister again was exciting.

So many emotions whirling around in one brain, at least when the journey was under way, she could settle for a bit and put Pete to the back of her mind. She could see him tonight and finally give him the shortbread she had found still lying in her bag on her return home the night before. They had made love and he had held her, as if life had depended on it. She was in love with him and, God help him, he seemed to be in love with her too.

She remembered the way his body made her feel. When they touched, it was as if she was burning with a sensual fire. It melted her and shot sparks through her veins, right to her heart. She had been cautious about sleeping with men over the years, but even from her limited experience, it had been... spectacular. She sighed, determined to put her niggling doubts about their future to the back of her mind and be content at least with the present. Now to sort out the past.

The station wasn't a long walk, so she bought her ticket from the machine on the wall and wandered onto the platform to wait.

The train pulled in and a gust of wind brushed across her face, disturbing the dust around her. It was almost empty and so, walking along the centre aisle, she found a nice spot with a table and sat down. She hadn't done much reading of late; couldn't seem to concentrate. At least now, with her love life finally blossoming, she might be able to try and so she reached for her book and waited to set off.

As the train pulled out of the station on the shorter stretch to Birmingham, Jenny settled in to her story. Ah yes, John was just keeping watch on the crows' nests for the sign to come and rescue his love...

Before she knew it, Jenny was changing trains and after checking with a guard that she was on the right route, she settled down again for the longer part of the journey.

It was a lot busier by then and it wasn't long before there was standing room only. Jenny was starting to get peckish, so she bought some crisps and a sandwich from the lady with the trolley and put her headphones in her ears. The fields that passed brought some tranquillity with them as she ate her meal and listened to Patsy sing. But the words were seeping into her, reminding her of her loves: of Simon and Clara, and Pete. Nobody in between had meant half so much. But Simon had prized his career over her and even his own child. He didn't deserve her sadness. Pete. She hoped for so much more from Pete. It made her ache just to think of him.

She couldn't think about Clara for now. Not in public. Not on a train. There would be time enough for that later. She blinked back the tears, removed her headphones and then hurriedly finished the last of her food and settled back into her story.

By late morning, the train driver was announcing the approach to Oxenholme and she packed her things back into her bag and alighted onto the platform. Home. Jenny braced herself. In - photo shoot - visit the grave - back on the train again. That was the plan. Her memories fell back to the rows they had had before she'd left that still stung sharply. Focus, she thought. She was there to see Clara and Lizzy. As for the rest? She would smile for the camera and take each breath as it came.

It didn't take long to find a cabby and she was soon winding through the countryside back to where she used to live. Her nerves were rising, even though she tried to ignore them. She had barely spoken to her parents since the day she left. What do you say after 14 years?

The stile at the bottom of the garden and then the horse chestnut came into view. It would soon be laden with conkers, ready to split open on the ground and be treasured. Then there it was, the house she had called home for 17 years. It looked exactly the same as when she had left it. The front door in the middle of an L-shaped house, with a porch and a pillar and giant sash windows. The trees in the garden were bigger now and, actually, now she looked closer, the front door was a different colour too; red, where it used to be green.

She opened the window and leant out at the sun. It smelled... fresh. A floral scent she recognised from her childhood brought back happier times as she pulled back a memory from the early years.

A minute later, the taxi stopped and Jenny got out. A dog bounded up to her, barking. She had totally forgotten the puppy they had bought six months before she'd left. He was an old dog now and he didn't know her. A man appeared, calling the dog to heel. "Charlie. Here boy." Obediently, the dog walked away and then there he was.

"Jennifer?"

"Dad?" My God, he was *old*. She hadn't even considered that. He had to be almost 60 by now. The sudden panic inside her made her want to run. She was disturbed by the emotion in his eyes, but she held strong and, paying the cabbie for her fare, she hoisted her bag onto her shoulder and walked across the gravel driveway to meet him.

Tears were in his eyes by the time she got there and holding out his arms to hug her, she went to him and he gave her a force of embrace she had never expected. It was as though he never wanted to let go again. Hesitantly she hugged him. A call from within the house pulled him up and he answered it. "It's Jennifer. She's here," and within seconds, her mother was there in the doorway too. Her look was more uncertain, but the same tears shone in her eyes.

"Jenny? My little Jenny? You came home," and she seemed overwhelmed with emotion. Jenny had not in a million years expected such a welcome as this. She had thought it would be awkward, cold and unsettling, but all everyone seemed to want to do now was cry.

"Hello, Mum." For a moment, she forgot to be angry, she forgot all the bitterness and pain and before she knew it, they were all in a huddle, and her parents were crying, and Jenny couldn't help but notice their pain.

The photographer pulled up and the three of them parted as Charlie went nosing around somebody new, barking at the car and wagging his tail excitedly.

Her mother took Jenny off indoors and showed her where to put her things while the two men talked. They walked into the living room, where the photos were going to be taken, and fresh furniture stood in place of what had once been. The walls were a different colour and almost everything in there was new, new to her at least. This wasn't her home. She felt awkward again. She was a stranger here.

A woman walked in carrying a tray of tea and sandwiches.

"In the dining room, I think, thank you, Susie," her mother told her.

Jenny glanced around. "What happened to Mabel?"

Pity showed on her mother's face. "Mabel died, darling." Her voice had gentled to break the news. "She retired a few years after... She passed away about six years ago now."

Life had moved on. Jenny had never thought about this place existing without her in it. In her mind, everything had stopped, suspended in time, just waiting for her spell of forgiveness, which would never come. But they had lived, lived and breathed and worked each day as the one before. Feelings of resentment stirred within her, confusing her emotions. Had she really mattered that much to them after all?

Stoically she lifted her chin. Her dad walked in and introduced the journalist and photographer, who had both arrived by now. "Where's Lizzy?" she asked and her mother told her she was in the study, working. "Can I see her?"

Her mother's brow twitched. "She'll join us in a minute. Let her finish what she's doing."

They adjourned to the dining room for a light lunch and she noticed numerous photos and accolades, won by her sister, pinned up along the walls. All of Lizzy, none of her. She tightened up her defences. Had they wiped the place clean of her? Her mind was working overtime. Had she not done the same to them?

Jenny thought it odd that her sister wasn't joining them. Surely she had to eat at some point, but as the time was ticking on, they soon broke away to freshen up for the shoot and reconvened in the living room shortly after.

And then she walked in. A woman so aloof and sophisticated, Jenny felt quite plain. She glanced at Jenny without expression and then smiled at her parents. "Where would you like me?"

Was this really Lizzy? Her Lizzy? When had she got so cold? What had she ever done to her? Jenny was quite at a loss. Lizzy had been the only one she had wanted to see and she wasn't even giving her the time of day. She didn't understand it. Did she not know it was her? What was wrong with them all? Everything was so topsy-turvy.

She tried her best to smile for the camera, but her heart wasn't in it now. Her mind was going in circles, trying to make sense of the day. Finally Charlie was let in and he trotted around to sit next to Lizzy. He looked up at her and she fondled his ears affectionately. Not so frosty then, just cold towards her.

Jenny wanted to talk to Pete. She wanted to run away up to the end of the garden and ring him in private and make him explain to her what was going on. But he would be in work now. She was on her own.

When the photos were finished, the journalist took her dad off to interview him, leaving the rest of the family to themselves. The photographer started to pack away and put the room back how he had found it and Lizzy made a move to leave.

"Lizzy. You've grown," Jenny said in a panic. What a dumb thing to say, but at that moment she could think of nothing else. Lizzy turned around. There was something cold in her eyes and Jenny felt their sharp gaze cut into her. And then she turned her back again and walked out. Jenny turned to her mum. "What did I do?"

"Don't worry, love, she'll come round. It's a shock, that's all. Give her some time."

"A shock?"

"Seeing you again."

"I know it's strange, it is for me too, but there's no need to be rude."

Her mum moved over and took her by the hand to sit down. "It hurt her when you left, my darling. She took a long time to come to terms with that. She felt abandoned. I'm sure she'll be okay. Just give her time to get used to you. It's so lovely to see you again. How have you been? How is the nursing going?"

Jenny couldn't understand it. Lizzy had been hurt by her leaving? But why? She had only been young when Jenny left. She would have thought she'd have been grateful for the lack of shouting and happy, suddenly getting all the attention to herself. She had obviously done well on it, whatever she had made of her life. Why had it affected her? "I thought she would have been pleased to see the back of me?" she said.

Her mum leaned forward over her knees and took hold of Jenny's hand. "She loved you, Jenny; we all did. We still do."

Jenny pulled away.

"It hurt her that you left without saying goodbye. She blamed herself for driving you away."

"But it had nothing to do with her."

"She was too young to understand that. We could hardly tell her about the baby."

"You could have."

"She was barely nine years old, Jenny. She loved you. She couldn't understand why you left her. And why you never even sent her a note again."

Jenny was distraught. She had never meant to hurt her sister. She hadn't given a second thought to the way she would have seen it. Lizzy had felt abandoned, rejected and *she* had never even considered that. How could she have done that to her little sister?

She shook her head, trying to shake the thoughts free. "Why didn't you tell me?" They had been the ones to send her away. They should share in the responsibility.

"You wouldn't speak to us."

Jenny was suddenly on the defensive. The pain was still hurting. "You sent me away! You sided with Simon's parents and then sent me away!" Her temper was rising. She had hoped not to cause a scene, being back for just a couple of hours, but this was unfair. "You ruined everything. You smothered me, never letting me out of your sight for weeks on end and then you turned your back on me altogether."

"We did no such thing. You wanted to go."

"I was 17. I had just lost my baby and I was devastated. Why couldn't you see that?"

"We did see that, darling. That's why we let you go. We thought you needed a change of scene, a break away from us, from here. We never thought, for one minute, you'd stay away from us forever."

Her dad walked in. "Is everything all right?"

Jenny looked at her mother and then to her dad, shaking her head. "No. No, it's not. I've got to go." She stood up and walked out to collect her things. "It was a mistake, coming back here."

Her mum hurried after her. "Don't say that, Jenny. It's been wonderful to see you again. Please stay a little longer. You haven't told us anything about yourself yet."

"No. I've got to go." She started walking towards the front door.

"But it's miles to the station," her father told her.

"I'll walk."

"I can give you a lift," the journalist said as he wandered into the hall.

"Great."

Her mother approached her, but stopped a short way off as Jenny looked into her eyes and let the anger and confusion show on her face.

"Don't leave us, Jenny, not like this. Not again. Please, my darling."

Jenny's heart was aching. She needed to get home. She needed Pete. "I have to," she said, her voice a little sadder now, and she closed the door of the car and looked straight ahead at the road.

To say that she had a lot to think about on the train back home would have been an understatement. Jenny couldn't settle to read or rest in any way. Nothing had been at all as she'd expected. Even *she* hadn't been how she'd expected.

By the time she arrived back at Duxley Station, Jenny was in bits. She looked at her watch. Pete would still be in work. The only other person she could confide in, and who might even have some answers for her, was her auntie, so, on impulse, she took a bus to her aunt's in the next town, grabbed a burger from a van along the way and went in search of some comfort.

Jenny felt a welcome sense of security wash over her as she arrived in her auntie's street. Her aunt would know what to say to ease her and she strode up to the door and knocked. She was just about to knock again when the door opened.

"Jenny! How wonderful to see you. I was just going out."

"Oh. But... I really need to talk to you." She felt her eyes beginning to glisten.

Another woman appeared behind her aunt at the door and her aunt looked at Jenny and turned to the lady behind her. "Frances, I think I'm going to have to sit this one out, love. You don't mind, do you?"

The lady called Frances gave her aunt a hug and left and Jenny walked in.

Auntie May settled her into the little living room and went to fetch some tea. "Have you been?" she asked, returning a few minutes later with a pot and a packet of Rich Teas.

Jenny nodded.

Her aunt passed over a cup. "Take a deep breath," she said, "and then tell me all about it."

Jenny felt safe there. She had come to think of it as her home a good many years ago. The knick-knacks around the shelves and the flowery walls were familiar to her and she felt wrapped in its safety. Jenny let her guard slip and her emotions unravel as, bit by bit, she told her aunt about what had happened that day. And when she had finished, she looked up into the warm blue eyes of the woman who had loved her at her worst and silently pleaded for understanding.

Her aunt pulled her into a hug and held her against her, soothing her back and her hair with her ageing hands. "And you want to know what happened. What *really* happened, not what you think happened in that lost, lonely teenage mind of yours that brought you to me?"

Jenny nodded, unsure if she was going to like what she heard, but determined she had to hear it.

And so her aunt told her everything. She told her how a brilliant, strong, teenage girl had fallen in love and found herself with a baby growing inside her. She told her how her mother and father had gone to see the boy's parents and that they had wanted nothing to do with it. They had decided to send their son away, away from her, to achieve great things and that Jenny should get rid of the baby.

"They said that?" Jenny asked, appalled.

"Apparently. Your mum and dad were terribly upset. And when the boy did as his parents told him, they were just as cross with him too."

"They never told me any of that," she said to her.

"No, well, they loved you. They didn't want you hurt any more than you had been already and you had enough on your plate coming to terms with the baby."

"But I thought *they* had told him to go."

"I know you did."

"Why didn't anyone correct me?"

"We tried. You were 17. You loved him. You didn't believe any of us. You were so angry after he left you. Understandably so. And then, losing the baby..." She shook her head. "You were devastated. You were just lashing out, everywhere. They knew that. So they asked you if you would like to get away for a while, a change of air, if you like, and I had a room free at the time.

"My Donna had left home a few years before and I thought I could use the company. It was only ever meant to be for a couple of months. But when it came to it, you couldn't bear to go home. You stopped reading their letters, taking their calls; you wanted nothing to remind you of home. You completely shut them out. Shut it all out. I tried, for a while, to talk you round, but then you started pulling away from me too. So we had to let it drop."

"But there was nothing of me on their walls. It was all Lizzy."

"That only happened much later on. She was having her own problems and having reminders of you all around the walls wasn't helping."

"Problems caused by me?"

Her aunt didn't answer. She didn't have to.

"It was all just a sad situation, my love. Nobody was really to blame."

But Jenny realised now that there was. It was her. All those years she had been blaming them, not even considering Lizzy, and all the time it had been her. Her teenage rejected self, lashing out at the unfair world around her. Her parents had been left to deal with the mess she'd trailed behind her and she hadn't even thought to care. If there was a medal for regret, she would own it.

She could still clearly remember the pain she had felt and the loneliness echoing around her. It had been at the forefront of her mind when she'd arrived there that day. Was this really what had happened? It did have a ring of truth about it, but it was completely at odds with what she remembered. If this *had* been the case, why hadn't they tried harder to reach her, or waited till she was older and then tried again. She was 31 now; there had been plenty of time to approach her calmly.

Jenny stayed for a while after that. Her aunt rustled them up another pot of tea, but as dusk fell, she realised she had better be heading back. There was so much to think about, so much at stake, but she needed to talk to Pete before she turned in. He would want to know what had happened.

By the time she got back to Duxley it was nearly ten o'clock at night. She took a taxi from the bus station, stopped briefly at her house to pick up the biscuits and went straight over to Pete's.

She didn't pause in her mission. She needed to speak to him. Taking the stairs two at a time, she knocked on the door, not even considering that he might not be in. Of course he would be in. He knew she would be needing him. She knocked again, harder this time, until she heard him respond.

"I'm coming, I'm coming. Hold your horses."

The door opened and Jenny's heart filled with joy. Pete; her handsome hero; he would settle her. But Pete wasn't smiling. She looked into his eyes and was disturbed by the turmoil raging there. And then, from behind him, she heard a woman's voice.

Chapter 12

"Who is it, babes?"

Jenny leaned to the side and looked past him, and there, as plain as day, lounging on his settee in the shortest skirt and cropped top imaginable, was Tina, a nurse she recognised from theatre. This could not be happening.

Jenny took a step back in shock. She had been the same as all the rest. One night, that was all you got with Pete, and now she was just another notch on his bedpost. And as the light flickered out in Jenny's tender heart, her eager smile faded and crumbled to dust.

She looked up at him and he must have known how it looked, because after a few seconds of feigned innocence, he couldn't even meet her gaze. What had she been thinking? She had caught him with his hand in the cookie jar and she had only herself to blame. He hadn't promised her anything. He hadn't even told her she was different. Her mouth opened, but she couldn't find the words to say, so she simply put down the box of shortbread and as a tear began to trickle down her cheek, she closed her eyes, blocking him out of her heart, turned and walked away.

"No. Jenny, don't go. It's not what you think," he called after her, but there was no point; she would not hear him. She had been a prize fool. You could have asked anyone in the hospital if it was wise to sleep with Dr Florin and not one of them would have said she should. And in amongst all the images of seduction and betrayal Jenny was repeating inside her mind, came the fact that *she* had been eating Jenny's cakes! Why the hell that upset her so much when all else had turned to pain, she had no idea.

Unable to process such a torrent of emotions, Jenny's heart shut down. She walked home down the night's streets. The shadows and crisp air were a godsend as they swallowed her tears and hid her from view.

How had she fallen under his spell? She had stood there, in his doorway, willing it not to be true, when all the while she should have been expecting it. Did she think she was so different from every other girl he had been with? No. It had meant nothing to him.

Humiliation tore through her as the sudden realisation that she had made the same mistake all over again squeezed the air from her lungs and rung tears from her eyes. She hadn't learned, and now she felt physically sick.

Her guts coiled, threatening to humiliate her. He no longer needed her. His life had turned around. He was on his way to making consultant and now, had even ticked her off his list. What an achievement that must have been!

Back in his flat, Pete quickly dispatched his visitor whilst fighting the urge to run after Jen. He hated the thought of her out there, upset and walking home alone late at night, but the last person she wanted now was him. He had seen that clearly in her eyes. Her box of shortbread lay open on his kitchen counter as the guilt threatened to choke him with every breath that he took. Wasn't this what he had wanted, even if it had not been of his doing?

He had considered setting her free of him, so she could find someone more worthy. It would free him of such expectation. But having happened now, he felt desolate. His life's blood was ebbing away from him and it was following her back to her home.

As the misery of the situation settled in, he remembered the photo shoot. Tomorrow he would have to go to her. She had wanted to speak to him tonight, of course she had. She'd had an exhausting, probably painful, day and she had come back to this. She was probably about to tell him everything that had happened and suddenly he wanted to know. He wanted to hear every detail of her life and her day and hold her close to him and make it all better. She had seemed so pleased to see him, at first; hopefully that meant it had gone well. He couldn't bear it. He couldn't bear hurting her, so he sent her a text.

JENNY WREN, NOTHING HAPPENED, I PROMISE. I MISS YOU. I HOPE IT WENT WELL TODAY. I'LL SEE YOU TOMORROW. I'M SORRY.

He didn't expect an answer, but at least she would have heard him.

Less than two weeks to go to the exam. He would have to try and put it to the back of his mind and study for the rest of the night. She would come round when he explained it. If he was going to make something of himself he needed to pass this final exam. He would never be able to hold his head up in front of her if he didn't.

He was on call the next day as it happened, but by the day after that word had got around. Looks of distaste followed him into theatre as the morning list passed very slowly. Only one theatre assistant was prepared to help him, not a woman, of course, they had all closed ranks and not one of them was going to speak to him unless a patient's life depended on it. He made his own coffee and found his own kit. And did he deserve this? He probably did. He had been a fool to open the door to Tina. He felt the pain of his guilt like a knife in his side and it seemed everybody *wanted* him to.

He didn't run into Jenny at all that day, but it was a warm evening and so, after freshening up, he threw a jacket in the car and headed over to see her. He picked up some flowers from the petrol station en route and turned up at Jenny's a little after seven. He knocked on the door.

Flis answered. Oh, yes, *she* lived there, he thought. He had forgotten. "What do *you* want?" she snapped.

"It's good to see you too, Flis."

"She's not well."

"Where is she?"

"I don't see how that's any of your business, but if you must know, she needed some air." She shook her head at him. "You couldn't help yourself, could you? The girl looked awful when she came back the other night. It's a knack of yours, isn't it, spreading misery like that? And not just misery this time; the poor girl spent most of the day with her head down the toilet, thanks to you."

Her words could not have been barbed more acutely. Pete felt them and each one cut deep. Yes he had hurt her, he realised that, but he had never intended to. He was actually trying to *not* hurt her; it had just somehow gone horribly wrong. And the sickness...? "Did she say anything about her parents?" he asked.

"Why would she have said anything about them? She only went up for a photo shoot. Probably had a whale of a time."

Flis didn't know! She didn't know about Jen's family and *she* was one of her best friends. She must have really trusted him. "Can I wait?"

"You can wait out there," she said, "but I doubt she'll want to see you." And so he nodded and walked back along the pathway to the little wall at the front.

The door behind him closed and he set himself down on the brick wall to wait. Flis would be in there texting Jenny right now, he was sure of it, but the sun was still shining warmly, although it was turning now from gold to pink. A bird-filled sky above him chirped a merry sound to his sorry soul below. Cars drove past in the close of the day and dogs came out to walk. A bee buzzed around him, in search of nectar, and he watched it pass on its jagged route, listening to its hum. The last wisps of summer, he thought. Soon it would be all gone. And so would he.

Footsteps walked softly in from the left and he looked up and saw her rounding the corner towards him. She was pale and drawn. She stopped a short distance off and looked at him.

Pete stood up. "Hello," he said.

"You know, I didn't think you'd actually have the nerve to come round here," she told him and continued to approach.

"You got my message, though?"

Jenny raised her brow. "Yes."

"I'm sorry. I forgot I was on call last night. Can we talk?"

She looked at him. "I'm tired, Pete."

"Jenny, look, I know you've been ill, but... Don't shut me out, Jen, please. I didn't do anything. I promise. She just turned up." His shoulders sagged. What was the point? He could see from her face that she didn't believe him. "I needed to make sure you were all right."

"I'm fine."

Like hell she was. "You don't look fine."

"Yeah, well, apparently burger vans don't agree with me."

"Oh." He winced. "But I meant with your family."

She searched his gaze, seemingly assessing his worth. "You expect me to believe you care?"

"I do care. Jenny. Please. Talk to me."

Jenny's gaze was caught by something behind him at the window and he turned to see Flis watching them. He looked back at Jenny. It was punishment enough to see her this way; surely she would still speak to him?

"Shall we go for a walk?" she asked.

Pete was pleased to be allowed time with her. Their closeness was something he was already missing, but it was clear she no longer felt the same.

They walked the short distance along the road to a park. The children had all gone now, their bath and bedtime stories calling them, so she sat on a swing and Pete took the one next to her.

He was the first to speak. "I got you these," he said, suddenly remembering the forgotten flowers in his hand. He held them out and Jenny took them. Her sad eyes regarded the blooms. "So how was it, with your family?" he asked.

Jenny started to swing, ever so slowly. "Awful."

Pete wanted to scoop her up and hold her, chase away anyone who would hurt her and let her mend, but he couldn't. Her body language was closed off. Only her voice was reaching out to him and for that alone, he was still grateful. "What happened? Did they upset you?"

"Worse," she said. "I upset *them*."

"I don't understand. Why does that bother you?"

"Because I think it's all my fault. All these years I've been blaming them, keeping them at arm's length, and all the time it was me. I messed everything up. All they did was try and protect me, look after me, and I pushed them all away. I punished them for things they had no control over. Lizzy most of all." She looked at him with pain in her eyes. "She hates me, Pete. I never once considered how my leaving would have affected her. I was so selfish, so wrapped up in my own problems that I didn't even think about *them*."

"So how were they? Did they have a go at you?"

"They broke down in tears the moment I arrived there."

"So it went... well, really?"

"No. I..."

He took hold of her hand and felt physical pain at her flinching. "What actually happened, Jen?"

"I think I messed up again. I don't know. I was angry and... I felt foolish. I ran." Pete just held onto her hand. She was defeated. "I went to see my aunt before I got to..." Her eyes fell away. "I asked her."

"That's why you were so late back that night?"

She nodded, an accusing look flickered across her gaze and Pete felt he had to try and explain. "I'm so sorry you came back to that, Jen. But it was nothing, it really was. *She* was coming on to *me*."

"It doesn't matter."

149

The hell it didn't! It had hurt her and suddenly all he had hoped for had gone. He shook his head. She would never believe him; why would she? "I didn't *do* anything."

Jenny's voice was strained. "Why was she there, then, Pete? Either you did, or you were going to. It makes little difference. Surely you don't expect me to believe she just popped round for a cup of sugar?"

Yes, he did. And then she would be happy again and he wouldn't feel so guilty. And for the first time in his life he actually had no reason!

It was starting to go dark. It was only the two of them there and the odd person walking a dog. He needed her to know it wasn't like that. And that he hadn't always been so shallow and small. He started to swing, gently, like her. "I'm going to tell you something now, something I've never told anyone. But I'm telling you because I need you to trust me."

Jenny looked across at him and stilled.

"It's about Ali."

Jenny nodded and continued gently swinging.

"She grew up on the same estate as I did. She was a few years older, but she was good to Jimmy and me. When we were out there, in the den, she would sneak us food. She tended to us when we had cuts and bruises and she stood up for me at school. But then she went away to university. I was 15. It was around the time my dad left home, after all the police and the scandal had died down. By then I had made up my mind what I wanted to do. I wanted to be a doctor, like her. So I studied as hard as I could and we were doing better at home. At least when I left I knew Jimmy would be safe.

"She was in the fourth year by the time I arrived, so we spent a couple of years at the same university and she kept an eye on me there too, lending me books and helping me out. By chance I landed up in the same hospital as her a couple of years after I qualified. That's when the accident happened. She'd married Adam by then and she looked completely happy. I knew I shouldn't, but I still wanted to spend time with her. I couldn't bear to just let go, after all we'd been through. Not just like that. That was why I persuaded her to go to the party with me that night." He stared up at the evening sky. "So you see, it really *was* my fault, I wasn't being overly dramatic, I actually *was* responsible for her dying. If I hadn't have been so selfish, she would still be alive today."

Jenny looked at him. "You loved her," she said, her voice calm, but not unfeeling.

"No."

"Yes, you did. You loved her. Oh, Pete. How could you not? She was the only one who showed you kindness. She was there for you. She was your lifeline through the dark times. Of course you loved her."

Pete's head dipped in defeat as the truth in what she was saying sought him out. "I suppose I did."

"And that's why you torture yourself over and over again. Because you feel responsible for the death of the woman you loved. That's why you used to let Adam treat you so badly."

He looked up.

"We could all see it. He was horrid to you. He was pretty foul to a lot of people back then."

He nodded. "I deserved it."

Jenny got off her swing and stepped around the bar to look at him. He stilled the swing before her and her eyes opened up to him.

"It hurts, doesn't it, feeling the burden of guilt?"

Pete reached out with his heart and met hers. "Yes. It does," he said.

"But I can't help you with that, Peter Florin. You are going to have to learn to forgive yourself and then one day, you might be able to move on, properly."

But he *was* moving on. He cared now, and that hadn't happened for a long time. But he could see in her eyes that she had left him. She was battling demons of her own now. She didn't need any more trouble from him.

"It's getting cold," she said.

It was over. What more could he do? "I'll walk you back and then I'd better get off home and do some more revision before this nurse I know gives me grief for slacking off," he said and he stood up.

"How's that going?" she asked him.

"Good, I think. I hope so, anyway."

"You'll do fine. I know you will," she told him.

They walked back to Jenny's house in a more companionable silence. At the path, he turned to her. "I think I'll say goodbye here. Not sure I'm up to another showdown with Flis," and Jenny smiled.

"Okay."

He could see the wind blowing through her empty gaze. To be the least tortured, that was a new experience for him. He would have to keep an eye on her now, make sure she didn't slip any further away. "Don't be too hard on yourself, Jenny Wren. You were very young and things are rarely as one-sided as they seem. I'm here if you need me," he told her and she just smiled sadly and walked inside and all he could hear was goodbye.

I thought that I knew which way I was facing, Jenny wrote that night. After the trials and revelations of the past 48 hours, I thought things couldn't get any more complicated. I wish that that were true. My body aches, but more than that, my heart aches. It aches to be with him, to hold him against me and lose myself in his touch, but I cannot go there again. After his sorry attempt to deny what was happening in his flat on Wednesday evening, I have resigned myself to the fact that he will never change.

So much about him is exactly what I've wanted, what any girl could want. He is kind, considerate, hardworking; he has the capacity for so much love, but he has been wounded and his wounds have changed him. I could wish until the sun refused to shine that he would feel the same way about me, but he cannot and I must learn to accept this. I need someone who really needs me, who wants me, whose world will not exist unless I am in it.

And I had that sorted in my mind, and then tonight he turned up and reached out to me in a way I knew he had in him, but dared not hope. And I wanted him, so badly it hurt. It is the agony of life to love and not feel love in return. All the great tragic love stories have heard of this pain. Authors and poets have written about it. They could understand how I feel, but sadly I cannot.

Still, he is doing well without me now. Soon he will complete his exams and move on to be a consultant somewhere else and I will... What will I be? I will go under... for a while, but I am a fighter and I am strong and I will survive. I hope.

Jenny decided to let herself mourn, for just one night, the loss she felt too deeply. She silently wept as the moon turned silver and the owl cries withered on the wind and in the morning, it was another day and she was determined to move on and be the person she knew she could be.

Her past was still in limbo. She could no longer ignore it, like something you might place in a drawer just in case. She had been at the very least partially responsible for the family's woes and she needed to put things right in her mind once and for all. She had failed Clara too, perhaps most of all.

It was time to start anew. Jenny searched her heart for what would make her happy. Lizzy was a priority. To try to reach out to her again was something she felt she had to do. She wanted to face her mother and father again too. They deserved to be heard and to be forgiven. She needed to go back to where it had begun, to see Clara and accept her past and then, when that was accomplished, she would try and move on. It was something she had to do. It was the *least* she could do.

As for her future, it was time to bite the bullet. With her holiday a little over a week away, she needed to sort things out. Grabbing the most recent copy of her writing magazine, Jenny flicked through to look for the getaways. One of them must have a place still begging. She was finally going to go on that writing break she had always dreamed of, be it success or disaster. At least then she would know.

That weekend she took the train back up to the Lake District and, more humbly than before, returned to her childhood home. She didn't ring to tell them to expect her. She couldn't speak so easily over the phone. But this time she was willing to stay, however hard it got, for she needed to understand what had happened so long ago.

Her mother was out picking raspberries in the garden when she arrived. Jenny walked slowly over to see her as the dog started barking from beyond. Her mother looked up and saw her over the top of the bushes. She looked so uncertain that an ache settled in Jenny's heart and, with her lips beginning to tremble, she forced herself to smile. As she got closer, though, she crumbled. "I'm sorry, Mum."

Her mother put the bowl down on an empty plant pot and hurried over to her, folding her in her arms. They held onto one another, without any words, and stayed like that for some time.

"I've been praying that you would come home again," she said to her. "It was so wonderful to see you the other day and… I've missed you, so very much."

Without the long-held walls to protect herself, Jenny suddenly felt the full turmoil of her teenage departure and she found herself openly weeping at last. And it was then that she knew, without a doubt, that she *had* been the one to cause all the fights. She remembered how hurt and rejected she had felt and how angry she had been at the world around her. This was a pain she needed. And the realisation of that pain could have suffocated her, but for the surge of love and forgiveness she felt implicit in her mother's arms. She was on the road back home and she had her compass.

"I'm so sorry, Mum. For everything," she said as she filled her

154

lungs with air.

"It doesn't matter," her mum told her. "You're home now. I should never have let you go in the first place. I blame myself. I should have trusted you, that you were strong enough to cope. And now look at you! You're all grown up," she said, pulling away. "Let me look at you. You're so beautiful. And a nurse; how wonderful." Then she straightened. "I've got to find your father." She turned around, looking for her husband in the garden. "John! John! Jenny's back. She's come home to us."

A moment later, her dad appeared from behind a hedge with a fork in his hand. His face lit up. "Jennifer," and he walked over to see her. He paused and for a moment Jenny didn't know how he was going to take it. "I'm sorry," she said and he wrapped her in his arms.

"I'll tell Susie there'll be one more for lunch, shall I? You *are* going to stay, aren't you?"

Jenny nodded. "Would it be all right to stay overnight? I think it would be good for me to spend a little time back here."

Her mother beamed. "I would love that, darling," and they wandered in to clean up.

At lunch, Jenny told them about everything she had been doing since she left so many years before. Then she remembered something she had spoken to Pete about. "Something has been troubling me that I need to know. How much has my training cost Auntie May? I'm going to have to pay her back somehow."

Her mother looked towards her father and Jenny followed her lead. "Dad?"

"You don't have to worry about your aunt, Jen, we made sure she had enough to see you through."

"*You* paid for me?"

"As soon as we realised you weren't going to come back to us we started paying into an account she set up for you. We couldn't have asked her to support you for nothing. Things were tight for her when your uncle got sick."

"You sent her money?"

Her mother seemed uneasy with her response. "We would have sent you anything you wanted, my darling. What we really wanted was to have you back here with us, but…"

"I was too wrapped up in myself to see."

Her mother reached out a hand and squeezed one of hers. "You were only young and you had been through so much. You can't blame yourself."

"Can't I?"

"No," her dad said quite firmly. "And I won't hear another word said about it. You're back with us now and that makes me very happy."

Jenny had spent so much of the past few days crying she found she was easily back there again. She sniffed and wiped her tears away. "Look at me. I'm a mess." She forced herself to smile and tried to eat the food set out before them.

That evening her mum took Jenny up to her bedroom and she placed her bag on the bed. Looking around her, she noticed the walls were covered with pictures. They were of her in various places: her graduation, in her first nurse's uniform, a seaside holiday and just sitting in the garden. She turned towards her mother. "But…"

"We weren't with you all the time," she told her. "It was hard to be, but we *did* manage the important things." She pointed to a graduation picture.

"You were there?"

"Wouldn't have missed it for the world. We were so proud of you."

Jenny was speechless. She had never even considered. She looked along the walls at the other pictures.

"Your aunt sent us that one in the garden," she told her. "I always loved that one."

"She kept you up to date on what I was doing?"

"You were our baby girl. We missed you."

Jenny turned back round and sat down on the bed. "What happened with Lizzy, Mum?"

Her mum came and sat down beside her.

"After I left."

Her mum smoothed at the creases of her dress as if thinking about how to begin. "She took it hard, your leaving, poor Lizzy. Suddenly her world, as she knew it, turned upside down. You disappeared and we missed you so much. She was only nine, you have to remember. I think maybe we didn't pay her enough attention when it first began. It was a harrowing time for everyone. You mustn't blame her, but she came to resent you. That's why all your pictures are in here. This is where we came to spend time with you. Bringing you in here, it was the only way to get her back to being the little girl she used to be. You do understand, don't you?"

"I never even thought about how she'd feel." Jenny shook her head. "The ironic thing is *she* was the one I came back for. I was determined to keep you two at a distance, but I wanted to know Lizzy. And then you took me back with open arms, and *she* could barely look at me." She longed to make things right between them. "What can I do to make it better?"

"Give her time, darling. We can begin to talk about you when she's around. She's a grown woman now. She'll have to accept it. You have managed such a turn-around, and you were always the stubborn one. She was our placid little thing. Times change. She'll have to too."

Her mum hugged her then and kissed her on the forehead. "Goodnight, my darling," she said and she left Jenny to go to bed.

Jenny sat there for a while, surrounded by memories, not all of them unpleasant, and then she found Fluffy, her cuddly rabbit from her early years and she tucked him up next to her and went to sleep.

The next morning Jenny felt like a baby lamb taking her first steps. Everything was new, full of hope, and although the same, it felt different. She revelled in the closeness of her mother and father and joined in the gardening she'd interrupted the day before. They collected berries for jam and freezing and enjoyed the last of the summer sun, but she still hadn't faced up to one thing.

After lunch, when they were sitting resting in the conservatory, Jenny started to play with her earring. "Would it be all right if I went to see Clara now?" she said quietly.

Her mother sat up, concern filling her gaze. "Of course," she replied. "We've been expecting it. Would you like us to go with you?" Her father looked up and studied her.

Jenny nodded, all at once afraid to face the even harder emotions awaiting her there, but the time was right and she had to do it.

"Come on, then," her dad said and he set down the pen and paper from his crossword and stood up.

Clara had been buried on the far side of the hill, in the grounds of a little chapel, where the sun never set, only slumbered. It was situated just beyond the reach of their land and it had been Jenny's decision to bury her there, in a place that had inspired countless imaginary adventures for her as a child. And it had been such a beautiful day when they had said their goodbye.

They pulled on their boots and jackets and all three together, they walked out across the garden to the stile on the far side and over into the field beyond.

High up on the top of the hill, a small clump of trees gave shelter from the harshest wind and just beyond this, Jenny saw her first glimpse of it. There, as the slope fell away from her, sat the simple stone chapel and nestled at its feet, were the handful of graves that accompanied it.

At the edge of the low stone wall, Jenny stopped, afraid to go closer. She had not seen her daughter's grave since the day she had left home, more than a decade before, and now the mere sight of it sliced her in two. It had been just a simple wooden cross when she'd left and now it had a gravestone, all worldly, and weathered with age.

Filled with a powerful remorse, she walked across and sank to her knees. She read the beautiful inscription through tear-flooded eyes: *Too heavenly for this world. Too sweet to last. Remembered always, our beautiful baby girl, Clara Louise White.*

"Is it all right, Jenny?" her mother asked, coming to stand behind her. "We wanted it to be perfect."

A small spray of pale pink hydrangeas lay at the foot of the headstone and with trembling limbs, Jenny reached out and plucked it from the ground. She held it to her lips and then looked up at her parents. Her dad sucked in a deep breath and, turning, he walked a few steps away.

"I come here when I need to think," her mother said, laying a gentle hand on Jenny's shoulder. "We have a chat, Clara and I." She looked over towards her husband, love filling her eyes. "Your dad comes here more often, I think. He always brings her a flower. Even in winter."

Jenny rose up, her soul crying out in pain and she walked over to her father. He understood her suffering, they both did, and it touched her so deeply that she wept all the more.

At the touch of her hand, her father turned. She opened her arms and he came to her. "Thank you, Dad," she whispered and she felt his body shudder with the tears he could no longer contain.

Jenny left them at the station at the end of the afternoon. She had made peace with the world; she had gone home to Clara and reclaimed her past. She would keep in touch with them now and be back again often, if they would have her, and hoped that one day soon, she and Lizzy would be able to rebuild their relationship too.

A single flower from the small sprig of the pale pink hydrangeas now nestled within the pages of her book, along with one from the spray she had picked to lay beside it, and it brought a small amount of comfort for her to know this.

As she boarded the train back at Birmingham, her phone buzzed in her pocket.

NEEDING SOME HELP WITH MY STUDIES. ARE YOU FREE TO DROP ROUND?

Jenny thought for a while. She couldn't see him that night. She doubted he really needed her anyway; he was probably just feeling guilty, so she told a white lie:

VISITING PARENTS. NOT BACK TILL LATE. SORRY.

She thought about it for a minute and then, satisfied it was for the best, she pressed 'send'. No good could come from being with him now. She was just tormenting herself. Truth be told, she didn't trust herself to behave around him, even now, and she definitely didn't trust *him*. That was why she had to distance herself.

Her phone didn't ring again that evening. She arrived home and then set about tidying. She wanted nothing of her dark times staying with her now. Nothing she couldn't mourn, anyway. She was loved and she was turning over a new leaf. From now on, she was determined to make those around her happy, and for as long as she possibly could.

Pete sat alone in his flat. He couldn't see her, or she didn't want to be seen. It amounted to the same thing in the end: he was back on his own.

Chapter 13

Pete closed his books at the end of a long evening's studying and leant back in his chair. He had come to terms with it now. Jenny had been right. He had loved Ali. There, he had said it, and still the walls of his existence had not tumbled in. He had loved Ali, first like a sister, but later as something far deeper. Maybe he had hero-worshipped her for a while, but in the end it had been love. That was why he had tried to deny it for so long, for fear that if people knew, if they even had a suspicion that he had loved her, they would have seen him for the selfish being he was. He had known she was with Adam, but he hadn't been able to let her go.

But now he was ready to move on. He had buried himself long enough. It was time to be more than his looks and his skills. Love had been offered to him and he had been too blind to see it, too afraid, anyway. He may have lost all chance with Jenny, but he owed it to her to help her be happy. He wanted to be the man she had wanted him to be, the man he *could* be again if he tried.

He wasn't promising success, he might not even be capable, who could say? But he was determined to try.

Jenny was hurting and he wanted to be with her. He wanted to wrap her in his arms and take away her burden. He wanted to give her all that she needed, so that there was no room in her life left for pain. His world had had sun in it for a while. She had been that sun. He needed to give that back to her now. He felt capable of achieving anything when he was with her. It was probably thanks to her he was even here. She had been the one to go looking for him, to realise he needed someone and to stand by him, however much abuse he hurled at her, because she had cared.

He had screwed up by being afraid and now he was paying the price. In hesitating about wanting her, he had only managed to make *her* not want *him* and she'd been retreating from him ever since. He was a fool if he thought he could change that. But she had confided in him and for that he couldn't account. Maybe he was all she had, and she thought she was safe to speak to him, just not to love him.

It was now his turn to be a hand to hold on to. He had to put his own needs behind him and concentrate on her. What did she need to get through this? What could he do to make her life better? He had to think of what he could do that she wouldn't find threatening.

He had a little over a week till his final exam, and he needed to sleep. It was almost midnight, but he hadn't seen her all weekend. He pulled out his phone.

ARE YOU OK, JENNY WREN? It was a pathetic opener, but at least he would know if she was awake. He waited. A minute later his phone bipped in reply and his pulse awoke.

CAN'T SEEM TO SLEEP. WHAT'S YOUR EXCUSE?

He replied. STUDYING HARD, LIKE A GOOD BOY.

His phone bipped again. GLAD TO HEAR IT.

His fingers hovered over the keys… CAN I SEE YOU?

There was a pause before her reply came in. NOW?!!!

He smiled. If only. NOT NOW! TOMORROW?

ON LATES. CAN DO THURSDAY?

Thursday would have to do. HERE?

PIZZA HUT. 7?

In a public place again. He sighed.

I'LL BE THERE. He switched his phone off and then thought

162

better of it and turned it back on, just in case she needed him. Time for sleep, he thought. Stretching, he filled his lungs with a deep yawn and walked into the bedroom.

The two days that followed, Pete filled with work and studies, leaving little time for self-recriminations. He had a goal in sight and was determined not to mess it up this time, so he did what he had to do, to the best of his ability.

Thursday evening was hers. Since the night Tina had effected his fall, Jenny had been building walls with him. It was plain she no longer considered him more than a friend, not *even* a friend in some respects. He had proven himself shallow in that one stupid mistake, but he couldn't bear her coldness towards him. He'd had no idea Tina was going to walk in that day. She shouldn't even have known where he lived. He had to try and win back Jenny's friendship at least, he needed her, or there was no hope for him anyway.

Jenny was waiting outside when he arrived. Pulling up in the car park, he noticed she seemed miles away. She was sitting on a low wall, reading a book and he watched her for a few minutes, just revelling in the sight of her, undetected, undone. She was everything he could ever ask for and more, her fragile depth of compassion and the strength she found to stand up to the world. She was beautiful. Open, yet guarded, she was so strong on the outside, but so vulnerable beneath. He loved her and if loving her meant keeping himself away from her, then so be it, but she had to know he cared.

He opened the car door and got out. As the door slammed shut, he caught her attention and she looked up. He smiled. "I'm not late, am I?"

Jenny closed her book and hopped off the wall. She checked her watch. "Not at all." She smiled and he was in no way fooled that she felt it. Something was different. Maybe it was being with him, maybe it wasn't, but his normally strong-willed Jenny

Wren was nowhere near her usual self and he was going to try everything he could to find out why.

"I'm really sorry for the other night, Jen." It needed to be said again, so he decided to just put it out there. She had done so much for him and he had let her down. "I never meant to hurt you, I know you don't believe me, but it's the truth. I didn't even touch her."

She screwed up her eyes as if blocking out his words. "It's okay, Pete. It was my fault. I shouldn't have barged in on you. Shall we go in?"

She was dismissing it as if she hadn't cared. She was hurting and he hated that. They headed for the entrance.

"I heard you had it in the neck from the nurses in theatre," she said. She was trying to lighten the mood, but she still didn't believe him, and why would she? There was no light shining in her eyes for him any more, her shoulders were heavy and her smile was weak. Gone was the confident woman he knew her to be. Then he suddenly thought. "They didn't have a go at you too, did they?"

She shook her head. "It's more like a book of condolences for anyone who's been hurt by you." A small smiled creased the corner of her face and he was grateful for it.

He rubbed his fingers across his brow. "Touché."

The waiter appeared by their table and they placed their order and watched as he left.

"What's happening, Jen?" Pete asked her. "Tell me it's not just me who's made you like this. Is it something to do with your family?"

Jenny shook her head. "No. It's me."

"You?" What could be wrong with her?

She looked into his eyes and Pete thought the world had stopped spinning.

"All the pain I caused my family over the years. The troubles with Lizzy. Losing Clara. Everything. Even my aunt having to put up with me for so long. It was all my fault. I can't be that person any more. I don't want to be. It's made me determined to be far

164

more careful with what I say and do from now on."

"But I thought everything was sorted out between you now?"

"It is. On their part. But I can't help thinking over what a mess I've made of everything."

He reached over and took her hands in his. "No. I think *I* get the medal for that one." He smiled kindly. "Jenny, your aunt loves you. Your mum and dad love you. Your sister will too, given time."

"Will she?"

"Of course she will. Who couldn't love *you*?"

He watched as her eyes fell and he realised he had said too much… or too little. She pulled away. What could he say to her? "What would you say to your sister if you could speak to her?" he asked.

"I would tell her how much I love her and how sorry I am for hurting her. I would explain everything and beg her to forgive me."

Pete was floored. "Then tell her. You have to talk to her, Jen. Tell her how you feel and that you love her and that you wish everything had been so different, that she could have known you in a better time; a better you. Tell her you're sorry for everything you've put her through and that if she can forgive you, you would be so grateful to be a part of her life again." His voice trailed away and they sat looking into each other's eyes. The words he had wanted to say had finally been released. He rested back in his seat. "Or something like that." For a moment, he was unable to hold onto her gaze, too painful to see the defeat in her eyes, but then he made himself. "Write her a letter, Jen."

Jenny picked up her drink and sipped at it and Pete could see that her hand was trembling. He had been a fool, such a fool; he didn't deserve her anyway.

The food arrived and he was thankful for the diversion. Jenny looked up at him quizzically as she started to eat.

"What?" he asked, smiling gently at her.

She shook her head. "Nothing."

"Come on. Out with it."

"I was just thinking how different you are to the man I thought I knew."

To the man *he* thought he knew. But he was changing and it was because of her. "Is that good or bad?" he asked.

She looked thoughtful for a moment. "I think it's good. Although... I'm a little more cautious of hoping to influence anyone at the moment."

He smiled. "You've changed me, Jen."

"Have I? I don't think so. Besides, there's not much point in change if it's only fleeting."

What did she mean by that? Was she saying she didn't think he really had changed? Maybe she didn't, but he had. He fell silent.

"Do you think you'll be ready to do the exam on Monday?" she asked after a few windswept moments had passed between them.

He nodded. "As I'll ever be."

"I'm going on holiday at the weekend, so you're on your own now. Don't let me down, Peter Florin, will you?"

The rest of what passed for their dinner was a stilted attempt at ease. At the end of the night, Pete couldn't bear her to leave him, yet she seemed to have no more will to stay. This was not what he had hoped for. But maybe it was what he deserved.

Melt away as it must, he was sorry to see her walk away that night and it was the final nail in his coffin that she didn't look back.

The following evening, just as Pete was leaving work, his brother called. He wanted to see him, to wish him luck before his exam on Monday. So Pete got a takeaway and got back to his flat about half an hour before James was expected.

Rachel was with him when he arrived, which was a surprise for Pete. Excitedly, he looked around for his nephew and niece. "My mum's looking after them," Rachel told him. We're on a sneaky weekend away."

His face fell.

166

"You're welcome to come over as soon as your exams are through and see them…" his brother added with a smile. "But for tonight we are kid-free!"

"And you're wasting it here with me?" he asked in horror, disappointed not to have had a bit of playtime with the kids.

"Oh, we're not stopping long," James told him, winking at Rachel and making her blush. "Can we come in?"

"Of course. Come on through." He opened the door and let them inside. "I've got an Indian keeping warm in the oven."

"Then we'd better let him out!" James replied; an age-old tradition between them. They laughed and then James looked at his wife. "Well it *would* be a shame to waste it."

Rachel rolled her eyes at the two hopeful faces looking at her, imploring her to stay. "Go on, then."

They dished up, pulled a couple of cold beers out of the fridge (allowable under Jenny's revised regime that he stuck to even now) and sat down.

"So, how's it going, then?" James asked him.

"Good, yeah." He put another forkful of chicken bhuna in his mouth and tore off some naan. "Need to give everything another once-over this weekend, but it's been going pretty well. So, a whole weekend without the kids? What are you two going to do with yourselves? Or shouldn't I ask?"

James and Rachel smiled at one another. "We're too bloody tired for any of that. You make the most of it while you can, big brother. Tonight we're planning on a crazy debauched night of uninterrupted sleeping."

Pete laughed, but he was unable to muster the humour he'd had before.

"What's the matter, mate? No one keeping you warm at night at the moment? You must be slipping."

Rachel thumped her husband playfully.

Pete made a small, sad laugh. "Afraid not."

James and Rachel exchanged looks.

167

"What?" Pete asked, sensing some kind of conspiracy brewing.

"Whatever happened to that nice girl who came to look for you?" James asked, but his pretence of innocence was abysmal.

"Jenny, you mean."

"Yeah, that's the girl. It's not going anywhere with her, then?" Reaching forward, James took a poppadum from the plate on the coffee table and took a bite, before casually looking back toward Pete.

"No." Pete could see what his brother was up to and he didn't want to play.

"That's a shame; she seemed nice. Got some hot blonde instead, have you?"

"No." He wasn't enjoying this line of questioning. "I'm too blooming busy studying. I thought that was what you wanted?"

"Absolutely." James took a swig of his beer. "Still… I did think the pair of you had a… well, a bit of a… What's the word?" He turned to his wife.

"A connection."

"That's it, a connection."

Pete paused with his chewing and looked at them both. He swallowed his food. "Okay, what is this? What's with the sudden third degree about Jenny?"

"Third degree? That's a bit harsh. We only wanted—"

"She was good for you," Rachel butted in. "She took it on herself to travel across the country to hunt you down. You don't do that on a whim."

Pete slowly blinked his eyes and lifted his chin.

"She cares about you, Pete. Or at least she did do, unless you've managed to balls it all up already. And it *has* only been a few weeks."

Pete's brow creased.

"You haven't!?"

Pete pulled a hopeless smile, mocking himself, and then let the smile drop.

168

Rachel shook her head. "What are we going to do with you, Peter Florin?"

"She was too good for me, anyway," he added.

"Darn right she was! But that girl took care of you. She even bunked off work for you and she didn't seem like the bunking type to me," Rachel told him.

Pete looked up.

"You didn't know that, did you? Yes. She was meant to have been in work on the day she took you home. She was all set to leave us when we finally found you. She didn't have to do any of that for you. And, according to James, she's been baking for you and helping you work ever since. You don't do that for a guy for no reason."

Pete shot his brother a dark look. They were trying to say that Jenny had real feelings for him. Or, at least, had done. Way to stick the knife in! He thought back over their time together: every touch, every kiss, every look. She really had loved him, hadn't she? It seemed like the most obvious thing in the world to him now. But he had realised it too late and let another woman come between them.

No, that wasn't right. It had been the thought of such love that had made him afraid. When he had needed someone she had been there for him, but when she had needed him the most, he had let her down. He set his fork down on his plate and put it down on the table, his appetite gone.

"Still, I'm sure you could always win her back if you wanted."

Pete looked up. "I don't think so."

An awkward silence fell across them as each one seemed to consider what an idiot he had been. "Where are you two off to, then?" Pete asked, trying hard to focus on something else for a while.

"We've got a hotel booked in Duxley for the night and then we're off for a decadent stay at a swanky hotel in North Devon. Five stars, four-poster bed, full board, the lot."

His visitors finished their meals and rested back for a while chatting.

"Right then, push off you two. Some of us have got studying to do," Pete told them and they made their way to the front door.

"You're looking good," James told him. "Whatever it is you're doing, keep doing it. And good luck with the exam on Monday. We'll be thinking of you."

"Will you hell!" Pete smiled.

"We will on Monday. We'll be back to the grindstone again by then."

He gave his brother a slap on the back. "Have a good time."

Rachel moved up to stand in front of Pete. "Feelings like that don't just disappear, Pete. That girl loved you. Don't let her get away." She hugged him and then the two headed off on their adventure.

Pete closed the door behind them. Jenny probably *had* loved him, he realised that now, but he was never going to be the right man for her. If she was *his* sister, he wouldn't let her date him. Not until he could prove to himself that he was worth it, and he couldn't. He had never been able to keep safe the ones he loved. He had failed his mother and he had failed Ali and each time the pain of it had near-killed him.

Jenny had thought a lot about the idea of writing to her sister, going over it in her head to find the words that sounded best. She didn't want to come across as selfish, because she really wasn't, not any more. She just wanted to offer an olive branch, a big one, in the hope that Lizzy would take it.

So she wrote and she made certain to post it as she left for the airport for her week away, learning about writing in the far corner of France.

A whole week of peace and quiet and a real writer on hand to give her some help. She needed this. She needed some time alone to concentrate on something other than herself and everything she'd done wrong. Life could be far too busy and complicated at times. It was lonely, waiting to be loved. She wanted to create something. Something to help her through the days of muck and toil, to fill her mind with another universe and keep her occupied until he left again.

Tickets? Check. Passport? Check. Money?

Jenny fished around in her bag for the umpteenth time to make sure she had everything she needed. Keys, instructions, invoice. Stepping out of the taxi, she looked up at the airport entrance in front of her and felt a large weight lift from her shoulders.

Not having travelled for years, she found check-in fascinating and, waiting for her flight, she watched as aeroplanes taxied around the tarmac and roared up past her, on take-off. She was on her own and she was excited.

Sitting in her seat, she fiddled with the contents of the pocket in front of her. There was a sick bag – always a possibility – and an instruction sheet on the use of inflight services. She read the lists to see what movies, if any, they were going to be showing that day. None. Well what had she expected? It was a cheap flight and a short one. She noted the emergency exits, although if the plane was going down, she rather doubted she would be thinking clearly enough to remember them.

Jenny fished out her book and rested it in her lap. She looked around her. All life was here. People of all shapes and sizes herding into a tin can to fly across the sea and start a new adventure. She supposed some of them had already had their adventure and were returning home. She rested her head back against the seat and closed her eyes. She was changing, she could feel it. She was very aware of the importance of this trip and although sense should have made her terrified, her overriding feeling was one of release. She took a deep breath of the cool, dry air and opened her eyes again.

A woman approached her and excused herself to sit down on the seat beside the window. "Actually, you wouldn't mind swapping, would you?" she said. "Only I'm not great at flying and I don't think being able to see just how far up we are is going to help me."

"Of course. If you're sure?" Jenny said and moved across, pleased to be getting a view.

The woman held out her hand. "Helen Sinclair," she said.

"Jenny White."

"First time flying?"

"First time on my own."

"An adventure, then?" the woman asked.

"Yes. I think so."

"Good for you."

As the plane began to taxi for take-off, Jenny dug her fingers into the seat. It was like a rollercoaster ride, from what she remembered. Exciting and wonderful, yet a little terrifying too.

She was pleased that the woman next to her seemed happy to leave their conversation at that for the time being, setting her free to wander around the pathways of her mind. There were so many dark corners to visit there and she had a whole week alone to do it.

She hadn't told the girls why she was going, embarrassed perhaps. She just told them she was visiting an old friend, which she *was* in a way. She had loved writing from an early age and her diary was probably her best friend now. Nursing was her calling in life, but writing was... What was it? Her passion.

She was nervous that now she had finally decided to do something about it, she wouldn't be able to write. Surely she should have some idea of what she wanted to do while she was out there, but in all honesty, she couldn't think of where to start. She just hoped her tutor would know what to do with her. *If* she found her, that was. But today's worries were enough for today, tomorrow's would have to wait for tomorrow.

As the approach for landing was announced, Jenny stowed her book back in her bag and turned to the woman beside her. The woman was sleeping. Jenny touched her gently on the arm and woke her up. "We're coming into land," she said and the woman smiled and thanked her.

As the flow of noisy holiday-makers bustled her forward through the terminal, Jenny found herself at baggage reclaim and stood there waiting to spot her purple case. She waited while the muffled sounds of distant announcements and 300 different conversations all combined into a cloud of noise. And finally they started to appear.

At last, with passport and handbag in one hand and her case being pulled by the other, Jenny arrived at the gateway, with a sea of faces set before her. She stopped a short way off and looked at the instructions on her piece of paper. "Under the clock." Jenny looked around for any clock on the wall and after a few sweeps of the building, she spotted one over the far side of the terminal. Relief.

Pulling the case along the smooth, polished floor, she headed in that direction and right underneath it she saw a woman, possibly in her fifties, searching the masses before her.

Jenny smiled and quickened her pace and the woman noticed her.

"Are you Briony?" Jenny asked.

"I am, and you are?"

She held out her hand. "I'm Jenny White," she said.

Jenny could feel the tide of her life changing. She was moving on. Things were only going to get better, because from here on in, she was determined to set herself free.

Chapter 14

Pete was working hard, harder than he had worked in years. The thought that work was finally saving him was a strange one, but it kept his mind busy and helped him deal with the empty space left by Jenny. He missed her, though he dared not admit it. He was torn apart by the sight of her walking away from him and, riddled with guilt that he only had himself to blame. He had been a coward.

But passing his exam was something he *could* do, to show her that he was grateful for everything she had done for him. He hadn't heard from her in a few days and he doubted he was going to until Monday. On Monday she might ring. He couldn't remember if she'd told him where she was going, but if she *could* ring him, then, he thought, she probably would.

He took a deep breath and slowly let it out. Monday: the day of reckoning. He had to work as hard as he could until then, but as soon as Monday was over, he had made up his mind to make things better for Jenny. Until then, he thought, and he opened another textbook and turned to the index.

Jenny was riding down the country roads, away from the hustle and bustle of the urban streets, in the back of an old green Citroën Picasso with two other hopeful writers. Their mentor, Briony

Withers – multi-award-winning novelist and screen writer – was driving, as she tried to engage them all in conversation, but they seemed a little star-struck and it was awkward trying to get it going. Jenny leant her arm on the window edge and breathed in the warm country air. The view was a world away from her little town in England, it was big, wide and colourful and, in her eyes, exotic. She relaxed. For this one week, life was going to be good, she thought.

As the roads became narrower and the hills rose up around her, they slowed to a crawl down a long country lane. A beautiful old barn stood at the end. It had been converted into a house, its stone walls grey and solid, giving it a sense of permanence and tranquillity.

"Here we are," said Briony and they stepped out of the car. Jenny felt the soft, warm, evening sun touch her face as she breathed in the flowery scent of her surroundings. She looked around her. The building was tucked away behind high hedges and ancient trees, but the garden around it was awash with colour. Brilliant spurs of buddleia treated the breeze to a hint of honey, while clematis of all colours trailed their merry way up the side of the barn and pergola beyond. The sound of cattle lowing in the distance and the buzzing of the bees were all there was to trouble the peace of the still, late-summer's day.

The boot popped open and they each took their own bag. Briony was talking, but Jenny's head was in a dream. This was a place of angels, she thought. She could disappear here and be content.

"Jenny?"

Briony's voice was calling her and she realised everyone else was looking at her from the door of the barn. She hurried in behind them and focused on the conversation there.

They ate that evening with two others who'd joined them: Raymond, Briony's partner, and a woman who had driven over by car. Over cold meat, exquisite cheeses and fresh bread, they

175

introduced themselves. There were four of them altogether: Simon, an accountant in his forties, with a passion for blood, guts and gore; Naomi, a post-grad whose entire life so far had been working towards becoming a writer; Cynthia, a woman in her late sixties, whose husband had died the year before and was now determined to seize the day, and Jen.

When it got round to her, Jenny was embarrassed to admit how little writing she'd actually done, but not one of them seemed to look down on her. On the contrary, they seemed to think it exciting to be so new.

That night she settled into her little room in the attic, with sloping ceilings and dark wooden beams. She unpacked and set Mr Rochester on her nightshirt on top of her pillow and put her book on the little wooden table beside her bed.

In her diary lay the flowers, tucked in the crease and now worshipped with love. Here I am, in a pocket of heaven, she wrote. In a distant corner of France, my heart is at peace. The thought of what awaits me fills me with hope and I am excited to get writing at last. What I really wanted is lost to me now, but I always knew, deep down, that it would be.

I cannot think of what has been or is yet to be. For this week... for now, I am determined to be free.

The following day, they each had some time alone with Briony to talk about what they wanted to achieve in their stay there. In her time, they talked about what Jenny liked to read and what writing she had done so far and then they talked about what she might like to do. Jenny was struggling to come up with an idea, until Briony asked her if there was any*one* in particular she wanted to write for and in that moment she had the idea of writing a story for the little girl on the wards. She was going to write a story about a pink unicorn called Penelope, who guarded a beautiful princess. It was a manageable goal for a week's work and Briony thought it was brilliant.

Objective achieved, they made a quick list of all the things she would need to think about and then Briony left her to it and Jenny became the scribe to her imagination.

At lunchtime they came together to eat and then found their own spaces to hide away again. For Jenny it was bliss.

The second day they were encouraged to try venturing out, to take their thoughts on a wander, and Jenny found a field at the side of the barn that looked over a small lake in the valley beyond. She lay out on a blanket and listened to the sounds of the world around her and let her thoughts drift into wonderland.

In the evening they all helped out preparing the meal and enjoyed a barbecue as the sun set over the hills around them. Despite herself, Jenny's mind felt drawn to thinking about Pete and how he must be feeling. It was his exam the following morning and *she* may have been enjoying a rest in the land of beauty and serenity, but *he* would be nervous and needing her and sadness slipped in.

Jenny hadn't called. He had hoped she would, to give him a chance to speak to her. The whole aim of her being with him had been to get him back on track in order to pass his exam, and, pass or fail, she had done it. She must have really decided against him, not to have rung, and that hurt more than he thought it could.

It was a waiting game now. Eight more days till he could find out his results. He needed to vent his frustration. He couldn't see Jenny, but he didn't want anyone else. She had spoiled him for others, giving him all of her, and now he wanted nothing less. He gave Neil a ring and arranged to go sparring.

They met at the club and started with some training: skipping reps and heavy bag work and then they stepped into the ring.

It felt good to get back in there, good and bad. Fighting helped bring some release from the stresses he was battling, but it also served to remind him of why he had begun. It was a good session, though. He'd worked hard. Neil had given as good as he'd got, so they had both taken some punches. He was a mate, however,

177

so the reins were always on, just keeping him fit and ready in case he needed it; determined never to take a beating again without taking the other guy down with him.

When they had showered and changed, Neil invited Pete down the pub. It was his brother's birthday and they had arranged to meet in the White Horse for a couple of pints around nine. Pete thought about this. He had no studying to go back to and he would only have the one pint, maybe two. But then, what did it matter if he didn't? Jenny had given up on him. He no longer had to try to impress her, only… he *wanted* to… still. He wanted to be the person she thought he could be. "Okay," he said.

Pete gave Neil a lift to the car park a short walk away from the pub. They talked about his exam and their impending fights, only two weeks away, until they arrived at the door of the pub and the starkness of noise hit them.

Moving through a crowd unusually large for a weekday, Neil spotted his brother. "Jack!" He beckoned him over. Turning to Pete, standing just to the side of him, he whispered a warning. "Vomit alert," he said. "I'm afraid my brother's surgically attached to his new girlfriend and she's back off to university next week, so it's pretty full on between them at the moment." He rolled his eyes. "Jack! Happy birthday, buddy." He patted his brother on the back and turned to Pete. "This is Pete. I don't think you've met before. Pete, this is my kid brother, Jack. Mum and Dad have managed to rope him into the family business." Jack and Neil solemnly bowed at one another and then Jack laughed and punched his brother in the arm. "Jack, this is Pete Florin. He's a doc at the hospital and a sparring buddy of mine, so don't mess with him."

They laughed and Pete shook his hand. "Happy Birthday, mate. How many is it today, then?"

"Twenty-three."

"Twenty-three? Oh, to be so young again!" Pete sighed.

"Come and meet Lena. We've got a table over there." Jack

178

pointed to a pretty, dark-haired girl sat at a table in the corner, quietly watching them.

Pete saw Jack's face light up and Neil told him they'd be over in a minute. They were just going to get some drinks in. Jack returned to his table and Pete saw the look in the eyes of his girlfriend as she smiled up at him. Something pulled inside of him as he recognised what he wanted out of life. And suddenly he wished he was with Jenny and that she would look at him as Lena was looking at Jack and that he would know what it was like to be loved.

Pete said his goodbyes not long after his first pint. The company was not the problem. Jack and Lena, and, in fact, all their mates, had been fun, but he was pining for the one thing that he couldn't have, and the longer he sat there, the darker his mood became.

Sitting back at home, Pete allowed himself to wallow. He put on his Nina Simone CD and sat back. What would be the point of getting to consultant level, having worked as hard as he had, and having no one to share it with? His mother would be proud, certainly, but that was no longer enough.

He thought about his nightmare and realised he hadn't had it again since the night he had shared it with Jenny. It wasn't the longest he had ever gone, perhaps, but it was a good start. He needed to see her, to talk to her and not just in passing in the corridor where he couldn't say anything with meaning, but in private. He had to try and prove to her that he was not the man he had once been. He needed her to *see* him, to look at him with open eyes, if not an open heart. He had changed... not enough, perhaps, but she mattered to him and he wanted her to understand that.

But it wasn't just about him. She no longer wanted him. And if he couldn't make her happy, or she wasn't going to let him, then who could? And then it struck him. What she needed was a man who was worthy of her, of everything that was wonderful about her. This would be his penance. He wanted Jenny to be

179

happy; Lord knows, she deserved to be happy, and although it tore a hole a mile wide inside him to do so, he was determined to find her a man.

Grabbing a paper and pen, he tried to think up a list of contenders, but the harder he thought about it, the more difficult it became. Of those he knew well, he knew too much to see them as perfection, and anything less would not do for Jenny. For those he didn't know it was worse still. Unknown flaws could be more dangerous than those that were known. He might be shoving her towards a potential wife beater or a philandering cheat. Frustration made him angry, at himself more than anything.

As the days passed he found himself scrutinising the men he met and considering each as possibilities. And then, just by chance, on Thursday afternoon, he was introduced to a locum in the canteen. He had been brought in to cover some maternity leave, so he was going to be around for a good few months. A decent-looking chap, he had an honest way about him. He was fun and charming and genial to talk to. At last he could be onto a winner.

His single status was established early on, when a conversation about home was brought up and a light turned on in Pete's mind. This might actually work. All he needed now was an opportunity to get the two together and a whole heap of luck.

It was the last full day of Jenny's writing holiday and the first draft of her story was complete. Briony had been a mine of useful information, with little tricks and strategies for getting her creative juices flowing, and on their last talk together she had let Jenny read her work to her, and had guided her with pointers about how to finish it off. She had brimmed over with encouragement and Jenny's head was swimming.

Elated by her relative success and eager to push on, she was a little disappointed that they were going on an outing for the latter part of the afternoon, but piling into two cars, they plunged further into the countryside to take in the view.

The drive didn't take long, and before she knew it, they were stepping out onto a panorama that quite took her breath away. Lavender fields: beautifully fragrant rows of deep-purple flowers springing out from silver-greens and rust-coloured soil, with low hedgerows dividing them, like speckled hems on a patchwork quilt, and Jenny was in awe. It was stunning.

They set out a blanket and chairs and sat in the warmth of the afternoon sun, chatting happily together about what they had learned from their week and how they were going to change their lives to allow more time for writing. But change was coming to Jenny faster than most.

As she was packing her bags at the end of the evening, Jenny spotted her box of tampons still lying in her case unopened. She stared at it. Rapidly calculating, she tried to work out when she should have been due on. She was five days late. To some, this might not be an issue, but Jenny had taken the pill religiously ever since she had lost Clara. It was unthinkable that she could have caught again. There her mind screeched to a halt. No! The vomiting! She had forgotten about the couple of days she'd been sick after the day she'd gone home. The day *after* she had slept with Pete…

Jenny touched her abdomen and all the turmoil of what had happened before shook her. Suddenly her brain was numb. She couldn't think. She was frightened. She couldn't go through it all over again. She couldn't do it. How could life be so cruel? She sat back on her bed and thought about her reality. Not the romantic interlude in a beautiful place she was currently enjoying, but the nitty gritty of everyday life and how hard it was going to be, because it *was* going to be now; it was too much of a coincidence to be just a blip. She was pregnant and there was nothing she could do about it, nothing she could bear, anyway. She thought she had felt different, but had assumed that was merely her will to be free. Well that was a laugh; free was now the one thing she never would be again.

181

Tomorrow she was leaving and going back to her shared little house and her job. It was the life she had made for herself. But proof of her love was growing inside her, for she *had* loved him. She loved him still. And in his own way, she thought he had probably loved her too. What he would say, she wasn't sure. Was she going to tell him? She ought to tell him. But was that even fair? She could do this on her own. Soon he would be off and gone, to a future he had worked hard so many years for. It was a good future too. Oh, there was so much to think about. Too much for one night. So pausing briefly to touch the hydrangea now pressed within her diary, she wrote about her day and then went down to join the others for tea.

That night, she picked up her book from beside the bed and the photo slipped out. Pete. He was relaxing in his brother's back garden, seemingly at ease with the world. Carefree. She yearned for him. But 'carefree' was not what he really was, it was what he wanted people to see.

Pete... a father? No. No way was he ready for that. She wouldn't want to tell him until it was several weeks on, anyway, to be sure, and by then he would be long gone.

As the night wore on, a kind of peace settled over her. It wasn't something she had planned on, but it could be a good thing. She was going to have a baby and maybe in the hours and days before the wind of change blew through, she could finish her story for the little girl on the ward. Oh, she was sure there would be times when she would resent Pete's ability to float above the pain he caused around him, but, in the end, she was a grown woman, and she had gone into this knowing him.

And so she would take what life was willing to give her, and be thankful for it. She settled her hand on her abdomen again and thought about how pretty her baby would be with Peter Florin as a father.

By one in the morning, the panic was fading and she pulled out her diary and wrote in it anew.

Well, it's my last night of light in this piece of heaven. We have all swapped email addresses and promised to keep in touch. Cynthia has been my favourite, so down to earth and easy to talk to. I have told her about Pete and she wished me luck and then the strangest thing happened, she looked me in the eye and said, "Forgiveness is the greatest gift we can give each other in life," and she smiled at me and I felt... I don't know exactly... forgiven.

She put out the light and rested back on her pillow. At the airport tomorrow there was sure to be a chemist's. She would buy a test, just to be certain, and when she got back home, she'd make an appointment at the doctor's. She was stronger now. She could do this and she had her family to support her if times got rough.

It was a windy day as they left the hills for the airport. Clouds were passing through, threatening rain. They'd had the best of the weather, not a bad day to leave.

Jenny waved goodbye to her friends and walked back inside the cool, bustling building. Noise surrounded her as children played, wheels squeaked and Tannoys called out their timely reminders. She looked around for her line to check in.

Duty free held little appeal and she realised she would have to start saving her money now, with circumstances about to alter.

She took her seat on the plane and rested her head. She spotted Helen Sinclair, the lady from the flight over, walking past.

"So how did the adventure go?" Helen asked, dipping her head to the side. "Life-changing or a bit of a damp squib?"

Jenny thought to herself and smiled. "Definitely life-changing," she said.

Helen looked at her closely and nodded. "I'm glad," and moved on past to find her seat.

So that was it. Back to the humdrum of daily life, although now life would never quite be the same again. In her darker times, Jenny had almost given up hope of having another baby. But what if it went wrong again? What if she could never have children? She just prayed to God this time she would get to keep her. Or him. A little Pete. She took a deep breath and let it out. She would like that.

As the plane settled in to its flight, Jenny pulled out her work and started to read it again. She was almost there now; just the odd tweak and it would be finished. Then she just had to type it up and print it out and possibly try to do a drawing for the cover. Maybe next time she would tackle an adult story, she thought. Far less cause for artwork there.

Time flew by as she concentrated on her writing and, before she knew it, they were coming in to land.

Back on the ground, the whirl of departure took over and she followed the convoy through the terminal and out into the cool grey of the British day.

Boarding the train back to Duxley, Jenny realised she had forgotten to pick up a test. But the day was still young. It was only mid-afternoon and the shops would be open in town when she got back. So she dropped in to a dispenser a few miles from home, on an estate where no one knew her and few people were around to see.

She was slightly disappointed at the lack of welcome at home. Nobody was in. They must have all been working. Jenny's mind focused on the side of her handbag where the pregnancy test had been stowed. Do it now and at least then you'll know, she thought.

She hauled her bags up the stairs with her heart rate pounding. Why was she so nervous? She knew what the answer was going to be. But feeling it whilst on a beautiful romantic holiday in the countryside was one thing, seeing it in black and white – or blue and white, in this particular case – was quite another.

Dumping her things in her bedroom, Jenny grabbed the box from her bag and hurried to the bathroom. She read the back and worked out what the exact indication would be and then ripped open the box. She looked at it. Hard. This piece of plastic was going to decide her future. Fear gave her stage fright and she had to run the tap to help her pee and then she waited, stick in hand, staring at the little window, daring herself to blink. Within seconds a bold plus was showing. She blinked and checked the box and then looked again. It was true. She had been right. She was definitely pregnant.

Dazed, she ditched the evidence in the bin and piled some tissues on top. She walked out and into her bedroom in silence. No thoughts crammed her head now, no sounds battled to get in, just silence all around. Empty. She sat on her bed and unzipped her case. Mr Rochester came out and she hugged him. After years of anxiety and denial, she was having a baby. Again.

Chapter 15

Monday morning, Pete was feeling good. He had spent the weekend cranking up his efforts with Rich, his trainer, in preparation for the fight he was booked in for the following week. His exams were over, good or bad, and Jenny would be back from holiday.

He hadn't seen her yet, hadn't heard a thing since before she left, which had been a disappointment for him, if he let himself think about it, which he was trying hard not to.

Neil had helped out with his sparring and worked with him for their fitness. He was ready and focused and eager to win; all he needed now was to be happy and he was hopeful that if he could find a way to make Jenny happy, then that would be enough.

In his mind he had analysed every word the locum had said during the weekend and the more he thought about him, the more he was convinced he was right. The guy was cheerful enough to make her happy, intelligent enough to understand her and he was sure to be a trusted provider. To all outward appearances, he seemed ideal; a far cry from a man haunted by a past that threatened to topple any good intentions he might ever feel.

He needed a way to get them together. Surgical nurse and medical doctor? It had to be something sociable. Maybe he could manufacture something. If he passed, *if* he passed, he could throw a party to celebrate and he could make sure they both came. But that might be too late. He was finishing in a matter of days now; what if one of them couldn't come?

His next patient was wheeled into the anaesthetic room and Pete refocused on the job. He smiled. "Mrs Simpson, how are you? Come on in. I've got a vial of gin and tonic lined up right here with your name on it."

Jenny walked back into work on Monday lunchtime, a more reserved and subdued woman than the one who had flown out the week before. This was real life. Gone was the carefree woman of the holiday in France. There were worries clambering at the door to get out. Her new reality scared her. Her career, her future, whether she could even face Pete, all was so uncertain and she couldn't talk to anyone. The girls would never understand. Flis would go ballistic. Her mum and dad had suffered enough with her drama for one lifetime and Auntie May, well... Jenny was going to have to work out in her own mind what on earth she was going to do before she talked it over with her. So, for now, she was determined to carry on as if nothing whatsoever had changed.

Several colleagues asked her if she was all right on her first day back, which surprised her; she thought she had been doing a good job of pretending. A few of them said she was looking very healthy and asked her where she'd been, and it reminded her to enquire if the little girl was still around on the wards.

That night her protective cloak began to show cracks. The others were sitting around the TV when Jenny got in. All three of them. They looked up.

"Good to be back?" Flis asked her.

Jenny smiled and let out a short laugh. "Absolutely." She hung up her jacket. "I'll just get out of this and then you can tell me all about what's been going on since I've been away," and she went to her room and got into her fluffy socks, her old jogger bottoms and a jumper and then walked back down to the living room.

187

The girls budged up and made room for her on the settee. "What are we watching?" she asked them and was immediately hushed as the final scene of a film was revealed.

Lots of sighs and chatter later, the TV was turned off and they asked about her time away. Time to be a bit brave, she thought. "It was a writing break," she told them.

"A writing break?" Flis was shocked. "What on earth made you go on one of those?"

"I loved it," she told them all. "I learned a lot and it was such a beautiful place. So peaceful and the people were so friendly."

"And you actually did some writing?" Chloe asked her.

Jenny nodded. "I wrote a story for a little girl who's having chemo on the children's ward."

"Can we read it?" Heather asked.

"Ooh, yeah, please," Chloe echoed.

Jenny looked from one to the other. Eager faces pleaded with her to submit. She had read it aloud to Briony on holiday, so maybe she could do this. It might be good to get some feedback before she handed it over, so she agreed. "Okay."

Jenny trotted back to her room to fish the story out of her drawer and then returned, a little anxious, to the living room, where three different faces met her. Heather seemed curious, Chloe delighted and Flis couldn't have looked more sceptical if she'd tried. Jenny took a seat.

"I haven't had a chance to type it up yet and my writing isn't very legible, but... here goes. It's called, 'Penelope, Champion of the Ward.'"

Jenny read her story and tried not to look at their faces as she did so. She put as much expression into it as she could manage and told them the tale of a magical pink unicorn, who came to life at night and protected all the poorly children of her realm, especially Lauren, her best friend, from the nasty germs who tried to attack them. She had found out the girl's name when she'd ventured to the children's ward to ask earlier that day.

When she'd finished, all three of them looked stunned. They broke into a round of applause and Jenny blushed and felt happy that she must have actually done a good job.

In the ensuing conversation, it turned out that Heather was a dab hand at drawing and Jenny asked her to have a go at doing a cover for her. "So you think it's okay?" she asked when the fuss had died down.

Chloe sighed and looked at her. "You'll make a wonderful mummy one day," she said.

Jenny felt the blood drain from her face and all of a sudden she wanted to burst into tears. She excused herself and hurried off to her bedroom, on the pretext of putting her work away. What had she done? She was having a baby. She was going to be somebody's mummy and she was all alone. She didn't want to be alone. She wanted Pete by her side. Her courage was failing. She wanted him to step up and be the man she knew he was capable of being, to protect her and care for them both, her and the baby. Was it a foolish hope? Probably. Pete had never wanted more than he could handle, and unbidden tears began to flow.

There was a knock on her door and a face peeped round. Flis. "Are you all right?" she asked.

Jenny immediately wiped her hands across her face and sniffed. "Fine. Fine. Just a bit of jet lag, probably."

Flis sat down next to her. "Because you will be a mum one day, if that was what was bothering you? I'm sure you will."

A sorry laugh escaped her at the irony of it all. She shook her head. "Ignore me. I'm just tired. I've probably been a little too much in touch with my emotional side this past week, that's all." She took a deep breath and let it out. This was neither the time, nor the person, for disclosure. She smiled.

Flis gave her a speculative look and then got up. "It's a good story, Jen. You should think about doing more. You could write an adult one, if you like. I'd read it."

Jenny smiled, grateful for the support and relieved to have

189

shifted the spotlight away from being a mum. "I might just do that," she told her. "But I think I'll get some sleep now. You on an early?"

"Yeah."

"See you in the morning, then, and... thanks."

I'm home, she wrote in her diary that night, and it's only you I can talk to now. I thought once I was back I would start to make sense of what was going to happen to me, but it's too big, too massive to get my head round. I'm desperate to see Pete. I want to look into his eyes and feel if he's missed me half as much as I've missed him. But I'm so afraid. What if he's all but forgotten about me now? What if he's moved on and had half a dozen women in the time since I've been away?

But, then again, would the loss of him be harder than having him obligated to a child he never asked for, never wanted? Wouldn't that be worse? Oh God, I don't know. Perhaps when I see him I'll know what to do. What I mustn't forget to do is book in at the surgery. I know they said Clara's problem was a one off, but... they might be wrong. They might have just been saying that. Oh God, I don't think I can do this.

And yet... here I am, doing it. Again. Knocked up by a man who can let me go as easily as leaves on a breeze.

Beany, I'm going to call you that, because you'll probably look something like that at the moment. Beany. It's just you and me now, kiddo. It's just you and me.

Wednesday evening, on her break in the canteen, Jenny heard about a party at a function room in town. She was beginning to feel a little queasy, but it was Emma, one of the nice lady doctors, who had just got engaged to an engineer, and she was having a do to celebrate. Invitations were fluttering around and Jenny was half tempted to go. She wasn't going to be able to drink, but it might at least cheer her up and take her mind off things. And then she saw him.

190

Pete walked into the canteen, obviously on call and he looked amazing. His eyes were brighter. He looked healthy. She hadn't heard any more scandal about him, not since Tina. She sighed. She wanted him... still. She thought about him every morning when she opened her eyes and every night before she closed them. For a short time he had been her world, and she his, perhaps. It was just a moment, really, but it had been enough to let her see how good it could be between them, sowing the seed of hope that had echoed within her ever since.

He looked over and saw her and their eyes met. Nothing was said. A brief smile touched the corners of his lips and then his attention was diverted by the woman at the till and, with one backward glance, he was gone.

She'd had time now to reflect on her change in circumstance. She didn't blame him. She had fallen for Pete, though she had known from the first that he couldn't commit.

Maybe if she hadn't felt the need to confess her past so openly, only minutes after they had shared such an intimate connection, maybe then they would have stood a chance.

This ache was going to take a long time to burn out and there was nothing she could do about it. She had been a fool, the biggest fool of all. She had been drawn to the man before she had ever really known him, sensing something deeper lurking within, but had never known quite how deep that person lay.

He was incarcerated behind walls, a million miles below the surface, with just the smallest gap to see the sun. She had reached him for a while. Their fingers had touched. His heart had begun to beat again, she was sure it had, but she'd been unable to get a firm grip to help him up, and then the ground had been pulled from beneath her and he had disappeared again.

Only Mr Rochester was waiting for her up in her bedroom when she got home. She had no reserve left for small talk; she needed to be alone. She needed to think, so she pulled out her diary.

It's his results tomorrow. I wonder how he's feeling. He seems happy around the hospital, but you never know what's going on inside with him. He has layers of defences built up over years. I wonder how deep I even got.

I miss our closeness. I miss the friendly banter and ease with which we spoke, the intimacy of our hearts. I miss him.

"Plenty more fish in the sea", people would tell me if they knew what I was feeling. "He's never been a keeper, anyway." *I know this.* But knowing that has never stopped a girl from dreaming. Lorna was never meant to be for John Ridd, but they got their happy-ever-after. It was a bit of a bumpy ride, of course, but they got there, in the end.

The next day, the ward was busy. An influx of cases over night had seen them full to capacity. Nurses off sick added weight to their load, but Jenny was relieved, as it left little time to wallow.

With the drug round done, she went back to check on the woman who had come in from an assault. She was out of danger now, since coming back from theatre, but she needed regular obs, having been stabbed repeatedly and left for dead in a back street. Jenny shuddered at the thought. Was pregnancy making her more vulnerable to her emotions? She gave herself a stern talking to and moved on with her day.

She was unsure about going for a run that afternoon, but she decided it would probably be all right, as long as she didn't push herself too hard. As she got ready, she was thoughtful about how Pete was doing and desperately wanted to go round to his flat to find out if he had passed, but she wasn't sure of her welcome. He might wonder what on earth she was doing there, so she sucked it up and went for the run instead.

Her feet pounding the earth felt good. It focused her thoughts on the next step. Sisters, babies and loves were banished from her mind as she pummelled the unforgiving pavements, trampled the fading earth and concentrated on the path in front of her. Autumn colours were moving in, painting the leaves with their palette and time was suspended for a while in the rhythm of her life.

An hour later she arrived home, breathless and spent. She showered and changed into something comfortable and then, lying on her bed, she pulled her phone out of her pocket. She looked at it and toyed with the idea of calling him. Surely he wouldn't mind that? She tapped her nails against the warm, purple plastic casing and then, scolding herself, put it back in her pocket and got up to make some tea.

Pete had seen the pass rate and he was uneasy. It was just over 50 per cent. He had worked harder this time than before. He had had reason. He didn't know what he was going to do if he didn't get it; his rotation was almost at an end and he wasn't sure he could face trying again, not if Jenny wasn't beside him. He needed this to prove he could make something of himself, that he wasn't just a mess-up holding on by a thread.

He logged onto the website that morning and there was nothing. By lunchtime they should have been posted. Something was causing a delay. He was obviously going to have to wait for them. His pain clinic that morning had been interesting and had kept his mind busy for the most part, but now he was eager to know... but not to fail.

With a cautious heart, he walked out into the car park at the end of the day, took out his mobile and checked again. He waited. He couldn't breathe, and then... up popped the list. He scanned down and... he had done it. Elation swept through him as the end of such a long, hard journey was finally in sight. He had got it and he was almost free to make consultant. He punched the air around him and whooped, grinning like an idiot at patients and relatives passing by. But then he became thoughtful. Jenny had kept her side of the bargain. Now it was time for him to keep his.

Pete had been asked to an engagement party by one of the doctors. He knew Jenny knew her too, surely that meant she'd be going, if her schedule allowed, of course. It was the night Rich had lined up the fight, so Pete knew he couldn't go, but Phil, the locum he had in mind for her, could get there, *if* she was going to be there. He needed to find out.

With a reputation like his, asking after a particular woman was tantamount to a declaration of intent. And not the intent he was thinking of. He had to be more subtle. Sneaky, even.

On his next few visits to Aintree Ward, Pete tried to be observant and spot where the nurses kept their rota and then he waited for a moment when he was alone and scanned for the 19th of September. His heart was hammering inside his chest as his eyes darted across the paper. He had to find out before somebody came and interrupted him. And just as a nurse was coming into view, he saw it. Jenny was on an early. She was free. He turned away and walked off to find his patient. Now he just had to find out if she was going.

He needed to talk to Emma and make sure Phil had an invite for Wednesday and, if he was lucky, work out if Jen did too. It was almost the weekend. If he didn't find out soon, he would have only a couple of days the following week to discover if she was going. Maybe it was time to be blunt.

He was in luck. Emma had been distracted and offered up the information willingly. Deed done, he returned home that evening, content that his plan was starting to take shape. There was an event, they had invitations and, best of all, he wouldn't have to be there to watch them. So, with his job done, Pete headed off for his training; he needed to be ready to give his all if he was going to win the fight the following week.

*

Jenny's head was hurting, so she leant back against her chair and breathed. She looked up at the clock on the wall beside her. It was a little after six in the morning. Her husband's footsteps were making their way along the landing towards her and she had no excuse for being there, other than she wanted to be.

She didn't think he understood just how important this was to her, to get it all down in writing. She wanted to purge her soul of demons and confess her sins to the world. She understood that he was only tolerating this for her sake, but he wasn't going to be happy with her pushing herself, not when he was trying so hard to protect her.

She reached for the cat, busy purring around her feet, and lifted it onto her lap. "You'll save me, won't you, Twinkle?" The cat padded around in circles, but then seemed to think better of it and hopped down, trotting out of the door. "I guess not."

The door opened wider and disapproving eyes looked in.

"I couldn't sleep," she got in, before he had a chance to scold her.

His eyebrows rose. "Is it hurting?"

"Not too bad."

He walked over and crouched down before her, looking at her hands held tightly in his. "I just worry about you. I'm afraid you will make yourself worse if you push yourself too hard. You need your rest."

"I'll be getting plenty of rest soon enough," she told him. "I want to finish this. I need to." She looked at him and waited for his tender gaze to hold her. "Please."

"Promise me you'll stop if it gets too bad, though. Promise me, Jen."

"I promise," she told him and he rose up, kissed the top of her head and left her to it. Within a few minutes, she could hear the sound of the kettle boiling downstairs and birdsong starting up in the trees.

*

Saturday morning the post dropped through the door and plopped onto the mat. Jenny looked up from where she was sitting, trying to get into a new book. She got up off the settee and picked up the mail and, rifling through, she noticed a handwritten letter for her. She didn't recognise the writing, so she flipped it over and then turned it back and looked at the postmark beside the stamp. It was blurry. Walking back to her seat on the settee, she opened it. She unfurled the letter. At the bottom she read the name, "Lizzy".

Fear and excitement rose suddenly within her. She had spoken to her mum and dad a few times since they'd last met, which in itself had been a mixed blessing. Talking with them again had cheered her up, but the thought that she was going to be disappointing them again so soon was now pressing down on her again. She had told them she'd sent a letter to her sister and they were prepared, but they hadn't wanted her to get her hopes up, and yet here it was.

With fingers beginning to tremble, she took a deep breath and started to read.

Dear Jenny,

Let me start by saying I am sorry for the way I treated you the other week. It was just a shock, seeing you after such a long time. You seemed well, very together, and the fact that Mum and Dad were so pleased to see you made my childhood resentment overwhelm me for a while. I apologise. I'm glad you have made a good life for yourself and that you are happy. My life too has been a trial at times, but I think it is in order now. My wonderful husband, Jeremy, is a barrister in Edinburgh, where I am busy working for an events team. We have a little son called Alfie. He's two.

Lizzy was married! She had a little boy! Jenny had a nephew! All these things she had missed. And for what? Because she had turned all her bitterness on the ones she should have loved. A moment passed deep in thought. She wanted to see them.

Blinking back the tears, she read on.

196

*It is a bit of a long way for us to meet up on a regular basis,
but perhaps it would be good to try soon, and see each other
as adults, putting the past behind us.*

*I cannot promise we will end up the best of friends; there
may be too much water under the bridge for that, but
maybe family parties could have both of us attending under
the same roof and getting along. That might be nice.*

*Thank you for writing and for your words of regret. They
mean a lot to me.*

Your sister,

Lizzy.

Silent tears crept out around the corners of Jenny's heart as she
read and reread the letter. It was less than the total forgiveness she
had hoped for, but it was a start, a good start. She had written.

Chloe came in from shopping and saw Jenny crying. "What's
wrong?" she asked. She put her bags down and hurried over to
Jenny's side.

Jenny folded up the letter. How was she going to explain it
without telling her everything? "Family problems," she said. "My
sister's not really been speaking to me, but this letter makes me
think that she might be coming round."

"Well, that's *good,* then, isn't it?" Chloe asked.

Jenny dried her eyes. "Yes. Yes, it is." She put on a smile. "Did
you get the outfit you were looking for?"

Chloe beamed and held out her bags. She pulled out the little
black dress she had described to Jenny earlier that day. "Ta-dah!"
She stood up and held it against her and Jenny oohed apprecia-
tively. She sat down. "So have you decided if you're going yet
or not?"

Jenny pulled a face. She had thought long and hard about the
pros and cons of being sociable. "I'm not really in a party place

at the moment," she said.

"Oh, come on. It'll do you good. Have a dance and a drink. You've been in a mope ever since you got back from holiday." Her tone changed. "There might be some nice men who don't work at the hospital there. Emma's other half is an engineer, isn't he?"

"Life outside the hospital?" Jenny said, feigning shock. "Well there's a thought."

"Go on, Jen. Let's see if we can set you up with a nice non-medical guy for a change."

"Absolutely not! No matchmaking!"

"But what if there *is* a great bloke there?" Chloe pleaded.

"Then I'm sure I can manage on my own."

"Oh, you're no fun," Chloe scolded, winking fondly and she picked up her bags to go and show the others.

Pete woke up on Sunday morning with renewed purpose. The exam had gone well, and now it was time to sort out his life. He had spent the night before thinking about how to achieve this and it came down to one thing: he was going home.

He had training in the morning and he needed to get his hair cut after that, but by two he should be finished and ready to go.

Arriving in Upper Conworth at half past four, Pete went straight to the florist's. He chose a pink rose – Ali's favourite – and then his feet trod a path to the edge of the church yard, on the far side of town and that was where they stopped.

He looked inside. The sun was heavy in the sky and the birds had left the air for the evening. All around him was still. The gate squeaked on its hinges as he stepped inside and up above him the clock began to chime the hour. He took a deep breath and walked in.

Ali's headstone was in the corner of the plot; back home, because Adam and she had not yet set down any roots. Adam was no longer around to bring flowers to her grave, but her family obviously had.

It was tended and clean. He read her name: Alison Jane Elliott - Ali Taynton, as was; his first love. Not that he had understood that until it was too late. But Jenny had seen it; she had heard it in his heart.

He knelt down and laid the single pale rose at the base of the stone and his heart spoke out. *Thank you, Ali, for everything you did for me. You were the kindest of girls and a beautiful woman. Forgive me for loving you, for wanting to be with you. I should have taken more care. But I need to move on now. I need to be free to love again, in the hope that one day I may be worthy. Goodbye, dearest Ali. I miss you.*

He stayed there, thinking about his lost love for a few minutes more and then, standing up, he brushed the dust from his knee and smiled fondly at her grave. And then he turned around and walked away.

At James's front door he knocked. Rachel answered. She was surprised to see him and quickly invited him in.

James appeared at the living room door. "Pete. You okay, mate? Let me get you a drink. Beer? Wine?"

"Just tea, please. I can't stop long." He walked inside. Rachel clipped on the baby monitor and they wandered out the back, into the kitchen.

An expectant silence hung between them as James poured the teas and they all sat down around the kitchen table, waiting to hear the news he seemed determined to bring.

"I've been thinking," Pete began when they had all got their drinks.

"Well, that's a first," James teased and Rachel thumped him.

"Go on," she said.

Pete looked at them. "About Jenny."

"Yes."

"When you said you thought she might have had feelings for me."

"Yes." Rachel was taking over the reins of this conversation.

He took a deep breath. "Did you really mean it? Only, I've just been down to see Ali," he told them. "I decided it was time to let go."

Half an hour later he was driving away from Teak, back to his little flat in Duxley. Maybe it wasn't totally hopeless. His dad hadn't loved him, Ali hadn't loved him, but, if Jenny had managed it, maybe it could happen again. He had a clear purpose in mind now. He was becoming the man he wanted to be. It may be too late for Jenny, but it was not too late for him.

On Monday lunchtime, Pete spotted Phil in the queue for the till. He managed to catch his eye and beckoned him over. Phil sat down opposite him.

"Hi, how are you settling in?"

"Good, thanks. Everyone seems really friendly around here. I've already been invited to a thing on Wednesday evening. Bit bizarre. Not sure I'm going to go."

No, he couldn't do this to him. "Oh, no, I think you should. It sounds like a great idea; you'll get to know a lot of people really quickly. From what I've heard, everyone's going."

"Are *you* going?"

"No. I can't. I'd love to. Some pretty hot girls going, from what I've heard. But I'm already booked."

Phil shrugged and carried on eating his sandwich.

He had to make this good. He had to bate the hook well. "Have you met Jenny and Kim from the surgical wards yet? They're both going." He pulled a face to show how hot he considered them. "Wouldn't mind getting a chance at either of those two. Not much hope with Jenny, though. Classy girl, that, but not that keen on me. Very choosy, I'm told. Hot as hell. Still, if I win my fight that night, I think Kim might be up for it." He looked over to his side, where a couple of consultants had just walked in. "You might want to keep that in mind. Excuse me, I need to speak to a man about a bone."

Chapter 16

Jenny emerged from the ward on Tuesday afternoon and there, in front of her, was Pete. He was passing by in the corridor as she came out, talking to a new face she didn't recognise. He smiled at her and waved and the new face looked too. Obviously no great rush of longing there, she thought, just a smile, like he gave any other, as he walked along, relaxed and happy in his emotionless little world.

She took a deep breath and let it out. So that was that. She was back to being 'one of the nurses' again, as though those few weeks had never happened. How could he do it to her? She had his baby growing inside of her and she fought the urge to run over and scream that at him. No. She could handle this on her own. She couldn't bear the humiliation of his not caring. Not again.

When she got to the canteen, a group of nurses called her over. She grabbed something to eat and walked across. Kirsty passed her an invitation, beaming with delight.

"It's just the party," Debbie explained. "Are you going?"

Jenny wasn't convinced there was a point. She couldn't drink, shouldn't be flirting and she had never been a good dancer. But she wasn't about to admit that now. "I don't know, but I'll definitely think about it."

The following afternoon, Jenny was feeling low. She finished her shift, promising to be at the party that evening, but she was still unsure whether she might claim a migraine and duck out. She decided it would be easier all round to act as if she *was* going and then make a decision at the last minute. So she had a shower and washed her hair. She picked out a long skirt and jacket, something she hadn't worn for a while. She used the hair dryer and painted her nails and then sat on the bed wondering if she could muster up the enthusiasm.

It was a celebration of an engagement; it was bound to be lovey-dovey and there was only one man she wanted to dance with and he would soon be gone. But then it was Emma, and Emma had always been kind to her.

She had heard Pete's good news. That he had passed. She had managed to smile and say how pleased she was, but it had also signified that he no longer needed her and that thought had brought her down. His eyes had been soft and welcoming when she'd passed him, but that had just made it even harder to walk away. It reminded her of what might have been. But she would never know that. Would anyone? Ever? Maybe one day he would learn to forgive himself, to trust in love and settle down. She hoped so. To be loved above all others, that was her goal in life. That was what she wanted. And she wanted that for him too.

As if to reinforce her tumultuous emotions, Cynthia chose that day to make contact again. She asked how the writing was going and if she had given the story to the little girl yet and lastly, she asked how it was going with Pete. Jenny stared at the screen for a while. It was easily summed up: nothing happening, and there probably never would be.

Heather and Flis were working and were going to try and make it after their shifts, so the beginning of the night was down to Chloe... and her, if she decided to go.

Chloe knocked on Jenny's door and asked if she was ready.

"Yes," she said. "But I might not stay till late. It depends what it's like. Have you been to this place before – The Nifty Goat?"

"Yes. My best friend had her 18th birthday there a few years ago," Chloe told her.

Eighteenth? Jenny felt old. She was 31 now and still smitten with the same guy she'd been in love with since her early twenties. How sad was that? And now all her thoughts of getting over him once he was gone had been blown out of the water. She would have a permanent reminder. Every day she could look at her child and think of him. She heaved her weary frame up to standing. "Is it walking distance?" she asked.

"For you, maybe, but not for me. And definitely not in these heels." Chloe lifted her foot to show off her new sexy shoes.

"Shall I call a cab, then?" Jenny asked.

"No, I saw Soph in town this morning. She's offered to give us a lift."

"Soph's coming? But isn't she ready to burst?"

"Exactly. It's her final fling of sociability before the baby arrives, and she can't drink, so she's offering to be our taxi for the evening."

And with that Jenny was decided. To spend a couple of hours catching up with Soph would be worth it. She hadn't seen her in ages. She was definitely going to go.

Sophie parked the car and the three of them got out. It was a warm evening and they linked arms and headed for the back door of the pub.

Disco lights and loud music hit them as they walked in and peered around to see who they could find. Nobody was dancing yet; they were all milling around the edge, drinking and having fun. For a moment Jenny wondered what on earth she had agreed to – standing in a gathering of eligible men – but then Emma walked over and started to talk to them and introduced them to some of the other guests. Jenny forced herself to forget about her woes for a while and soon she began to calm down.

Once they were settled in, Sophie regaled them with tales of

Kate and Adam and the highs and lows of how they'd got together. She kept on the breezy side, never making it too gloomy, but inevitably it brought Jen's thoughts back to Pete and his battles and she looked around to see if he was there.

"Looking for someone?" Sophie asked when the two of them found themselves alone.

"No. Not really."

Sophie looked at her.

"I was just wondering…" She shook her head. "It doesn't matter." What if she never saw him again? Surely it couldn't be long now before he left? A day or two, maybe more. Jenny bit on her bottom lip and then a smiling face appeared before her.

"Hello. I'm Phil. I'm new at the hospital, but I've seen you around, haven't I?"

He held out his hand and Jenny felt inclined to accept it. "Jenny. Yes, I think I spotted you the other day in the corridor."

"I was probably looking lost."

Jenny smiled. "Well you did pretty well to blag an invite to this so quickly. How did you manage that?"

"That's exactly what I was wondering." He smiled and Jenny immediately took to him. "It must be my natural charisma."

This was a nice man, she thought. No arrogance about him. He seemed very natural and he had a kind face, a handsome face. She looked around to introduce him to Soph, but Soph had slipped away quietly. She smiled up at him, easier now, as she knew there was no hope of anything happening. She was pregnant with another man's child. But she would enjoy the attention for a little longer.

"You have a beautiful smile," he said. "And your eyes… What colour are they?"

After a while Phil offered to get Jenny a drink. She asked for an orange juice and he smiled and promised to return in a few minutes.

205

Tina walked up and Jenny wasn't sure what to say to her considering the last time they'd met.

"I thought I should come over and apologise in person," she said. "I told Flis to let you know, but... I'm sorry, Jen. I wasn't thinking. Can you forgive me?"

Jenny was confused. "Told her to tell me what?" she asked.

"About the Pete thing. To be honest, I'd really just like to forget about it."

Why wasn't this making any sense? "What about Pete?" What hadn't Flis told her?

Tina frowned. "Didn't she tell you? I told her to let you know that nothing happened between me and Pete. Not for the want of trying, I'm sad to say." She shook her head. "How depressing is it to be the only woman that man has ever turned down?" She let out a breath in exasperation. "I found out my husband was having an affair. I was angry. It was stupid. We're dealing with it now, but... I just thought you should know, just in case." She smiled a sorry little smile and touched Jen's arm tentatively. "He's in love with you, you *do* know that?" She looked into Jenny's eyes, her face full of honesty and meaning and then she let her hand drop and walked back over to her friends.

Phil appeared with a drink and a ready smile and they began to talk once again. Kind blue eyes twinkled down at her as she tried hard not to think about what she had just learned and wonder at why Flis hadn't told her. The way Phil's mouth quirked as he smiled managed to distract her for a while. But slowly she began to feel that everything was wrong. She needed to see Pete.

Like a flame building rapidly inside her, suddenly it became all-consuming. She made an excuse and hurried out of the bar. She needed to go to him. She needed to be with Pete now, whatever happened. Her rejection of him had been unfounded. He had been honest with her. She was to blame, but this time she was going to do something about it. And so she stole out of the party and moved into the shadows to walk the two short miles across town to his home.

Whether it cost her her pride, whether he turned her away, only his feelings on the matter were unknown now. She had to go to him and look into his eyes and tell him that she loved him. Only then would she know.

Pete stood in the shower having beaten the champ. Hot water poured all around him, cleaning the dusty sweat from his skin. He should have been feeling elated. His finals were in the bag, he had proven himself in the ring and Jenny was getting her man. Why, then, did he feel so wretched?

He walked out into the bar and a cheer went up. Neil called him over to a group of three women, all painted up and dressed to impress. Eyelashes fluttered as he was introduced and Neil called to the barman for another pint for Pete. This was his home turf, women ripe for the picking, hot and willing and up for a good time, but this was not him any more, not what he wanted to be. It was all wrong. He thought about the words Rachel had said to him. That Jenny had loved him.

Zoning out from the chatter, Pete looked deep inside himself. Something was building inside his guts and it scared him. Jenny had loved him. He tried to picture her smiling at Phil and his muscles tightened. By now he might be slow-dancing with her. Pete's fingers dug into his skin. This was what he had wanted... wasn't it? For her to be happy? But it was with another man. Another man holding her, touching her, looking into her big, round eyes as he carried her off to bed with him...

"Are you all right, mate?" Neil asked, and Pete could feel that his jaw was clenched.

Chills shook him. He had made such a huge mistake. Could she still love him, given half a chance? Could he fight for her and win her back? And then, standing there in that bar, he suddenly understood what love was and he knew that he loved her. He wanted her. He needed her, every second of the day, and right now

207

he was throwing her at someone else. Something akin to blind panic wrenched at his soul as he urged himself to feel what he'd dared not feel before. He loved her. He *loved* her. He loved Jenny White, his beautiful, independent, soulful Jenny Wren. He loved her and, feeling unworthy, he had done everything in his power to serve her up to another man. A better man; but it wasn't him.

"Yeah. No. Actually... sorry; I've got to go."

He wanted her far more than any new pretender could. He needed her, like he needed the air to breathe. His time at St Steven's was almost over. He might not get the opportunity to see her again. He looked at his watch. It was almost ten. Maybe it was already too late, but he had to take that chance.

With the chorus of cheers and chanting ringing out behind him, he threw his kit bag in the boot of his car. Everything else could wait. He had to find her, and he raced off in the hope that it wasn't too late.

As he pulled up in the car park behind the function room at the back of The Nifty Goat, Pete's heart was pounding. He jumped out, not sure if he was elated or terrified, and marched around the corner to the main door.

Inside, the party was in full swing. He was immediately welcomed in by some rather inebriated lads and he smiled and laughed and chatted, while his eyes searched feverishly behind them. He managed to pull himself free and spotted Kim, centre of attention in the corner of the room, queen of all she surveyed. A pile of guys hung around the bar waiting for their orders, but there was no sign of Jenny. He moved around, trying to scan the room and then he saw Sophie under an open window, resting on a chair. He walked over.

"Soph. Hi. How are you doing? You're looking radiant."

"I'm looking fat." She smiled. "Congratulations on your exam, by the way."

"Thank you. Um... You haven't seen Jenny around anywhere, have you? I need to have a quick word with her."

"Last thing I saw she was getting very friendly with that lovely locum chappy, Carl, is it?"

"Phil."

"Yes. That's the guy. Nice man."

Pete bristled and cursing under his breath as he walked away, he left Sophie commenting on his rudeness.

Phil was nowhere in sight and nor was Jenny. What the hell had he done? Fear coursed through his veins as he was overtaken by the urge to yell out. It couldn't be too late!

Striding up to the DJ, Pete grabbed the mic and called out her name. The talking hushed as only the music played on, and puzzled looks flittered around the room. His eyes darted around as the DJ brought the music to a stop. Whispers mingled as his search became more apparent. He asked again if anybody had seen her, but there was nothing. Pete shoved the mic back at the DJ and stormed out of the building to search outside. At the doorway he spotted Phil coming out of the gents. He grabbed him. "Where's Jenny?"

Phil looked taken aback and tried to unhand himself. "I don't know. I was talking to her, we were dancing and then she just took off. I've no idea where she is now."

Concern gripped Pete. "When? When did you see her last?"

"Only about five minutes ago. Ten, maybe. I don't know. Why? What's the matter? I thought you weren't going to be here, anyway."

Kirsty, a nurse, walked passed in the direction of the toilets. "She's gone," she said. "She left a few minutes ago. Seemed to have something important on her mind. Not sure what. She didn't stop to talk. But from the look on your face it's not a long shot to believe it's got something to do with you."

Pete wasn't going to waste time arguing. "She's gone? Out? In the dark? You're sure she didn't call a cab or something?"

"Jen? Unlikely. You know what she's like. If it's that important to you, you could probably still catch up with her, if you try."

Pete thanked her and hurried out to search up the road for

Jen. He strode out under the streetlights until his fears made him impatient and he broke into a run. The wind was whipping about him as a rising tide of concern made him peer into every darkened side road as he passed, half afraid of what he might find.

At the end of the street was a crossroad. His flat was off to the right and her house was a mile or so to the left and he was just about to head off in that direction when a sudden noise and a crashing of bins caught his attention back on the right. He heard a scream and although desperate to speak to Jen, he could not ignore what sounded horribly like a woman crying out for help. He looked one way and then the other. He heard another sound of a man shouting. Jenny would still be there when he got back, and he ran off in search of the disturbance.

A short way up the road he slowed down and listened. A muffled cry had him around a corner and into an alley. It was lit at one end by a streetlight, but darkened as he walked in. He called out. Silence. A few steps further on, his body braced as he came face to face with a man. There were two of them. They must have been late teens, early twenties perhaps. A quick review of his surroundings and he knew it was going to be better to talk them down. A blade glinted in the half-light and adrenaline began to surge.

He held up his hands. "Is everything all right, lads? I just heard a cry, that's all."

A mouthy youth approached him, trying to stare him down. He was shorter than the other and wiry. He looked as though he hadn't had a good meal in weeks. "It's none of your business, is it? So get lost."

Pete wasn't afraid of them, but with the possibility of a third somewhere lurking in the shadows, maybe more, he couldn't be sure, plus their weapons if they all had them, it was going to be a big ask. He took a single step back. "I'm not after a fight here, lads. Just wanted to check everybody was okay."

"Get him out of here, Rigsy," a voice spat, moving up out of the shadows beside him.

Pete heard a struggle beyond him and then a high-pitched voice yelped out. They had someone. He tried to keep his voice calm. "Let her go, lads. Don't be foolish. Let her go and nobody has to get hurt." He moved cautiously towards the place where he had heard the noise, but the bigger lad blocked his way.

"You're going to regret this, pretty boy," the lad said to him and he lunged at Pete, the punch missing him by a fraction of an inch. Pete dodged past and quickly turned the second lad against the first, blocking his attack. He was running on instinct. Years of training and a childhood living on his nerves were going to be invaluable to him now. In a blink, he had the second lad with his arm locked behind his back and his wrist flexed, yelping. Another moved about in the shadows with the woman in his grasp. He heard the man cry out in pain and then the woman screamed out his name.

All of a sudden, Pete's world hit a flat spin. Jenny. It was Jenny, and a rage took over him. "Jenny!"

Pete launched the second lad at the first, taking out his feet as he shoved him. The first lad, Rigsy, quickly recovered and pulled his blade into the game, a slow, arrogant chuckle dancing in his voice. He broke into action, swiping at Pete repeatedly. Pete jumped out of reach and took the opportunity to disarm him. It was a blind fury that spurred him on. Trying to block out all thoughts of what they might already have done to Jen, he concentrated on staying alive and annihilating the opposition.

Untrained, another lad swung. He overshot and Pete took the advantage, locking his knife arm back across his body and slamming his elbow down across his knee. The lad screamed out as his elbow snapped sickeningly, leaving the knife clanking to the ground as Pete quickly kicked it away.

Alert to the sounds of Jenny being grappled by whichever one he had left to maim, he poured every ounce of strength and cunning into destroying them. He felt flesh cave as he sank the back of his fist into a guy's face and, with a sickening thud, he crumpled and staggered away. He was machine now.

Movement came from behind him as he was caught around the throat and Pete braced himself for escape. His hands grabbed the arm that held him, flipping it over his head and spinning him into a lock. He launched the lad at the brick wall in front of him and it made a hideous crack that echoed in the darkness around them. Pete was all out of sympathy. He drove his fists in hard and the lad collapsed at his feet. There was someone in the shadows, someone else, and he prepared to strike. Jenny called to him. "Look out!"

Pete spun round in the dark and took a blow to the face. He recovered and found himself in a bare-knuckle fight with a much meatier guy. But the man mountain's reactions were slow, infuriating the oaf, who then pulled out a blade. Pete's side took a swipe before he could make out the direction. He was cut, but he could barely feel it. He had to protect Jenny. He rallied and launched a right hook and a cross to the big lad's face and followed with an upper cut. The lad was reeling. He spun him by the arm and shot a kick out so fast and so hard that the lad went toppling like a tower and fell crashing forward against the wall.

Pete spun around again to check on the others and scanned for danger. His mind was working at a frightening speed, but they were moaning where they lay and were no threat to anyone any more. He stood over the last one and knelt on his neck. He increased the pressure. "If I find out any of you have harmed a hair on her head, I will find you and I will kill you," he said and then he smashed his fist into his face, knocking him out.

Jenny rushed up and they fled the alley. She fell against him, crying and calling his name. She was there, beside him, her body shaking, but alive. He had to gather his senses and get her out of there.

"Are you hurt?" he asked as he held her away from him and peered in the half-light to try and make out her injuries.

"I'm okay. But *you're* bleeding. Give me your phone, Pete, they took mine."

He wrapped her in his arms and then they ran out across the street to get away.

Stopping a good distance off, Pete found a place where he could keep an eye out for the attackers while keeping Jenny safe.

His body began to shake as the adrenaline was crashing, but he was still at the ready, still vigilant.

Jenny was talking to him. He focused in on what she was saying. "Your phone, Pete. Where's your phone?"

Pete handed her his phone and watched in a daze as her trembling fingers tapped in the numbers and her voice asked someone for help.

Chapter 17

Pete was trying to move her further away from danger, but Jenny knew they needed to stay put. The emergency services were coming and she had given them the address on the road sign close by. His eyes were wild and not really seeing her. She had to try and make him connect. "Pete. Look at me. We have to stay here."

"It's not safe. I need to get you away."

"No. The ambulance will be here any minute. Just hold on. I know I can trust you to protect me if they show up again. In fact I can hear the sirens now. Listen."

The ambulance arrived and a police car close after. Jenny directed them to the alleyway while the ambulance crew took a look at Pete and loaded him on board.

In the back of the ambulance, the paramedic tried to take his details and another pressed a pad against his wound, laying him on the trolley in an attempt to calm him down. Pete struggled, trying to see the street outside, calling out for her with such anguish. Jenny tried her best to reassure him she was safe and she would see him at the hospital, but he wasn't settling. A policeman went inside and explained that they would take her with them, but as they closed the back of the ambulance, she could still hear his cries calling her name.

In the back of the police car, half frightened to death by what she had seen him throw at them, and still shaking from the attack, Jenny began to realise she was safe. She had witnessed a young boy fighting for his life… for her life, and now he needed the reassurance that everything was okay.

In A&E they were separated again. She could hear Pete creating hell over the other side of the department, but the police arrived and calmed him down, reassuring him that they would be staying with them both until they were free to leave.

Jenny tried to help, calling out that she was fine and telling him he needed to get seen to. It was as if the world around her was moving at a hurtling pace and she was inside it, in a bubble, watching it pass by.

A numb kind of peace took hold of her as she settled in for the wait to be seen. Half an hour or more rolled past before she was called. Moving through the process, she tried to answer where she could, but her only real concern was the baby.

She told the nurse and they arranged for a doctor to do an early ultrasound scan. But this would not be for a while, so she was asked to wait back outside in the waiting room until they called her name. So there she sat with the policewoman who had been drafted in to sit with her.

"Have you got them," Jenny asked, looking through the half-open door into A&E to see if they were inside.

"I believe we have three males in custody, yes," the police woman said.

"Three?"

"I believe so."

"But there were four of them, I'm sure there were," Jenny said. "What about the other one?"

The woman called to a colleague to radio in. "He must have given them the slip. I'm sure they're out looking for him right now. Try not to worry."

"Where are they?" she asked her, for Jenny was certain they would need attention.

"They took them to Garnley General," she replied. "So you didn't have to see them."

Jenny was grateful. "Thank you," she said and felt her tension ease just a little. She looked around her, reading the posters on the walls, but taking none of it in.

It felt like an eternity before Pete was ready to be released. When he appeared, he had a bandage just visible through the ragged slit in his shirt. He gazed at her and his golden eyes were full of such intensity it took her breath away.

"Are you okay?" she asked and he nodded and reached out a hand to pull her to him. He squeezed her tightly and she looked up at him. He was her rock in stormy waters. She might be battered from bumping up against him, but he was strong enough to lift her above the waves and keep her alive.

"Can we go?" he asked, calmer now that he had seen her.

"Miss White hasn't been discharged yet," the WPC told him. "But as soon as she's cleared, we'll take you both back to the station to make a statement. If that's all right?"

Suddenly, concern furrowed his brow. He looked at her. "You're hurt? I thought you were okay." His voice was urgent, needy, angry even. "What is it? What did they do to you?" His gaze was searching her rapidly, looking for evidence of what he had missed.

She stepped away from the others, just slightly, and took hold of his hand. It was time for the truth. "I'm fine, Pete. It's not me." She swallowed the lump in her throat. "It's the baby."

She watched as his face paled. "Baby?"

She nodded. "They said they would scan me to make sure I haven't... That it's..." She couldn't even bring herself to say the words.

Pete was dazed. "You're... pregnant?"

"Yes."

He took some deep breaths. "And is it...?"

She nodded again. "Of course it's yours, Pete. Who else would there be?" Jenny thought for a minute he was going to pass out, but she needed him to know. And with the tiny part of her that wasn't praying for the life of her unborn child, she started praying that Pete would be pleased.

Furtive looks passed between the police officers until a nurse appeared and called her name and Jenny turned to see.

"Jenny White?"

"Yes."

"If you'd like to come this way, please."

Jenny turned back to the WPC. "I won't be long," she said and she made to follow the nurse. But Peter was still with her. She stopped. "It's an internal thing," she said in dismay. "I'd rather go in on my own."

But he looked at her. "No. I'm coming with you. This is my baby too. Please, Jen, don't stop me."

Jenny let out the breath she'd been holding and met his gaze, searching for the answer she had hoped to find. Had she seen it in there? Or did he just need proof? "Okay," she said and he took her hand and they walked in together.

On the trolley, the doctor inserted the probe and uncomfortable, both physically and mentally, Jenny stilled. She held her breath as she waited for the news. Any second now she would know if her baby, *their* baby... Tears threatened to fall from her eyes as the tension and worry sank through to her bones. The world about her froze as the clock on the wall ticked on. Pete squeezed her hand and as the fuzzy screen pitched and swirled, the doctor finally peered closer. He pointed. "There," he said and a tiny, funny-shaped blob appeared through the fog and in its centre was the miracle of a ticking heart.

Relief the size of a tidal wave crashed over her as she saw her baby for the first time and, filled with hope, she plucked up the courage to turn to Pete. He was staring at the screen, open mouthed. What was he thinking?

"Safe and sound," the doctor added as he withdrew the probe and covered her up. The nurse let her get herself straight and

217

then showed them back to the waiting room. All this time, Pete had said nothing at all.

They were put into the back of the police car and driven to the station and still he was silent. It had not been the finest way to find out you were going to be a father, she conceded, but he knew now and Jenny was on tenterhooks to know how he felt.

The police interviewed them to get a formal statement. They gave descriptions of the men, as far as they had been able to determine in the half-light and agreed to come back to identify the attackers at a later date.

"Have you found the other one yet?" Jenny asked when they were just about to leave.

"You haven't got them all?" Pete asked.

"We have three of them. The other one must have got away. But with your descriptions, I'm confident we'll have our man very soon."

"Then she's coming home with me," he said.

Jenny wasn't used to being discussed in the third person. "I'll be fine at home," she told them. "One of the others will be there."

"No," Pete insisted. "You're coming home with me. Then I'll know you're safe."

If she had been in her right mind, she would have argued. She'd never been one for being bossed around, but she realised, after all she'd been through that evening, that she *would* feel safer with him. She *wanted* to be with him. So she agreed.

A policeman drove them to Pete's place and promised to let them know as soon as they had any news. They took the details of his car to make sure it wasn't clamped overnight and escorted them up to his flat.

Inside, Pete locked and bolted his door. He quickly checked around the rooms and then took a deep breath and slowly let it out. They were safe.

The events of the day suddenly took over and Jenny burst into tears. All the fear and the turmoil of the past few hours had caught up with her and her features crumpled, her limbs started to tremble and the tears erupted into shudders, engulfing her entire body.

Pete rushed over and folded her in his arms and they sat down on the settee. He cradled her against him, smoothing her hair and whispering comfort in her ear.

After a while, she was worn out from crying and he just held her still, his face in her hair and his hand stroking her back.

"I'm sorry," she said.

"What on earth for?" he murmered.

"For getting you into all this. You're injured. If I had just stayed at the party, this would never have happened."

"You're wrong. It would have happened, only to somebody else. I heard the police talking. They think these guys could have been responsible for a couple of other attacks across the county. Nevertheless, selfish as it may be, I wish it hadn't happened to you. Why did you leave the party, anyway?" he asked her. "You obviously weren't on your way home."

Jenny hesitated. "I was coming to see you." She felt him take a deep breath.

"You were?" His voice was calm, giving nothing away.

"Yes."

"Why?"

His chest stilled beneath her. What could she say? Because she wanted him? Because she needed him? Because he was the thing she thought about every minute of every day? Because she had just found out that he hadn't cheated on her? She needed to know how he felt first. There was too much at stake. "I wanted to tell you I had heard back from Lizzy."

His lungs filled with air once more. "In the middle of a party?"

She shrugged. "Yes."

"And was she friendly?"

"Not bad," she told him. "Not as good as I'd hoped, but... probably better than I deserve. We're going to arrange to meet up soon."

"Don't talk like that, Jen. You are a kind, beautiful, amazing person. She'll see that. She just needs to get to know you."

Jenny sat up and looked at him, wishing with all her heart that he wanted her half as much as she wanted him. She noticed his right hand, now resting in his lap. It was swollen and bruised. She looked at the other one and it was in a similar state. His face was marked where he had been bleeding; only his knife wound had been significant enough to be tended to in the hospital. Her brow crinkled as she felt the weight of his injuries. "Look at the state of you."

In a minute she was back at his side with a bowl of warm disinfectant she'd found in his bathroom cabinet, some cotton wool and a towel. "Take off your shirt," she said and his eyes met hers. He slipped out of his ruined top and he was magnificent. Jenny bit her lip to focus her attention and then started at the top.

Bathing the scrapes and cuts, she caught a look in his eyes that was dangerous to behold. Her mouth went dry and her breathing hitched as she wiped the dirt from his bloodied lip.

She took hold of his hand and bathed the dirt and blood away, her touch gentle in case she hurt him. "Who taught you to fight like that?" she asked, having waited till they were alone to find out.

"I needed to learn how to protect us," he said. "My dad didn't get to me often, but I had to be able to stand up for myself in case he did. And the others needed protecting too. Ali's brother did karate, so she got him to teach me everything he knew. A couple of times Dad got the better of me and it made everything worse, but in the end I knew enough. And when that day came, he started laying into Jimmy and I finally had the guts to call the police on him. That was when he left."

She was looking at him. What this man had been through was enough to make her cry. He was a hero, to her and his family, but he obviously still couldn't see that.

"After he left I took up boxing, to make sure he never came back. That's where I was this evening. That's why I was late to the party."

She took hold of the other hand and washed the dirt away. Her gaze moved to his chest wall, as she let her finger trail over his beautiful skin, searching for any injuries. The bandage was over his left side, where the knife had caught him and she stopped as she approached it. She looked up at him.

"It just needed a few stitches, that's all," he murmured. His eyes were on her now, his body still and his breathing shallow.

She rested a gentle hand on his thigh and then leaned in and kiss beside his injury. "Thank you," she said, "for saving me," and he looked at her with such adoration that she would have given him the world.

"You were *always* worth fighting for, Jen" he said. "Why did you not find me years ago," his voice croaked and she looked up at him.

"I did," she told him. "But you weren't ready." A long moment hung between them, laden with the loss of unspoken words.

Pete's phone rang, breaking the silence, and he stood up to fish it out of his back pocket. He answered it. "Hello. Yes. You have? Thank you," and switched it off. "They've got him," he said. "They've got the last one."

Jenny took a deep breath and shivered. Suddenly she thought about her own skin. "I need a shower. I feel dirty."

"You're beautiful," he told her.

"I need a shower, Pete. I need to wash him off me." Just the thought of that man's foul hands on her, around her throat and in her mouth when she bit him, she needed to be rid of that. She got up and started searching for his towels.

Pete's face changed. He took a step toward her. "Jenny, he didn't… They didn't… They didn't hurt you in any other way, did they?"

Jenny's mind reached for something to connect with. She remembered the woman on the ward. She had been stabbed and… and raped. "No!" she said. She shook her head vigorously, walking towards him. He didn't look convinced, so she gently took hold

221

of his battered hands. "*No*... Thanks to you." His expression eased. "I just want to feel clean again. Is that all right?"

Pete took Jenny into the bathroom, fetched a towel and his largest t-shirt and then left her to wash the grime away. He stood in the living room and looked around and then turned the thermostat up to make sure she didn't get cold.

He needed to take care of her. Jenny would need to eat. He had to feed her. They were out of danger now, so they could have a drink too. Except *she* couldn't, could she? Nerves gripped him. The baby. He was going to be a father and that scared him more than he had ever thought it could. Would he turn out to be like his own father? That was at the heart of it. It appalled him to think that he ever could, but how could he be sure? Was he too much of a risk? And did she *really* want him? She hadn't told him about the baby. Would she have... ever... if this hadn't happened? Perhaps she was wise enough to know better.

He had never put his heart on the line like this before and it scared him. Would she take him, if he asked? Would she believe in him, that he'd changed? He had to try. Living without her was no longer an option. He loved her. He wanted her. He wanted both of them.

Everything in his life had brought him to this moment. Everything he had been through seemed to have led to this. His terror and need to protect as a child had made him strong, had made him a fighter. The love he had for Ali and her affection for him had brought him to this career, and the torment he had battled to get over her had brought him Jenny. She was meant to be with him. It was obvious to him now. He just hoped it was obvious to her too.

By the time he had found something for them to eat, Jenny had emerged and was standing sheepishly in the door of the bathroom. Her hair was damp and scruffy, she had no makeup on and all she was wearing was his navy blue t-shirt and the wind was knocked clean out of him. She was… stunning.

He licked his lips to help them move and took a deep breath. For what felt like a lifetime, he couldn't say a word. Then she walked over and looked down at the kitchen counter.

"Sandwiches?" she said and smiled at him.

He couldn't move.

"May I?" she asked and he nodded. He cleared his throat. "Yes. Of course. I made them for you."

Jenny picked up the plate and walked over to the settee and put them down on the table. She curled her legs up beside her as she sat. "Come on, then. You need to eat too," she told him and obediently he went to join her. But he couldn't bring himself to sit, suddenly too afraid to touch the thing he wanted most in the whole world.

This was it, crunch time. He had to say something. He had to know. He watched as Jenny took a bite of her sandwich and looked at him. She swallowed.

"What? What is it?" Jenny held one out to him and, like a fool, he just stood there, anxiety growing like frost through his veins. He couldn't breathe, he couldn't think. He had to act.

Quickly, he took the sandwich and put it back on the plate, he took her by the hand and pulled her up to stand in front of him. There was a question in her eyes and he answered it. Gently taking her face in his hands, his gaze fell to her lips, which seemed frozen in anticipation and he leaned in and kissed them.

Tantalised by the delicate touch, his kiss deepened. He wanted to taste her, to know her again, to feel what it was like to be with a woman he loved. There were no words to describe how much he needed her now. It was more than he had ever known. He *felt* more, he *wanted* more, he wanted her to know how utterly loved she was. But she had to feel it too.

She was moulding herself to him. She fit so well against his body. His hands began to explore her. The touch of her naked thigh, her waist and the side of her breast. Any minute now he expected her to pull away and turn from him. But she didn't. She pulled him closer and a soft moan escaped from her lips. God help her, she wanted him! She had to know he wasn't going to leave her ever again, not if she'd have him. He was different now. His life was going to be different too.

He pulled away and gazed into her kaleidoscope eyes. "I love you, Jenny Wren." He smiled. "I want you. I want you forever. I want to hold you in my arms and never let you go. Life is wonderful when I'm with you and it's hell when I'm not. I have been a fool, Jen. I love you and I want you to be with me always." He waited for her reply, his heart racing.

Jenny's gaze fell away, as if looking for the words to let him down gently and he was afraid.

"You might *think* you love me, Pete, but you can't go saying things like that on a night when everything has been so intensely emotional. You'll only regret it. You'll wake up in the morning when the dust has settled and you'll just think: 'What have I done?'" Her gaze dropped to her fingers, intertwined with his. "I love you, Peter Florin, with all my heart, and I want to be with you, but this is all new to you. I've had time to come to terms with it. I've never asked for anything from you. I've never expected—"

"You think I'm just rushing into this because of what we went through this evening?" he asked.

She nodded.

"Did you not wonder how I came to find you tonight? I wasn't meant to be there at the party; I came to look for you."

Jenny gazed up at him and his world appeared in her eyes and then her eyes filled with tears once more.

"I'm serious, Jen. I love you. I was coming to find you this evening to tell you that. To tell you how much I love you and that I want you to be with me. I want to marry you, Jen. The merest thought of you being with someone else, it was killing me. It's only ever been you, since you cared enough to find me."

"I know you didn't sleep with Tina," she told him.

"I couldn't. I never even wanted to." Pete looked quickly around the flat and hurried out to the kitchen. He found a bag tie and fashioned it into a ring. He took it back to her. "Will you take a risk on me, Jen?"

Seconds ticked by like hours before she smiled and said, "So you really think you can do this?"

Pete looked down at her. "I know I can. You've changed me, Jen. I'm not the man I used to be. I want more. I want everything. I want you."

"Okay then," she whispered.

"Okay, you'll marry me?"

She grinned and then nodded. "I fully expect you to regret this by morning, but… yes, I will marry you."

Pete slipped the ring on her finger and his heart rejoiced. He kissed it in place and pulled her into his arms, crushing her against him. And in that moment he knew she was safe, he wouldn't let her down and he would always be there to protect her.

With each kiss came a caress and each caress became a hunger. Passion that had been suppressed for too long found a way to shine and they moved slowly across to the bedroom, revelling in their love. Pete laid her gently down on his bed, touching, learning, exploring sensations and as their bodies joined together, their hearts became one.

The moon smiled down on their naked forms, intertwined and spent in the early hours of the morning and Pete turned to look at Jenny. She wanted him, and sweeter words he had never heard… until morning.

Jenny woke up in a foreign land. Furniture she didn't recognise sat plainly against a weathered wall. Pete. She had been rescued by Pete. He had saved her and loved her and *made* love to her. But it had been so much more than that. She uncurled her left hand and saw the homemade ring still resting there. It was beautiful

225

as it was. *They* had been beautiful. He had told her he loved her and asked her to marry him, but now it was morning.

Taking a deep breath, she stretched out. Her limbs ached as bruises from the attack began to make themselves known. No limb bumped into hers, so she reached around. She couldn't feel him in the bed beside her. She couldn't hear him around the flat. Her mind spun into action, preparing herself for impending doom.

She swallowed. Maybe she could just lie there a little longer and pretend that everything was still as wonderful as it had been the night before. If she closed her eyes again, she could even see him smiling down at her, whispering words of love and devotion. But illusion was no use to her now. She had to face the day and whatever came with it.

Lying quiet and still, she took her courage in hand and rolled over... and there he was, on the far side of the bed, propped up on one elbow, looking at her. He was gorgeous, love flowing from his smiling eyes.

"Good morning, beautiful," he said. "So, do you still respect me?"

Jenny smiled at him. "I love you, Peter Florin," she murmured. "I always will."

*

Jenny typed the word 'End' and sat back in her chair. It was finished. She looked out through the window beside her desk and watched as her husband and children played happily on the back lawn.

Taking a deep breath, she let it out as she felt the anxiety she had put on hold for the days and weeks leading up to this, creeping back in on her. She had done it in time. Tomorrow morning her editor would find it in his inbox and know that she was ready.

226

She had so much in her life to live for now, so much love. Pete looked up from where he was kneeling, under the apple tree near the bottom of the garden, and although she couldn't see him clearly, she could feel his loving gaze upon her, and her heart swelled. She could not have loved that man any more if she'd tried. The sound of her girls playing brought joy to her heart, their laughing eyes blissfully unaware of the importance of the day, perhaps their last day of carefree existence.

Pete was desperate of course, she understood that. She had tried to talk to him about what might actually happen, but he hadn't been able to bring himself to discuss it. He'd understood her need to write the story down, only didn't want to believe it would ever see the light of day. She hoped it wouldn't, not yet. But what could she do? He was everything to her, a hero, even if he didn't think so himself. And now there was a blip that he couldn't help her over, and it was killing him. She would give anything to make her life different. And there she paused her thoughts. No, she wouldn't. She wouldn't change a single thing. She just wanted more of it.

Jenny had spoken at length with her editor and he understood that if the worst happened, he would publish. Nobody need ever know it was them. That it had happened. That the story was real. She had even enjoyed picking out names. Eloisa Woods. She liked that name. She thought it suited her. It had something poetic about it. She smiled. The pain was building again, so she breathed in, deep and slowly.

Martin would amend any errors she had missed and wait for her to call. She had left a reminder on Pete's mobile and her laptop to prompt them if they forgot, and if not...

Her bag was packed and waiting in her wardrobe upstairs along with a list of last-minute things, like her wash kit, comb and books. Books. As if she was going to be in a fit state to read any books! But they comforted her. She would get the girls off to school in the morning and... Here her world caved in. How was she ever going to let them go, or say goodbye.

Time. It was such a precious thing, she thought. There was no controlling it, whatever you did. It slipped through your fingers like grains of sand, until all you had left was a pile on the floor.

Pete's mum would be there to collect them at the end of the school day. They'd like that. A bit of spoiling from their gran.

They were playing hide and seek now and she loved to play with them, so she saved the file onto her laptop and wrote her final note.

Dear Martin,

Well, it's done. I'm attaching it to this email for your safe-keeping. If all goes well, I'll call you in a couple of days. Then we can file it away for a rainy day and maybe make it into something special, something beautiful. If not, you know what to do.

If what I fear most happens, Pete will need time to come to terms with things, but he knows I want it to be published and that the names can be changed. Please don't pressure him if you need anything from him, give him time. He's stronger than he thinks. And who knows, if all goes well and I pull through, one day he might actually let me publish it as it should be, as us.

I'm relying on you to come up with a great title. And I'd just like to thank you, from the bottom of my heart, for everything you've done for me over the years. You made my silly dream come true. (But if I make it through tomorrow and am back at my work by next week, I will deny ever having said that!) Think of me, at a quarter past eleven in the morning. And send up a prayer. I think I'm going to need one.

Wishing you all the best,

Jenny.

Jenny attached the file, braced herself and pressed 'send'. It was done. She was ready. Or was she? She looked down at her trembling hands and bit back the urge to retch. No. Not now. She wouldn't let it. Today… This afternoon… Now, had to be perfect.

Looking back at the scene outside her window, she smiled. The sun was shining down and she could hear her children's laughter as they played with their father, the man that she loved. The man who had brought her peace and who set her heart aflame every time he looked at her. Still. After all these years. And now she wanted to be with them, to be surrounded by those who meant more to her than life itself. What better way to spend a final day? And she closed up her laptop and walked out into the sun.

Epilogue

For four days Pete sat in a white room and looked at the woman behind the tubes. The love of his life was lying there fighting for her own and he could do nothing but wait, and hope, and tear himself apart. He should have spotted it earlier: the headaches, the nausea, even the blurred vision. He had thought they were just migraines. He had *hoped* she might be pregnant. Now he would give anything to be lying there in her place.

Her head was bandaged where the surgeons had been and the monitors bipped quietly around her. Tubes were running out of her mouth, her neck, and her arms. He nodded to the nurses who crept quietly on and took over her care.

In the days leading up to this, he had tried to prepare himself for its coming. He had been through every scenario in his mind. They had not spoken of it, of course. Too painful. Too emotional.

He had expected her to pull through straight away. She was strong. Stronger than him. But he had also feared that she would not at all and he would have had to say goodbye. This, now, was almost worse. Almost.

They said there had been complications. The tumour, although benign, hadn't come out as easily as they'd hoped. There would be a lot of swelling to settle and after that, they would just have to wait and see.

Pete took hold of her hand, so frail and lifeless, lying over the crisp white sheet. It was warm.

There was too much emotion for him to let go right now, for then he would crumble and she needed him to be strong. But he needed to be there, beside her. Waiting. Hoping.

A nurse walked over and laid a gentle hand on his shoulder. He looked up. "Any change?" he asked.

"Not yet. It's still early days," she said.

She walked around and pulled over a seat next to him. "Jenny left something before she went down to theatre. She knew she would be coming here after and she wanted to make sure we had it to pass on to you, should the need arise. I think she would want you to have it now," and she pulled a white envelope out of her pocket, looked at it and handed it to him. "I'll leave you alone to read it."

Pete turned the envelope over in his hands. It was a regular white envelope with just his name in the centre: Pete.

He was afraid of what was inside. If it was a goodbye, he wouldn't be able to cope. He wasn't ready for that. He never would be. He stared at the envelope in his hands for a long while until finally he found the courage to open it.

Dear Pete,

Comatose Prose!

He stopped and smiled. Trust her to try and do that to him. Even now.

If you are reading this, I expect I will be lying close by.

He looked across at the bed and studied her. It was as if she was speaking to him from right there.

First, just let me say that I am still with you. And I know this is going to be hard for you, as it would be for me if our roles were reversed. But you are the finest man I have ever known. I know you have it in you to be strong for me and our girls. But I know, too, that you need me to stay strong for you. There is nothing else in this world half so worth fighting for as the love you have given me. You are my world and my harbour, my safe place to stay and the force that drives me on. I was empty without you and now I am so full that sometimes it makes my heart ache just to think of it. I am constantly in awe of Daisy's love for life and am moved every day by Lily's incredible heart. Thank you for being part of them.

I have written our story, as I told you I would, and sent it to Martin. I want him to print it. I want the world to know what a wonderful man you are. I have told them everything. If you can bear it, let him do it, and if you can't, he can change the names and no one will ever have to know. It's your call. He'll be in touch.

I don't know how long it's been since I spoke to you last, but know this, that it is as lonely for me in here as it is for you out there. Be kind to yourself. Don't blame yourself for any of this. I know you will try. We both knew it was going to be a journey; I've just had to make one more stop than most. But I miss you.

I have loved my life with you and I am nowhere near ready to leave it, so wait for me, my love; I will be there, by your side again soon.

You are my world, Peter Florin, so whatever the struggle, whatever the odds, I will be fighting my way to get back to you, through whatever darkness tries to claim me. And I will come back to you, I promise you that. However long it takes me, whatever hardships I face, I will get there. Keep waiting.

So smile at me now and take hold of my hand and tell me that you love me. Tell me about our girls and all that they have been through and tell them that I love them and that I will be home soon. Don't give up on me, my love. I'm coming back to you.

Yours, patiently waiting,

Jenny Wren. xxx

Pete looked up at her then, tears pouring like rain, and taking hold of her hand, he whispered, "I love you, Jen," squeezed it, and began.

Hard-fought days passed in that corner of the ward; painful days, where nothing else seemed to matter. Just him. And Jen. And keeping her alive.

Long days and nights were spent by her side, talking, whispering, praying, and then, on the ninth day, when Pete was at his lowest ebb, and all hope seemed to be lost, a hand squeezed gently back and slowly, on the wings of angels, the woman he loved came back to him.